I0824143

Praise for Jessica Guerrieri

Both Can Be True

"*Both Can Be True* is a beautifully written story of love, redemption, and resilience. Guerrieri explores what it takes to survive, and to thrive, and at what cost to ourselves and to the ones we love. A compassionate tale told bravely and honestly that will make many feel seen and understood."

—Amy Neff, international bestselling author of *The Days I Loved You Most*

"It's a rare novel that tells the hardest truths about motherhood and the reasons so many women feel a need to escape, even when they fiercely love their children—and *Both Can Be True* is that rare and bold novel. In prose that took my breath away, Guerrieri explores the bonds of sisterhood and friendship between women with an unflinching and generous eye, while also shining a light on the darkness of addiction and sexual assault. By turns devastating and transcendent, *Both Can Be True* had me turning pages late into the night."

—Kerri Maher, *USA TODAY* bestselling author of *All You Have to Do Is Call*

Between the Devil and the Deep Blue Sea

"Debut author Guerrieri draws upon personal experience for this nuanced story of a woman in crisis. Leah's gradual slide into alcoholism is sensitively portrayed, and her path to sobriety, with its ups and downs, is authentic. Leah is not always a likable character, but as readers follow her story, they'll root for her recovery. Readers of Marian Keyes will be moved by this family drama."

—*Booklist*

"Set in a coastal California town, Guerrieri's first novel examines the intricacies of motherhood, friendship, and the pull between perfection and self-identity. Leah, a professional artist and mother of three, navigates the turbulence of her personal life. Her relationships with her husband's close-knit family, especially as they collaborate to open a restaurant in honor of matriarch Christine, are fraught with tension. At the heart of the narrative is Leah's evolving friendship with her sister-in-law Amy, a bond forged through shared struggles and unspoken family secrets. Leah is a compelling protagonist whose internal battles—a longing for freedom, a phantom self lost to the demands of child-rearing, and an increasing dependence on alcohol—are achingly relatable. Guerrieri's prose conveys her protagonist's feelings of being a prisoner within her own life with piercing clarity. The men in the story take a backseat to the novel's true focus: the complex dynamics among women, especially mothers and daughters . . . A raw, honest look at the lives we construct and the pieces of ourselves we leave behind. This powerful debut is sure to resonate with readers who like complex family stories."

—*Library Journal*

"*Between the Devil and the Deep Blue Sea* examines the delicate balance between identity and obligation, exploring the quiet struggles and unspoken truths of motherhood. With piercing honesty and lyrical prose, Jessica Guerrieri illuminates the spaces between love and resentment, sacrifice and self-preservation, and the impossible choices women face in their quest to hold it all together while they secretly self-destruct. This is more than a beautiful novel—it's a mirror, a reckoning, and ultimately a lifeline for anyone who's ever felt like they are drowning under the weight of being everything to everyone."

—Lara Love Hardin, *New York Times* bestselling author and Oprah's Book Club pick

"Jessica Guerrieri's powerful debut is a deeply moving account of motherhood, addiction, and how we lose—and find—ourselves within family. I loved getting to know Leah, Lucas, and the entire O'Connor clan within the sweeping backdrop of a Northern California surfing town."

—Tara Conklin, *New York Times* bestselling author of *Community Board*

"*Between the Devil and the Deep Blue Sea* is an unflinching look at the perceived expectations of raising children and the emotional turmoil of trying to balance motherhood and identity, mirrored perfectly by the intense atmospheric imagery of the Northern California coast."

—Lindsay Currie, #1 *New York Times* bestselling author of *The Mystery of Locked Rooms*

"A brave confrontation of the distance between who we were and who we are explored with razor-sharp honesty. The relational complexities are written with breathtaking precision, and the intimate experience of Leah's journey into marriage and motherhood is book club gold. *Between the Devil and the Deep Blue Sea* is an urgent call to drop all pretense, stop numbing, and let the fullness of life come flooding in. The complicated but real loyalties within this family remind us that we are not alone."

—Sarah Damoff, bestselling author of *The Bright Years*

"Motherhood isn't necessarily every woman's dream. *Between the Devil and the Deep Blue Sea* tells the important story of a woman whose decision to marry and become a mother has been more complicated than she bargained for, leading her to feelings of self-doubt and guilt and addiction as escapism. This engaging and introspective tale expertly peels away the mysteries of addiction, painting a riveting portrait of how quietly it can start, persist, and destroy. A compelling story of vulnerability, family resentment, and second chances told in beautiful prose reminiscent of Ann Napolitano, Guerrieri's debut is not to be missed!"

—Jacqueline Friedland, *USA TODAY* bestselling author of *Counting Backwards*

"A powerfully written page-turner about impossible choices, motherhood and creativity, and the devastating results of using alcohol to fill the void. I read it in a single day, riveted by Leah's inexorable descent into addiction. A delicate and unblinking study of addiction and recovery, but most of all, an intense portrayal of the ways we lose ourselves to motherhood and how to find the impossible balance. A beautiful book!"

—Barbara O'Neal, bestselling author of *When We Believed in Mermaids*

"Every once in a while, a novel comes along that so completely encapsulates a piece of the human experience. Jessica Guerrieri's debut novel, *Between the Devil and the Deep Blue Sea*, does exactly that for both motherhood and alcoholism in a breathtaking story about the bonds and trauma of family, the struggle to retain a sense of self while parenting tiny humans, and the difficulties of marrying into a family with different values than the ones you were raised with. With a cast of characters so real that you'll swear you know them, this is the perfect read for fans of Celeste Ng and Liane Moriarty. Mothers of all ages will relate to Leah's desire to remember who she was before having children, as well as her perceived inability to live up to the standards of seemingly Stepford-perfect moms."

—Sara Goodman Confino, bestselling author of *Don't Forget to Write* and *She's Up to No Good*

"*Between the Devil and the Deep Blue Sea* is a powerful and eloquent novel that plumbs the depths of the conflicts between domestic tranquility—particularly parenthood—and a growing dependence on alcohol to fuel the creative life. This book is highly recommended and impossible to put down!"

—John Lescroart, *New York Times* bestselling author

"A compelling exploration of the human experience. This novel captures the intricacies of family dynamics layered with money, status, and the weight of expectation. Each page resonates with universal reliability that draws readers deeply into its story. The interplay between characters is so vivid and profound that I was utterly absorbed, losing track of time in the process. This is, without a doubt, one of the most impressive debut novels I've encountered—a remarkable achievement. I eagerly await

Guerrieri's next work, as this is only the beginning of what promises to be an extraordinary literary journey."

—Katherine Rhadans, quit lit writer
and addiction recovery advocate

"I read it in one sitting and loved it. Told in Jessica Guerrieri's inimitable voice, *Between the Devil and the Deep Blue Sea* is both real and unflinching. I was struck on every page by how painfully familiar it was, like I was reading my own story. Each chapter is both epic and powerful, causing the reader to root for Leah, while at the same time, quietly hoping that she gets the help she needs. A beautiful debut."

—Laura Cathcart Robbins,
author of *Stash* and *My Life in Hiding*
and host of *Only One in the Room* podcast

BOTH CAN BE TRUE

ALSO BY JESSICA GUERRIERI

Between the Devil and the Deep Blue Sea

BOTH CAN BE TRUE

A Novel

JESSICA GUERRIERI

Both Can Be True

Copyright © 2026 by Jessica Guerrieri

All rights reserved. No portion of this book may be reproduced, stored in a retrieval system, or transmitted in any form or by any means—electronic, mechanical, photocopy, recording, scanning, or other—except for brief quotations in critical reviews or articles, without the prior written permission of the publisher.

Published by Harper Muse, an imprint of HarperCollins Focus LLC, 501 Nelson Place, Nashville, TN 37214, USA.

This book is a work of fiction. The characters, incidents, and dialogue are drawn from the author's imagination and are not to be construed as real. Any resemblance to actual events or persons, living or dead, is entirely coincidental.

Any internet addresses (websites, blogs, etc.) in this book are offered as a resource. They are not intended in any way to be or imply an endorsement by HarperCollins Focus LLC, nor does HarperCollins Focus LLC vouch for the content of these sites for the life of this book.

ISBN 978-1-4003-4599-1 (ePub)
ISBN 978-1-4003-4598-4 (TP)
ISBN 978-1-4003-4600-4 (downloadable audio)

Without limiting the exclusive rights of any author, contributor, or the publisher of this publication, any unauthorized use of this publication to train generative artificial intelligence (AI) technologies is expressly prohibited. HarperCollins also exercise their rights under Article 4(3) of the Digital Single Market Directive 2019/790 and expressly reserve this publication from the text and data mining exception.

HarperCollins Publishers, Macken House, 39/40 Mayor Street Upper, Dublin 1, D01 C9W8, Ireland (https://www.harpercollins.com)

Library of Congress Cataloging-in-Publication Data

CIP data is available upon request.

Art Direction: Halie Cotton
Cover Design: Holly Ovenden, Ovenden Design, Ltd.
Interior Design: Jackie Alvarado

Printed in the United States of America

26 27 28 29 30 LBC 5 4 3 2 1

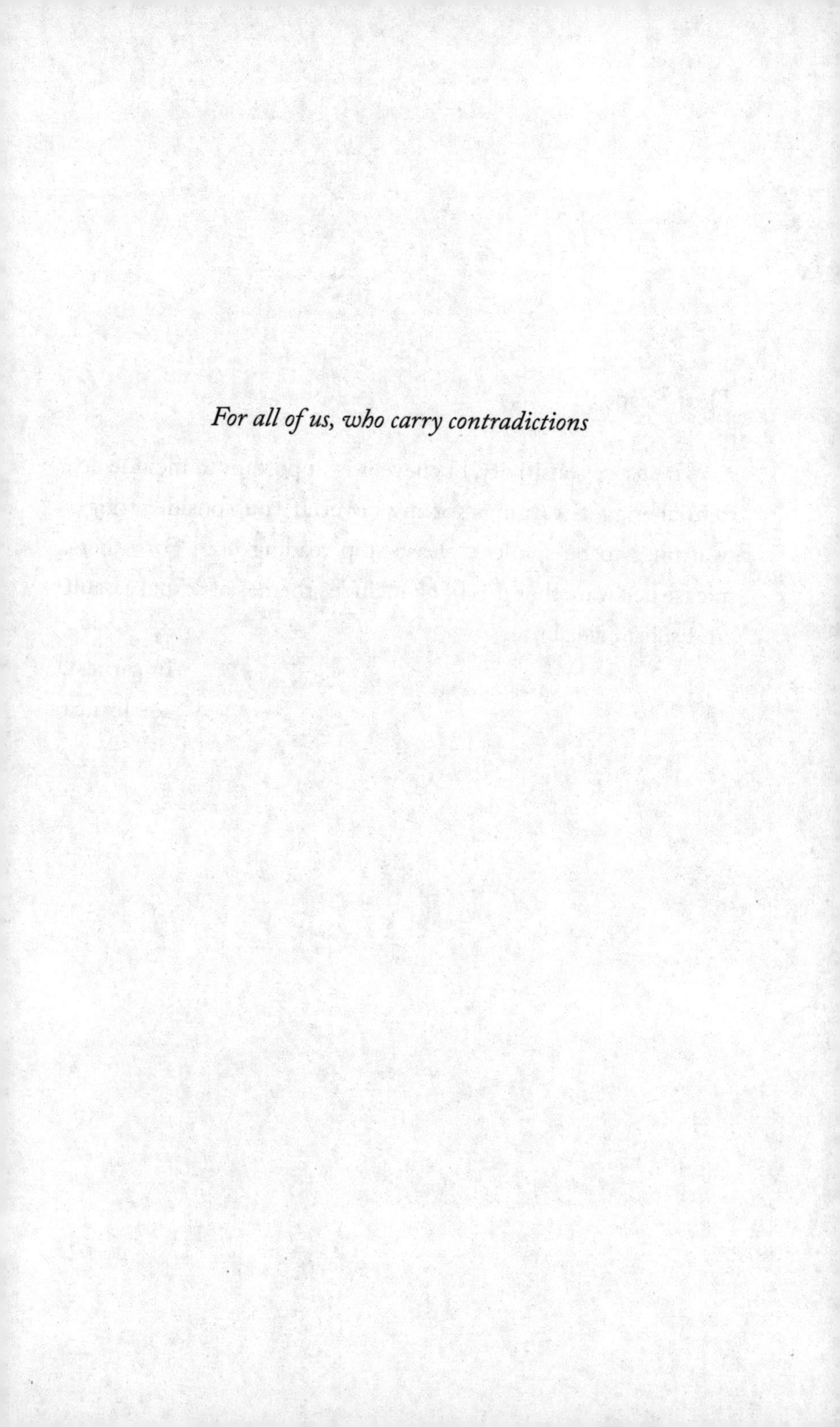

For all of us, who carry contradictions

Dear Reader,

To ensure sensitivity, I believe it is important to include potential trigger warnings for my novel. If you consider trigger warnings to be spoilers, please stop reading now. For others, please be aware that this book includes themes of sexual assault and substance abuse.

In earnest,
Jessica

PROLOGUE

There's more than one way for a woman to disappear. She can leave without packing a bag. Slip out so quietly no one thinks to follow. Or she can stay, stay smiling, stay small, stay busy, stay married, and vanish anyway.

She used to believe escape was a privilege. That only the selfish left, the ones who could afford to blow up their lives and start fresh in some coastal town, blending into the hum of tide and anonymity. Until she learned the truth: Sometimes leaving isn't a decision at all. It's the final, flickering instinct of a woman trying to stay alive. A quiet kind of survival.

There is almost always a moment in time. A threshold where a decision must be made. And even if the world leans in, offering its polite suggestions—*Be good, be grateful, be fine*—it's still hers alone to make.

But there's a part of her, a soft animal part, that still wants to run. That wants to fade into the trees or the lakes or the arms of no one at all. To stop performing. To stop explaining. To stop.

She began to wonder how long she could be gone before

anyone noticed. And she wasn't thinking about the version of herself who packed lunches and signed permission slips, who kept the calendar color coded and the fridge full. She meant the real one. The one who had already been missing for a while now.

Because sometimes the body stays. But the woman is already gone.

1

FRANKIE

Friday, March 15, 2024

Frankie found her beneath the incense cedars. Here, campus and community blurred at the edges, academia brushing against small-town living like colors bleeding on wet paper. The trees leaned close, weaving a canopy that softened the noise beyond, as if sheltering the secrets beneath them—a fragile kind of tenderness.

On a bench under the twiggy arch sat Brie, a waif of a woman whose blunt bob framed her face like parentheses. A pair of crutches slumped against the wood, an ACE bandage hastily wrapped and already loosening around her ankle. Frankie barely registered it—injuries happened. What held her was the smile: too quick, too brittle, the kind of expression she knew by now was a costume. Something slipped on, like dress-up.

She hadn't always known Brie well. At first it was in the shallow way that mothers tend to become acquainted with one another—faces recognized in pickup lines, hellos exchanged at birthday parties, small talk at school fundraisers. When their older girls became friends, forced proximity tugged Brie a little closer into Frankie's orbit. Then, finally, there was the unmistakable shift at the start of this school year, the night Brie showed up drunk to chaperone a school dance. Frankie had stepped in to help, and afterward, Brie asked Frankie to sponsor her. They'd been meeting weekly at the arboretum, usually just the two of them, and sometimes at Frankie's Sunday women's AA meeting when she managed to get Brie to come along.

Frankie had to remind herself constantly that a sponsor wasn't a savior or a warden—Frankie's own sponsor, Pearl, had been saying it for nearly a decade. A sponsor was a guide with a flashlight. *We cannot walk the path for one another, but we can light the way so none of us stumbles alone in the dark*, as Pearl would say. For six months now, though, Brie had been stuck at Step One: admitting she was powerless over alcohol and that her life had become unmanageable. Frankie understood; she, too, had choked on the word "powerless" at the beginning. For women, surrender was never neutral; powerlessness was too often forced on them by men, by circumstance, by the sheer weight of expectation. Still, Step One had to be faced, and Brie couldn't get past it.

So here they were again, sponsor and sponsee, seated beneath the cedars, their branches bowing toward each other in quiet surrender, mirroring the first step Brie could not yet take.

"What happened?" Frankie asked, tilting her chin toward Brie's ankle as she settled beside her.

"Can you believe I tripped going up the stairs? Apparently, aging is really agreeing with me." Brie's line sounded as rehearsed as her smile looked.

Frankie crouched down, tugging gently at the wrap. The ACE bandage made more of a fuss than whatever injury was hiding beneath it, all loose ends and overcompensation.

"I once painted my entire kitchen blackout drunk," Frankie said. "Fell straight off the ladder, tore up my knee in three places. When I got my brace off, I was practically an expert at using these things."

Brie laughed. The sound was sharp at first, but it soon softened into something real. Then she reached into her bag and pulled out a round metal object. A small tin dropped into Frankie's hands, the muted thud startling in the quiet.

"I don't trust myself. I need you to take these," Brie said in a whisper.

Frankie lingered on the packaging, too much like the candy her daughters once begged for at every checkout, sweet little bribes that clung to their teeth and filled the car ride with the wet sound of sugar being sucked clean. The THC leaf on the tin was so subtle, it could easily be overlooked.

"You okay?" Frankie asked.

"Fine," Brie answered, the word Frankie's daughters used when they were anything but. "I'm fine," she repeated.

Frankie knew enough from sitting around tables of sober women, from raising two daughters, and from her own lived experience that by the time a woman says she's fine, all her petals have already been plucked and she's a single sneeze away from being scattered to the wind.

"I thought I'd try a couple of gummies instead of the painkillers the doctor prescribed," Brie added, her voice sliding into false casualness. "You know, something more natural to take the edge off. But they didn't help."

"Your doctor prescribed painkillers for your ankle?"

Brie's answer came too fast. "Yeah, oxy. At home. Haven't touched any, though." She pressed her lips together, then added, "I just . . . wanted something that felt easier."

Frankie studied her, not sure if she believed it—if, in her vulnerable state, Brie didn't have the bottle stashed somewhere on her person, as physically close to her body as she could get the pills without ingesting them. The story wobbled at the edges. Why bring the gummies here and not also the pills? Why confess to Frankie in half-truths? She tucked the tin into her purse to throw away later. Whatever Brie's motive, at least she had handed over the gummies.

"I get it. Glad you haven't taken anything stronger," Frankie said carefully. "It's all a slippery slope, and together, we gotta figure out a healthy form of escape."

Frankie had sponsored other women before, but Brie was the most reluctant. Still, Frankie couldn't ignore how the injury and the tin didn't line up.

"Tell me how it's been since Margaret's surgery," Frankie said, wanting to steer them toward something brighter. Margaret, Brie's older daughter, had been born deaf, and just weeks earlier she'd undergone a cochlear implant procedure. "Chloe told me Margaret said it's been life-changing."

The dimness left Brie, replaced with a maternal radiance. "It has been. For our entire family. The first thing she said she loved was the sound of the coffee maker. Can you imagine?" Her laugh broke in the middle, turning wet. "*It's all so loud*, she said, and at night I asked if maybe she wanted to just switch it off, but she doesn't want to miss any of it. She keeps saying, *I don't want to miss a thing*." Brie took a deep breath, steadying herself. "The other morning, I was humming without even realizing it—just folding laundry, humming the Aerosmith song from that insane save-the-world movie where they blow up an asteroid—and Margaret stopped what she was doing and said, *That's you, Mama. I can hear you*." Brie blinked quickly, as if the memory itself might tip her over. "I've been her mother her whole life, but that was the first time she'd ever heard the sound of me. My voice. Not just the shape of my words on my lips, but the music of it. And she smiled like she'd been waiting for it forever."

"That's recovery too," Frankie said, barreling forward, excited to help Brie recognize the correlation between those precious moments she no longer missed out on. "Learning to tune in instead of numbing out. It's painful, yeah. But it's also—"

"No." Brie cut her off, shaking her head. "It's not the same. Margaret hears my voice now. My actual voice. You don't get that in recovery. You don't get back the thing you lost."

Brie was so wrong, but Frankie was losing the steam to fight her. Brie turned her gaze to the path, where a group of students drifted past, earbuds in, shouting, disrupting the entire ecosystem of the trees. "Margaret has spent her whole life longing for noise. But sometimes I just want quiet," Brie whispered. "To escape someplace with opaque water. No reception. A stack of the trashiest gossip magazines."

Frankie sighed, trying desperately to meet her where she was. "That sounds kind of perfect," she said. "You could find me on the beaches of Tahiti, in one of those enormous floppy hats that shades basically your entire body. From above I'd look like a giant tortilla chip and dip holder."

Brie closed her eyes, breathing deep as though she could catch salt air here in the middle of the Northern California mountains. For a flicker, Frankie let herself imagine it too.

"Do you ever regret it?" Brie asked, her eyes still closed.

"Regret what?" Frankie asked.

"All of it," Brie exhaled, sharp and unsteady. "Marriage, kids, the whole thing. Do you ever wonder if you missed a turn somewhere? Like it started out as the magic of sleepaway camp for grown-ups—messy, loud, fun—and then, without warning, something shifted. Or maybe it didn't. Maybe you did. And the drinking made it easier. It was always five o'clock somewhere because we were needed everywhere. And now it just feels like a place you can't ever leave. Like you're dissolving inside of it, piece by piece, until the person you were disappears."

The answer should have been a resounding yes—Frankie had felt that way a million times over—but she had grown weary of Brie's resistance. Frankie felt herself pulling away, saving what little stamina she had for later that evening, when she'd meet her sister, Mere, for dinner. It was the twenty-seventh anniversary of their mother's death, and still they kept the tradition, even if Frankie approached it with a kind of practiced restraint, the quiet distance she'd learned to keep so her sister could never again get close enough to wound her.

"I hope I see you Sunday morning," Frankie said, leaving it there like an open door. Another invitation to another Sunday women's group. Based on how their conversation had gone today, she wasn't holding her breath that Brie would accept it.

"Yeah, I dunno. It's hard to get around." Brie's tone was evasive.

Frankie was familiar with all the excuses; she'd used them herself from time to time, usually when she felt herself slipping out of that pocket of serenity. Sometimes it happened so suddenly she could hardly believe how quickly her "isms" from alcoholism could sink their teeth back in, like a rabid dog with a taste for flesh—relentless and unyielding, gnawing away at the marrow of bone until nothing was left of the good parts of her she'd worked so hard for.

"Still, you should come," Frankie said again, forcing herself to keep trying. "I'll pick you up."

Brie kept her eyes fixed on the middle distance, silent, while Frankie heard Pearl's voice in her head: *You can lead a horse to water . . .*

Frankie had bristled at that line her first month sober. *Isn't the entire point* not *to drink?* she'd shot back, all sharp edges.

Pearl had only laughed, her smoker's cough rattling like gravel in her chest. *Oh, I see how it's going to be with you.*

Frankie checked her watch. Pearl would be arriving any minute for their check-in, and Frankie swore she'd hand off the gummies before they piqued her curiosity any further. THC was a gray area she'd only dabbled in as a teenager, nothing she wanted to play around with now. Better to pass them on. She decided she'd bring Pearl along to dinner too—her own kind of emotional support person. Mere would be annoyed, but Frankie figured she'd survive.

Brie stood then, shifting her weight absentmindedly onto her bad ankle, rebuffing Frankie's offer. "If I'm coming, I'll get there myself."

"You sure you're good?" Frankie tried again.

"Fine," Brie repeated, gathering her things to leave.

Frankie studied her, tempted to push but knowing better. *Fine* was the armor you wore until it cracked. Brie was the most stubborn of horses.

2

MERE

Friday, March 15, 2024

Mere's cell phone rang, and she tensed the moment she saw Aunt Gina's name on the screen. A grunt slipped out, low and primal, a drumroll of dread.

"Hi, Aunt Gina. Is Dad okay?"

Avery glanced over from the driver's seat, one hand steady on the wheel, the other reaching across to brush Mere's arm. The gesture was small but grounding, reminding Mere she wasn't alone in the car, even if her mind had already started to spiral.

"I'm sorry to call you. I tried Frankie, but she didn't pick up. Yes, we are good here. Just wanted to check in." Mere knew there had to be more. Aunt Gina would be calling from Washington state, where she looked after Frankie and Mere's father, Ed, who had lived in a small cottage on her farm property ever since Frankie left for college. While they tried in their teens, neither sister had been able to care for him properly after their mother died. Her death hadn't just created a loss—it had removed the lid from the pressure cooker, unleashing the full force of Ed's mental illness, which their mother's presence had once managed to keep contained.

"I thought I would just pop him on the phone. He seems convinced that he's doing just fine these days and therefore doesn't need to continue taking his lithium." Aunt Gina's tone was even, unbothered—her unyielding patience for her baby brother the only gift horse the Gilmore sisters had ever been given.

Avery shot Mere a look of concern. She knew the whole saga: how Ed had lived for years with bipolar disorder and attempted to self-medicate with alcohol. Mere always wondered which came first, the drinking or the diagnosis. It was her family's own broken chicken-and-egg situation.

Mere's stomach dropped as she waited for him to come to the phone. She pictured him standing there, puzzled, as if it were the first time he'd ever been asked to speak into a small rectangular box with a screen.

If her dad was off his meds, it meant either she or Frankie would have to head up to Washington and have him placed on an involuntary seventy-two-hour psychiatric hold until he stabilized. It happened every few years—he'd convince himself he was fine without the medication, forgetting that the pills were the only thing standing between him and something reckless. Something like what had happened that one time neither she nor Frankie ever really talked about.

Aunt Gina had been their lifeline. Without her, their dad likely would've ended up on the streets—or one of them would've had to take him in. The small space on Gina's property gave him just enough autonomy to keep him content. He worked as the groundskeeper, and as long as he stayed on his meds and off the bottle, he could live a mostly stable life.

"Hey, Dad. I know you think that, but we've been through this before. You need your meds in order to keep living on the farm," Mere said, trying to match Aunt Gina's steadiness, though she wanted to scream. The monotony of always needing to repeat the same things—to her dad, to Lily, to Dale—made her feel like she was stuck on a merry-go-round, their selective hearing kicking in only during certain spins and never all at the same time. Which meant she was always on. On duty, on edge, on the verge of burning out.

"It makes my willy numb, and what's the fun in masturbating when my dingle dongle is asleep all the time?" Ed's tone struck a chord of urgency despite the absurdity of what he was saying and who he was saying it to.

Mere squeezed her eyes shut and quickly switched her phone off speaker, glancing at the kids in the back seat. Thankfully, they didn't seem to have been tuned in to the conversation. Noah—Avery's almost-five-year-old—was busy beaming at Mere's three-year-old, Lily, like she'd hung the moon. The two had known each other since Mere and Avery met at music class when Lily was only a few weeks old, and they'd been thrown together by their moms' close friendship ever since. Though they were both only children, their similarities ended there. Noah always seemed unfazed, all loose limbs and easy rhythm, while Lily was currently pressing her forehead against the glass, holding herself steady with the cool pressure.

Mere had been down enough internet rabbit holes lately to recognize it—her daughter's nervous system was asking for calm. The experts called it "stimming," but to Mere it looked like Lily's body trying to tell the world what it needed. Her OT had suggested squeezes or massages as a safer alternative to ramming into people like a tiny rhinoceros, which, while adorable now, was not something she could get away with forever. Mere had been trying to help Lily's sharp corners find a place in the world's smooth, unyielding roundness.

As her dad rambled on about his penis problems, Mere tried to tamp down her frustration so she'd be capable of crossing over into Frankie-mode soon. But her patience kept objecting that it was Frankie's week to field the calls from Ed, a system they'd carefully orchestrated with Aunt Gina, rotating the emotional labor like clockwork. She shouldn't be the one having to deal with this.

"Well, any and all conversations about your 'willy' should be directed to your doctor, not to your daughter—or your sister, for that matter. Okay, Dad?" Mere cooed, hating that she'd slipped into a toddler-friendly tone, but knowing sometimes it was the only way to get through to him.

"Okay, but I'm all backed up. A man must regularly be able to relieve himself. It's just biology."

Despite the crudeness, Mere felt a rush of relief. If this was his main complaint, he wasn't in any real danger.

"Continue to take your medication as directed. I'll email your doctor and set up a phone appointment so you can discuss your . . . uh, concerns. I'm doing it now, okay, Aunt Gina?"

"Thank you, Mere," Aunt Gina said, taking over the call once more. "I swear I didn't know this was the direction he would take this call. Love to Lily."

"Not a problem. Thank you for the call—and for all that you do for him."

"Bye now."

Mere waited to disconnect, still hearing her father muttering something indistinguishable in the background.

"Damn it," she mumbled once the line went dead. She signed on to their shared healthcare app and opened a new message to his doctor. "How do I convey via message that my dad wants to still have regular orgasms?"

"Probably title it 'Boner Emergency.' If he's male, he'll answer right away," Avery said without skipping a beat.

As Avery adjusted the air in the car, they passed the outskirts of Big Sky. When people heard the name of their small town, they usually thought of Montana—the ski town with overpriced cabins and celebrities tucked behind tinted windows. But their Big Sky was quieter, unremarkable in all the ways that made it lovable. Mere liked that—how two places could share a name and be nothing alike. The way she could love her daughter and husband, yet still sometimes want to flee.

Mere had picked the restaurant for its proximity to the park, so she could be close by if Avery needed anything while she was at dinner with her sister. Once a year, Mere and Frankie came together out of respect for their mom and who she had been to them when she was alive. It felt as if she reached from beyond the grave to hand them an excuse to set aside their resentments and wade, briefly, into something deeper—before retreating again to the shallow pool they had wandered into as adults.

"Just meet us at the park when you're done?" Avery offered as she pulled into a spot.

Mere exhaled. She was grateful. Avery never made her feel guilty about not being able to count on Dale to give Lily his full attention, especially during business hours. Frankie had insisted on meeting at five, and Dale would stay barricaded in his office until seven, unwilling to budge.

"Thank you so much for doing this," Mere said.

"It's the least I can do. I know how hard these anniversaries are." Avery's voice dipped to a near whisper. She, too, had lost her mother to cancer as a teenager, a haunting similarity that had bonded them. Mere didn't need to explain that there's a narrow window in a girl's life when only a mother can soothe the ache—lose her then, and something in you never finishes forming. That kind of grief carved out permanent hollow places. Avery understood.

Mere slid out of the car and opened the back seat passenger's door, instantly regretting it. Lily lunged for her, wailing and pressing herself against the straps.

"No, sorry, Lily. I'm going to head inside, and Auntie Avery's taking you and Noah to the park to go on the swings." Mere had already confirmed on an earlier drive-by that this park's swings were intact—especially the baby swing, the only one Lily couldn't tumble out of. Lily loved the gentle back-and-forth, but she wasn't steady enough to hold herself on a "big-girl swing" without pitching backward. The moving parts Mere had to align as the mother of a neurodivergent child were endless. Any one of them slipping out of place could bring down the whole house of cards.

At the word "swings," Lily's cries evaporated, her whole body softening.

"I got her, Mama. Go," Avery said, making a shooing motion with her hands.

"Let me at least walk you guys over to the park."

Avery rolled her eyes and said, "We can make it the hundred yards."

Mere knew Avery was right. As a yoga instructor at the downtown gym owned by Frankie's best friend, she could more than handle chasing after two kids. She was a godsend when it came to Lily. Mere was just stalling. She didn't want to walk into dinner already soured by irritation that Frankie hadn't been flexible with the timing to accommodate Dale's work schedule. And now, layered on top of that, the unsettling phone call with their dad, which Frankie should have handled.

Once inside the restaurant, however, she was comforted by its quaint rhythm—the shuffle of servers, the quiet clink of glasses, the soft lamplight catching on evenly spaced napkins. It wasn't grand, but it was predictable, and Mere needed that.

As she approached the table, Mere was taken aback to see Pearl, Frankie's sponsor, already seated with Frankie. This was supposed to be the one night all year reserved for just Mere and Frankie. Leave it to her lawless baby sister to once again assume that the rules didn't apply to her.

Pearl stood to greet her, pulling her in for a hug. Mere cherished the role Pearl had played in her sister's long and arduous sobriety journey, but she didn't appreciate her crashing their dinner.

"Pearl and I met before this, so I invited her along," Frankie said, standing to hug Mere too. With each passing year, Frankie looked more and more like their mother—not because she was aging poorly, but because she was aging beautifully. Their mother had been stunning, rail thin, model tall, with thick, wild hair that had never met a brush it couldn't destroy. The similarities transported Mere so much she tapped at her chest to remind her heart that Frankie was not their mother, who had been gone twenty-seven years now, and the time for this kind of wistfulness had long since passed them by.

When they took their seats, Mere and Frankie sat side by side, across from Pearl, and Mere immediately reached for her water glass. The configuration made it feel like the sisters were on an interview with Pearl.

"We ordered some appetizers already," Pearl offered to break the discomfort. "I'm so sorry to crash like this. I hope it's all right that I'm here."

Mere's shoulders melted down away from her ears. This would be fine. They could still honor their mother with Pearl here. "It's fine. I have a friend with her son and Lily just over here at the park—so if something comes up, I can always slip out anyway." The words were light, polite, but also a subtle jab. Frankie hadn't given her a heads-up, so she gave herself an out.

"Why couldn't Dale take her?" Frankie poked.

"He's working. You know he works until seven," Mere said dismissively. Frankie's lips pursed into a pinch and then opened as if to speak, but Pearl chimed in to keep the peace.

"How wonderful that you have such a supportive friend who can help out. How is Lily? And Dale? Tell me everything."

It felt odd to have Pearl speak about her family in a knowing way. Their time together had been limited to celebrating Frankie's sobriety anniversaries mostly, a few dinners at Frankie's house. Mere assumed Frankie had filled in the gaps about their relationship and in doing so would have revealed the complexity of their childhood.

"Lily, as I'm sure Frankie has told you, has recently been diagnosed on the autism spectrum." Mere paused, suddenly embarrassed that this was the first thing she had to say about her daughter. "She's just the light of our lives. Recently we adopted a therapy dog for Lily, named Pancakes."

"Pancakes?" Pearl asked, so gently and without judgment that Mere's eyes nearly welled. It was a silly name for a dog, but it was Lily's favorite food and what was on her plate when they asked her what they should call the cocker spaniel mix.

"How delightful." Pearl beamed, then leaned in, her voice

softer now, more maternal than probing. "And Dale? How are the two of you managing with this new development?"

Mere hesitated, the practiced answer on the tip of her tongue. *Fine, figuring it out together.* But under Pearl's steady gaze, the words stuck. There was something about her presence, the way she listened without rushing or flinching, that made Mere feel like she could unclench, like she could get caught in a slipstream of truth-telling.

"He's . . . good at some things," Mere heard herself saying. "He's such a hard worker, such a provider for us. But sometimes it feels like I'm carrying the rest of it all on my own, especially with Lily."

The pause afterward was too long, the silence too vast. Suddenly, Mere felt the urge rising in her chest, wild and uncontrollable, to share the secret that had been pressing at her for over a year. She wanted another baby. Not because it made any logical sense. She was already in over her head with Lily, but the contradiction of overwhelmed yet wanting more had her caught between the devil and the deep blue sea—the impossible pull of exhaustion and longing that only mothers seemed to understand. What she ached for wasn't just another child, but the hope that maybe this time, she could do it with less fear. Maybe this time, joy could take up more space than survival.

She wanted the chance at an easy child, if such a thing existed. The thought shamed her even as it burned inside her, because to say it out loud would make it sound like Lily wasn't enough, like she was wishing her daughter away. And that wasn't true. Not at all. Still, beneath the weight of Pearl's gaze, the ache of that wish pulsed through her, insistent and undeniable.

Frankie cleared her throat, reminding them both she was still at the table.

"Is this very hard for you, Frankie? Splitting my attention with Mere?" Pearl asked without missing a beat.

Mere almost spit out her water. Never—*never*—had anyone so blatantly called out her sister without getting scorched for it.

"Ha ha, very funny," Frankie muttered.

"All right, my dear, your turn," Pearl said brightly, reaching across to take Frankie's hand in hers. "And what are you up to?"

Wouldn't they have already covered this in their time together before? Mere wondered, secretly wishing her spotlight with Pearl could last a little bit longer.

Frankie used her spare hand to fuss with the silverware, sheepish, like her tail was between her legs. "The dads are actually planning a camping trip. Caleb and Jack. They're going to get out together for a weekend. So I'll be home with the girls."

"Dale loves camping," Mere slipped in quickly, taking advantage of Frankie's softened defenses.

Pearl brightened. "Oh, I bet the guys would love to have him along."

Mere didn't need to look over at her sister to know—Frankie would be shooting daggers into Pearl. Dale wasn't exactly Frankie's favorite person, or her husband Caleb's for that matter. They seemed to tolerate him in a way that had always stung, a paper cut that only flared when they were around.

It was the kind of tiny wound that didn't bleed but throbbed all the same, proof that they'd never tried to see what she saw in him.

Frankie sighed and tore a piece of bread from the basket, setting it on her plate. "He could come if he wanted. It's not like anyone would say no." Her tone was flat, not enthusiastic, but the offer hung there.

Mere jumped on it. "That would be wonderful. He needs more male friends—he really does." Dale was so reclusive in his habits, so solitary, that he had no real friends to speak of. Lately it had worn on her—spending hours with Avery, only to come home to Dale, who couldn't understand her need for companionship outside of their family. He was perfectly fulfilled in their small unit, even welcoming Pancakes into the fold, but his social life stopped at obligatory work functions and holiday gatherings.

Pearl smiled, nodding with approval. Mere let herself take it as permission, a reminder that wanting more for Dale, and for herself, didn't make her ungrateful. It just made her honest.

3

FRANKIE

Saturday, March 16, 2024

Frankie stood in the hallway, listening to her oldest daughter's voice drift from behind the bedroom door. Chloe was on the phone. She was always on the phone, whether it was pressed to her lovely, delicate ear—the one she'd begged to pierce with tiny gold stars at age nine—or gripped in her hand like a natural extension of her body. She texted with such speed, thumbs flying, that Frankie often wondered if they might detach altogether from sheer friction alone.

Chloe's low, sultry tone sent a pang of unease through Frankie's chest. It had to be Patrick on the other end of the line. Of course it was. Frankie should be relieved that her daughter's first real boyfriend was someone as trustworthy as her best friend Janey's eldest son. Frankie and Janey had once prayed for this very thing. When their children were toddlers, they'd put them in baths together, their chunky rolls all deliciously intermixed. But now as Frankie listened to Chloe's laugh, all flirtatious and feminine, she got an uncomfortable cinching sensation around her sternum. The drawstring clenched whenever Chloe seemed to slip into something too grown up too soon. Patrick, or the very act of being a teenager, had brought out a version of Chloe that Frankie both recognized and feared. Chloe's ability to captivate, her need for control—it all felt too hauntingly familiar.

Frankie moved quietly, the polished hardwood beneath her socked feet muffling her steps as she lingered by the doorway. She didn't need to hear Chloe's words to know their energy. The power she could wield over men's desires. The one-track mindedness of it all. Now that her daughter was becoming a young woman, Frankie feared every man would somehow smell it on her.

She forced a breath in, a breath out, reminding herself that Chloe was not her. Logically she knew that. They came of age under vastly different circumstances. The brokenness of Frankie's childhood wasn't something that could be inherited. Was it? She'd read that the body keeps the score, that trauma is passed through the generations. Was this how Chloe inherited her own intensity? That never-ending need to dominate a room or situation? Fears clawed at the edges of her thoughts: Chloe could spiral. Chloe could follow the same path she had. And Frankie wasn't entirely sure her sponsor was ready for the barrage of panicked late-night phone calls she was going to get the second Chloe inevitably came home plastered. Whenever Frankie shared her fears, Pearl would gently remind her to stop "future tripping" and trying to "control people, places, and things."

Frankie shook away the thought and knocked on the door gently before opening it. "Time to go," she said, trying for lightness.

Chloe snapped up her head, her expression flicking to irritation instantly. "Were you spying on me?" she accused.

Frankie raised a brow. "Always. It's my full-time job." Frankie wanted her daughters to think of her as home base—the place they could always return to. A port in the storm that offered them safe harbor, even when mistakes were made. But as Chloe depended more on her friendship with Margaret and grew closer to Patrick, the chambers in Frankie's heart felt like they were being pulled and stretched thin, as if they were made of Silly Putty.

Chloe groaned dramatically, sliding her phone onto the bedspread and crossing her arms. "You're the worst."

"That's how I know I'm doin' it right," Frankie said as she leaned a shoulder against the doorframe. "Come on, we need to get driving hours in. Your test is in two weeks, and you're not going to magically figure out parallel parking on your cell phone."

Chloe dragged herself off the bed with just enough theatrics to register her displeasure. Frankie trailed her down the hall, bracing for the bickering that driving practice would inevitably bring. She was in charge of teaching Chloe, while Caleb would eventually take on Rayna, their younger daughter, who at fourteen still had time.

Before they began this nerve-racking rite of passage, Frankie had insisted it made more sense for her to take the lead. After all, she understood how Chloe's brain worked, since it mirrored her own. Surely that shared wiring would be an advantage. She could anticipate Chloe's worries before they surfaced, ease her through them. In reality, they'd only managed to irritate each other—trapped in a metal box that, when mishandled or when Frankie lost her patience with Chloe, felt less like a car and more like a metaphor for parenthood: claustrophobic, volatile, and potentially a two-ton death trap.

The abandoned church parking lot had been their go-to since the start of driving practice. Despite the tension that simmered during every session, Frankie secretly cherished the forced alone time—no distractions, no outside noise, just the two of them sealed inside a bubble that felt, if not peaceful, at least contained. She adjusted her seat belt as Chloe, with exaggerated precision, angled the mirrors. With her driving test looming, Chloe had been practicing more on real roads, but Frankie much preferred the predictable emptiness of this lot. Out here, the only collisions they risked were the emotional kind, the kind that happened when mother and daughter were navigating more than just parking lines.

"Literally all my friends are learning on Jeeps or Range Rovers," Chloe said, her voice thick with teenage judgment. "A Prius is, like, the most embarrassing first car ever."

Frankie bit her cheeks to hold in her smile. "Aunt Mere and I learned to drive in your grandma's 1989 Dodge Caravan. We called it 'the Space Shuttle.' I promise you'll survive the humiliation." She paused, then added, "And by the way, the sooner you stop caring what other people think, the happier you'll be."

Chloe rolled her eyes and shot Frankie the look that had become a staple in their household. "Sure, Mom. Whatever you say."

"Let's start with some parallel parking between those trees. You've got this."

Chloe bit her lip, maneuvering the car slowly and deliberately. Frankie let herself relax into her surroundings. Last week, the air in Big Sky had shifted, as it did every March—not with the lightness of spring but with a charged stillness, as if the whole valley were bracing. The clouds had thickened into a dull, flat gray, heavy as wet wool, stretching over the basin in an unbroken sheet. Locals knew the signs. The wind, rising in erratic bursts, rattling the pines until they hissed their warnings. Birds flying lower, quicker. And the sun, no longer setting but retreating, swallowed whole by the horizon. Everything pointed to the same conclusion: A storm was coming.

Chloe continued to park and repark. The rear-view cameras made it impossibly simple. Frankie remembered having to place her right hand on the front passenger's headrest in the Space Shuttle so she could crane her neck around and see what was happening out the back window. *Proper hand placement is the only thing that separates us from all those other lunatics on the road*, her dad had insisted.

When Chloe finally spoke again, her voice was quieter in concentration. "Margaret's driving now that she got the implant," she said. "She shouldn't be too far behind me in getting her license."

"Oh, that's exciting!" Frankie said as Chloe eased into an almost-perfect parallel spot.

Frankie's thoughts drifted to Margaret's mom, Brie, and their meeting in the arboretum yesterday. She was still holding out hope that she'd be at the meeting tomorrow.

Brie's path through recovery had never been as linear as Frankie's. Before Frankie became her sponsor, Brie had another one, a woman with a few years of sobriety under her belt, but she'd left the program and never come back. Brie once remarked that she preferred her other sponsor's laid-back methodology for working the program. *And how did that work out for her?* Frankie had wryly commented.

When Brie showed up to chaperone the high school dance more than a little tipsy, Frankie had quietly asked another mom to cover for her and led Brie out to the parking lot. Brie didn't resist. She seemed almost relieved to be steered, as if temporarily the burden of what it took to hold herself up could be shared. That is, until she promptly threw up all over the passenger's side of Frankie's truck. As Frankie held her hair back into a makeshift side ponytail, she registered with a kind of dark humor how well the hairstyle suited Brie's neon pink, '80s-themed sweatshirt.

When Frankie followed up the next week, after Pearl's gentle nudge, Brie asked her to be her sponsor. At first Frankie considered tough love, warning that recovery would only work if Brie worked the program, and that Brie should call again whenever she was truly ready to surrender. But Frankie quickly realized Brie needed something softer. It was a balancing act—support without control, compassion without ownership. Whether Brie chose to drink again or not, Frankie had to remind herself, was never hers to carry.

Frankie reached for her purse at her feet and pulled out her phone. She wanted to text Brie and follow up. *How's the ankle? See you at the meeting?*

"I'm so glad Margaret will get to drive," Frankie said, then paused, letting the thought settle. It was strange to picture either of the girls alone behind the wheel, just them and the road. Nothing was more terrifying than the slow realization that Frankie would no longer be able to control every danger that darted into Chloe's path.

"I can't imagine how loud everything must seem to Margaret now with the implant. She told me that before it felt like she was in a video game or a simulation. Like everything was underwater."

Frankie held her breath, not wanting to interrupt a mini update, the snippet of teenage dialogue a rare behind-the-scenes pass, even if it was just a small glimpse.

"It's so weird. I got so used to needing to make it so she could read my lips. The other day we lay down next to each other on her bed and talked. That was the first time we could do that, where we weren't facing each other." Frankie smiled, picturing the girls in a warm tangle of golden hair.

Brie had shared on the group level during meetings the significance of Maragret's decision to go forward with the surgery.

When she did speak, Brie kept the focus on her children rather than herself—especially on Margaret, who was born deaf but had decided to have the surgery now, before she went off to college. Apparently, there was significant debate within the deaf community about the merits of cochlear implants, with strong opinions on both sides. One side viewed the implants as a kind of betrayal, an unnecessary medicalization of deafness that implied something needed fixing. The other saw them as a tool, a choice, a way to expand access without erasing identity. Brie had been careful in the way she spoke about it, always circling back to the idea of agency, of giving her daughter options, even if those options were complicated.

"But how's that been going? With driving. Is she learning with her mom or her dad?"

"Both. But mostly her dad. Her mom doesn't have the greatest track record for patience." Frankie tilted forward in understanding. While Frankie's own daughters knew she was in recovery and went to meetings, Brie had told her that she wasn't ready to be forthcoming with her girls, at least not about this. It felt like yet another way for Brie to keep one foot out the door of committing to sobriety, but Frankie knew the decision to be vulnerable with her family was deeply personal.

"I know it's been a lot, a big change with her hearing, and I really want to be there for her . . ." Chloe continued talking as she pulled into a spot and put the car in Park. "I think Mar has been feeling a little left out lately with me and Patrick, but it's hard. Of course I want to hang out with her, but I also want alone time with him." Frankie remembered she'd gone through something similar in high school with Janey and her boyfriend, feeling like the third wheel. It was a hard balance to get right, even without the raging teenage hormones.

The rest of the lesson passed in relative silence, Chloe focused on perfecting her parking while Frankie stared at the open meadows around the parking lot. The sky sagged low, promising snow before nightfall. Even from inside the car, she sensed the air outside was dense and waiting, the hush of it pulsing like the final days of pregnancy.

Having grown up in the Bay Area, Frankie was still getting used to the snow. It never got cold enough to snow in Belmont, where she grew up. Maybe a flurry once every decade, but never the kind that stuck. When the girls were younger, she'd been overwhelmed by the ridiculous fuss it took to get them all suited up: the hats and gloves, the puffer coats that made them look like overgrown toasted marshmallows, and the boots they could never tie themselves. If they bent even an inch, they'd tip over, and she'd have to start the whole process aga—

"Squirrel!" Chloe shrieked, slamming on the brakes about two feet after Frankie felt the distinctive crunch of the tires rolling over a speed bump of animal bones.

"Oh my god! Oh my god! Is it okay? Oh my god, Mom! What do I do?" Chloe's whole face tightened with panic, the worry in her voice pitched so high it felt like it might split Frankie in half.

"It's all right. Okay, um . . ." Frankie wished she could swap sides, take all the blame—teleport them back to when Chloe had been gullible enough to be appeased by misdirection. "So, honey, this sometimes happens while driving." She kept her voice steady. "You were going slow enough that the little guy clearly had a death wish. There wasn't any way to avoid it. Now we should get out and check that he's no longer . . . uh . . . living, or I can check if you want."

Chloe's hands gripped the wheel as she threw the car into Park. Her skin had gone pale, her face fraught with concern. "No, no. Let's just go. We can't look."

"Honey, that's not an option." Frankie softened her tone but held firm. "Part of being a responsible driver is taking accountability for our actions. It was an accident, and these things happen." Chloe's heart was too big for her body, and the depth of her feelings often exhausted them both. Frankie knew the next decision would impact Chloe's ability to handle moving forward with her lessons.

Frankie opened the passenger's side door and reached for Chloe's hand, giving it a squeeze.

"No, please don't. I can't." Tears were pooling at the corners of Chloe's eyes.

"I'll just make sure, and then we can go home. We can even donate your allowance this week to an animal rescue or something if you want," Frankie said, proud of her ability to improvise.

To her surprise, Chloe exited and followed around behind the car. Tiny guts were splayed out all over the cement. The bushy tail stuck to the tackiness of fresh blood, which thankfully helped shield a lot of the carnage from view. Chloe turned her body into Frankie's, her hands covering what had become full, wet tears.

Frankie couldn't help but recall her mother's death, the ways a body ravaged by cancer could be unbearably cruel. She'd died at home in her bed on hospice. Cancer had warped her color and caved her shape, stripping away her liveliness, her vitality—everything that embodied her essence—until she was nearly unrecognizable. Frankie felt powerless, forced to watch her slowly decay and vacate her own skin. Try as she might, she knew some sights couldn't be unseen. And in Frankie's fourteen-year-old mind that craved stability, this became the image that clung, with the same terrible finality as the squirrel on the road.

"It's okay," Frankie said softly, putting her arm around Chloe and pulling her in close. "I hear squirrel heaven is amazing. All the nuts they can eat, no cars, just endless trees to climb."

Chloe let out a shaky laugh, wiping her tears with the tips of her fingers, a movement so delicate Frankie wondered how she could have blinked her way to this moment where Chloe no longer depended on Frankie for every need. "Do you think so?" Frankie was grateful when Chloe still played along in childish things.

"I know so," she said firmly. "Come on, let's get some ice cream. I'm thinking rocky road. Though maybe too soon?"

Chloe pushed off her mom in playful protest. As Frankie started back toward the driver's side, Chloe dropped to her knees, her lips moving in what looked like a silent apology.

Frankie slipped into the driver's seat and let her daughter linger on the pavement a little longer.

Inside the car, Frankie checked her phone. Still nothing from Brie. In the rearview, Chloe's bowed head caught her eye, and that familiar unease coiled in her chest. In recovery, death was spoken of in a way that made most people flinch—studied too closely, named too plainly—because those who'd dodged it couldn't afford to look away. Frankie knew how thin the barrier was between living and vanishing. One moment you were here, warm and breathing, and the next a wheel swerved, a trapdoor opened, and it was over. The knowledge never left her: She and everyone she loved were all just living on borrowed time.

4

MERE

Saturday, March 16, 2024

Lily was nestled between Mere and Dale on the couch. Her small body was soft against Mere's side. Their dog, Pancakes, waited patiently at Mere's feet because she wasn't allowed up on the cushions. Pancakes was still learning the rhythm of their household but had eased into her role more seamlessly than any other member of Mere's family in the three months she'd been there. Mere hadn't been looking for a dog, but another mom in their community had posted in a Facebook group that their highly trained, ASD-specialized therapy dog needed a new home after her child developed an allergy to dander. Pancakes was the sweetest sixteen-pound, blond-haired, big-eared love bug who, almost unbelievably, had been trained to perform deep-pressure sensory techniques and offer emotional support to children with needs exactly like Lily's. Mere took it as a sign—this was meant to be their dog.

Dale had been hesitant at first, but after the initial introduction with Lily was a total and complete success, they brought Pancakes home that same day and let Lily choose her name. Mere reached down to scratch the soft spot behind the dog's ear. Dale looked down at them and smiled, reaching to pat Pancakes on the head.

"I don't see why they want me to go camping," he said.

Mere kept her gaze on the dog. "It's one night. You never go out and do anything. It will be good for you."

"What about food? Are they expecting me to cook? Because I don't like guessing what the rules are."

"Remember to keep your voice even," she told Dale, nodding toward Lily, who was fiddling with her dog's ear. "When she's focused like this, changes in tone can set her off. They've got food covered." Then she added softly, "Just show up."

"I don't like just showing up. If there are rules, I should know them."

"The only rule is that you go, relax, and have a good time. And honestly, Dale? It'll mean a lot to me if you do this."

Despite his hesitation, Mere had known last night when she brought it up that he would go. Resistance always came first, then logistics, then reluctant agreement. It was the same way with parenting Lily—he let Mere hold the responsibility until he couldn't avoid it any longer.

Dale began stacking wooden blocks in a straight line across the coffee table. Mere didn't have to ask what he was building. The formation was long and even. Stable. Structurally sound, as he liked to say.

Lily flapped her hands in front of her while Dale traced slow patterns on her cheek with one hand and kept arranging the blocks with the other.

Mere adjusted the weighted blanket over Lily's legs and nodded toward Dale's hand. "Keep the pressure steady." Mere knew better than to assume her daughter's movements were ones of joy. She'd learned to watch Lily's wrists. If they stayed stiff, it meant she was tipping toward overstimulation.

Several of Lily's most noticeable spectrum traits came in the form of repetition and the need for routine. This meant wearing the same dress every day—no buttons, no seams, no texture. Listening to "Defying Gravity" on a loop during bath time, though lately they'd been able to branch out to the entire *Wicked* soundtrack when they were in the car. And in public, when things got too loud, her hands would flap like a bird that had flown through an open window and couldn't find her way back out. Mere had worked tirelessly to protect Lily's fragile ecosystem, and it was difficult not to resent Dale's hands-off approach. He was content to let Mere carry the responsibility, just as he was content to let her coax him into going camping with the guys, as if he weren't a participant in their family so much as another figure she had to manage. Every time she tried to bring up ways for him to be more engaged, they circled the same loop: He worked full-time, so of course she knew best. She did the research, she made the calls, and he was happy to fall in line. Sometimes it felt less like a partnership and more like Mere was parenting two dependents instead of one, which only deepened the absurdity of her yearning for another child.

Mere watched Dale manipulating the wooden blocks, leaving a deliberate space between the two structures he'd created before gently placing the arch—the great connector of the two sides. He studied it, then shifted his attention to the room just beyond where they sat. He spent most of his hours there in the office, sequestered behind a sturdy red door.

Their home routine left Mere without a break, and the level at which Lily needed her sometimes felt like a wave crashing down upon her shore. Again and again. That was the problem, wasn't it? Not just the exhaustion, but the absence of partnership. Dale loved them both in his quiet, steady way. But he didn't know how to carry her too. Not emotionally. Not ever. And maybe she didn't know how to ask. Or maybe she'd stopped trying.

Mere never intended to be a stay-at-home mom. Before Lily, she worked for almost eighteen years as an elementary school teacher. The prospect of becoming parents had come and gone in her thirties and she thought, *Ah, well.* Every year she had thirty students who acted as her own children. She loved them just as much as any mother could—or so she thought. Until Lily came, and then she felt almost foolish for ever thinking that kind of love could compare. Maternal love transcended time and space. But it also made her bones ache for her own mother in a way she had managed to ward off for the past thirty years. And lately she wasn't convinced the doorway to another child was ready to be shut.

Mere picked up a block and tried to guide Lily's hand to build, but she swiped it away. Mere tried again.

Dale's hand stilled on Lily's arm. "She doesn't want to."

"I know she doesn't want to, but the OT says it's good for her fine motor development." Mere could hear the sharp edge in her own voice.

Dale's air of befuddlement had once charmed her, harmless in contrast to their father's unmoored aimlessness. Dale's professional drive gave him purpose, the kind her father never could sustain. As a civil engineer, he used mathematical formulas and principles from physics and materials science to ensure the structural integrity of bridges. Mere didn't understand all the equations, but she knew that most of his time was spent calculating how much stress and strain materials could withstand before they bent or broke. A metaphorical concept she was all too familiar with.

"Lately I feel like a bridge," she admitted quietly, "and I'm worried about my own structural integrity. I've been carrying too much, and I don't know how to reset."

Dale conceded then and leaned into her, which in turn made Lily press against her other side. Mere stayed upright beneath the combined weight of them both, her body holding even as something deep inside her wondered how much longer it could.

5

FRANKIE

Saturday, March 16, 2024

“Hey, where are the flashlights?” Frankie’s husband, Caleb, stood in the doorway with sleeping bags tucked under one arm and five different kinds of rope draped over the other.

“Why so much?” Frankie asked, raising an eyebrow. “Are there cattle where you’re camping?”

Caleb kept rummaging through the utility closet. He’d aged into an older version of the guy she’d met a little more than twenty years ago—same bone structure, just softened at the edges. Most days, she didn’t notice. But sometimes the thinning hair and the lines around his eyes startled her, as if the boy from Wellington Hall she’d first noticed on UC Blue Ridge’s campus had been covered in stage makeup to play an older version of himself, a strange sleight of time.

“Do you mind if Dale borrows your sleeping bag? He

doesn't have any gear, and since you're forcing us to bring him along, it's either your bag or he doesn't come."

She sighed as she pulled the emergency lantern from just inches beyond where he'd been looking and placed it in his empty hand. "It will be fine. Go and bond. Dale's your brother-in-law. Ask him how he's doing. See how it's been with Lily's autism diagnosis. Just . . . I dunno, communicate."

Caleb blinked at her, bewildered. "I think you might be confused about what a guys' camping trip actually entails."

"And I think you're all fools to go camping now. It's supposed to dump snow tonight." Janey's husband, Jack, and Caleb had planned the excursion as they did every few months. Both men were drawn to the outdoors, having grown up in similar situations with families who fished and hunted and did outdoorsy stuff that had never been a part of Frankie's childhood. Frankie had sexually coerced Caleb into bringing Dale along, implying she'd make it worth her husband's while once they got back.

In the parking lot after dinner last night, Frankie had picked up on Mere's discomfort. It was like a radar—no matter how far they drifted from each other's daily lives, she still knew the frequency her sister's body gave off when worry set in. Pearl's magical sway had made honesty feel easier, almost inevitable. Frankie really looked at her then, and the exhaustion was impossible to miss: the deep shadows under Mere's eyes, the way fatigue seemed carved into her face.

What is it? Mere asked. *Why are you looking at me like that?*

You look so tired, Frankie said, softening before Mere could grow defensive. *Does Lily let you get any sleep?*

Mere shook her head, eyes shining. *She still sleeps in the bed with me, Pancakes tucked up against her. Dale sleeps with fifty pounds of weighted blankets and it's like a coffin no one can penetrate.*

Frankie had tried to banish the image of her brother-in-law, stiff and vampire-like beneath his layers. *I'd love to take her*, she'd blurted. *Please let me. Dale can go camping with Caleb and Jack, and you can finally have a night to yourself.* She'd said it as if this were normal between them, the kind of sisterly favor that happened all the time. But it wasn't. Other families might have called it obligation, yet that wasn't the way the Gilmore sisters ever operated.

Oh yes, please, Mere answered too quickly. *I'll come get her before bedtime, but even if I could be alone in my home for a few hours . . . that would be really something.*

So now, the next evening, here they were—Caleb shrugging on his jacket, already planning for a tagalong, while brushing off Frankie's concern about the cold. "I dunno," he said. "There's something primal about sleeping outside, especially in the elements. Plus, we're going to a spot that's set up for it. Should be fine. I don't mind the cold."

Frankie rolled her eyes lovingly. "Yes, like true cavemen." She reached for the extra sleeping bag and put it down by the rest of the gear next to the front door.

"Did you ever call to confirm your oral surgery for Tuesday?" Frankie asked.

Caleb didn't look up. "Pretty sure they called me."

Her eyebrows shot up. "Pretty sure?"

He shrugged. "Okay, actually sure. They left a message yesterday, one o'clock Tuesday afternoon. It's all set."

"I thought it was in the morning. It got moved to the afternoon? And you didn't think to mention that?"

"I just did," he said, flashing the same charming smile Chloe had inherited, the one she used whenever she wanted to get away with something. "And what happens if I put it off again and reschedule?"

The oral surgery had already been delayed until the last possible second. The only thing Caleb hated more than missing work was a medical procedure. As a kid, he had meningitis, the bad kind, and nearly died from it. Ever since, hospitals, shots, and surgeries were all filed in his brain under one giant nope.

"First of all, you wouldn't be the one who would reschedule. I would have to do it for you. And if you even so much as think of canceling, I will rescind my chauffeur services and make you Uber both directions."

Frankie and Caleb were both fiercely independent. That balance was part of what made their marriage work. But this time, Frankie almost welcomed being needed. Not in the draining, everyday way parenting demanded, but in the way that made her feel steady and useful.

"You would not dare. Not when I am drugged and vulnerable."

Frankie knew he was teasing, though his words skimmed the bruise that pulsed just beneath her skin. Vulnerability sounded harmless in a man's mouth—a luxury—while for women it bore its cost in silence. She swallowed the urge to answer, unwilling to shatter the fragile lightness of their mood.

"You are not getting out of this," she said, leaning over to kiss his shoulder.

Frankie returned to the couch, picked up her phone, and resumed swiping through videos. She shouldn't be mindlessly scrolling. There was too much to do before Janey and her sons came over. Frankie worried the noise would be too much for Lily. Mere had given detailed instructions regarding Lily's sensory needs, diet, and evening routine. Mere also mentioned that Pancakes would need to come too, but that was fine with Frankie because their mutt, Ruby, got along with all dogs. Frankie assured her that she was a mother herself and was familiar with the basics of what it took to keep a tiny human alive.

Funny how Mere never thought to ask if she was capable when she left Frankie alone with their dad for those two years. Maybe that was why this new version of Mere—protective, checking in about Lily—scraped at something raw inside her. Back then, Frankie had wanted her sister's worry, her sister's care, but got nothing. She'd resented Mere so fiercely, knowing her neglect could have had dire consequences. Now she couldn't help but envy the maternal vigilance Mere poured into her child. Where had that care been when Frankie needed it most? The thought dragged her back to their last day at the Belmont house, the three of them together for the final time.

Their father had sat in the backyard smoking a blunt as Frankie and Mere packed up the house on that last day, preparing to take him to Washington state to live with his sister. The ivy had overtaken the backyard pergola, the one their father had built for their mother's birthday when she was dying, back when his manic phases led to bursts of productivity. Since it wasn't Frankie's responsibility to hire a gardener, the yard had long since been overtaken by weeds. It was essentially a giant tinderbox of kindling. By the time they smelled the smoke, the flames ran the length of the wooded structure. Frankie had found her father standing there, with the blunt in his mouth and the Zippo lighter still in his hands. She remembered thinking it all could have looked beautiful had it not been so terrifying. People often thought of fire as orange, but there were so many colors within the flames.

Even now, the memory clung to her, the way danger could look like beauty if you stared long enough. She carried that thought with her as she stepped into the kitchen, trying to shake the heat of it from her skin.

The snick of the door opening startled her, snapping her fully back to the present. When Janey walked in, Frankie almost didn't recognize her. Janey's hair was gone—cropped into a sharp pixie, the kind of cut that announces a shift, a woman cracking open and daring the world to notice.

"Oh my god!" Frankie exclaimed, rushing toward Janey, whose chestnut hair had never been shorter than her shoulders in all their thirty-five years of friendship. She reached out to touch it, half afraid this new version of Janey might forget that Frankie only ate grapes in pairs. Or she might forget how, during lightning storms, they were meant to meet on Frankie's deck and count the seconds together, waiting for the thunder. Frankie needed Janey to always be her North Star, unchanged and unwavering no matter what else shifted. "I love it! But oh my god, lady!"

Janey was grinning like a lunatic. "It's different, huh? I'm kind of obsessed with it. I should have done this years ago, but I never had the balls."

"And now you've grown said balls?" Frankie said, touching the base of Janey's neck, which she'd never studied this closely before. She noticed a tiny freckle there in the shape of a heart and pressed it lovingly with her index finger as if it were somehow lucky.

"With the separation, I figured it was either this or bangs, and bangs felt more like a pandemic solution—like sourdough starters or herb gardens. This," she said, pulling at the inch of hair left on her head, "feels like a fresh start of something for me."

Janey and Jack had been separated now for almost three months. They were calling it a trial separation, but Frankie wasn't sure how "trial" it really was. Janey had been unhappy in her marriage for years. Frustrated to the point of no return that Jack had never stepped up in parenting the boys the way Janey routinely asked him to. Even from the sidelines, watching their merry-go-round of empty promises and inevitable letdowns, punctuated by nagging and then more promises, was exhausting. While Frankie loved Jack, sometimes it felt like he belonged in Neverland with the other Lost Boys. On more than one occasion, Frankie had witnessed him come home after work, crack open a beer, and immediately start playing video games while he called over his shoulder, asking Janey what was for dinner. Janey blamed herself—they'd married young. But Jack still seemed to be waiting for his invitation to grow up. Caleb and Frankie were far from perfect, but from the beginning they'd mutually agreed to more of a partnership. Maybe it was because Frankie gave and then took in equal measure, while Caleb served as the steady, unwavering metronome she could set her heartbeat to.

"I think Jack hates it," Janey said, "but he hasn't said anything. He can't really say anything. It's not his hair, not anymore. Not that it was *his* hair." Janey's words were coming out all jumbled. She was nervous about what she'd done, so Frankie made sure the smile on her face could only be interpreted as sincere. Janey would be watching her intensely all evening, trying to read if Frankie was emitting even the slightest signal that Janey had made a huge, irreparable mistake about her hair, her marriage, or anything in between.

Janey was far too progressive a woman for someone like Jack, who grew up around Big Sky, where it was still expected that a wife prepared a hot meal at dinner, and women certainly didn't have hair that could cause others to mistake them for men. "I read somewhere that cutting hair helps heal past trauma," she added.

"Well, consider yourself completely healed," Frankie said, reaching out to tap the freckle heart on the back of Janey's neck one more time for good measure.

"Okay, we're heading off." Caleb walked in, coming over to kiss Frankie and then hug Janey. "Oh hey, I like your haircut."

Frankie beamed at Caleb, grateful for his ability to notice these things. Having two daughters had reshaped him, made him eager to stay in the loop about things the girls were calling "cool"—or whatever word had replaced it.

"So we'll be at Hollow Ridge. They've got the best setup for the kind of snowfall that's coming," Caleb said. Dale appeared from the hallway, and Lily followed close behind, tiptoeing toward the counter while clutching her globe—the one Mere had explained was her most prized possession.

Frankie had set out a big bowl of ice cream, and Lily made a beeline for it. Mere wouldn't love that Lily was being plied with sugar before dinner—but what Frankie's sister didn't know wouldn't hurt her. This was Frankie's first real chance to connect without Mere's watchful eye, and she was determined to graduate from a "fist bump" aunt to a full-on huggable one. With only a few hours to make it happen, she wasn't above a little strategic bribery.

"Is that the Golden Gate?" Frankie asked, pointing to the well-worn glass orb with San Francisco's iconic red bridge inside. When she righted the globe, the tiny cars began inching along the span. Frankie leaned her elbows on the kitchen island to meet Lily's eyes as the girl shook the globe and watched the cars crawl steadily across.

"Yeah." Dale's eyebrows lifted, a flicker of excitement breaking through his usual flatness. "I got that for her. You know the two main cables on the Golden Gate Bridge? Each one has exactly twenty-seven thousand, five hundred and seventy-two wires inside. Twenty-seven thousand, five hundred and seventy-two," he repeated, like the number itself should mean something to everyone standing in the kitchen. "They spun one wire back and forth over the towers more than two thousand three hundred times to help make a single cable. It's called cable spinning. The symmetry of it, the precision—it's . . . honestly kind of perfect."

Caleb made eye contact with Frankie, and the look on his face clearly said, *This better be the best damn BJ you've ever given me in exchange for babysitting Dale.* Frankie winked at him seductively to let him know she'd received the message loud and clear.

Dale was an odd duck. There wasn't another way Frankie could think to put it. He came into her sister's life immediately after Mere got out of a bad relationship. She had a pattern of dating guys who treated her like crap, and then Dale came along with his chinos and bizarre bridge knowledge and Mere swore he was the Second Coming. They'd met and married later in life—well, later in Dale's life, as he was eight years older than Mere—and he was approaching fifty by the time they had Lily. Frankie felt like she had lived a hundred lives before her big sister ever really started hers.

"Let's leave now. I want to get a hike in before it starts to snow," Caleb said, kissing Frankie quickly on the lips before heading out.

Ruby barreled in from outside, immediately greeting Pancakes as they launched into the compulsory sniffing ritual.

Frankie glanced at Lily, curious if she'd find it funny, but her face stayed neutral. So Frankie let it be, watching as the dogs spun in circles until Pancakes finally pulled away and curled up beneath the barstool where Lily perched, still working on her ice cream.

Janey set about making hot chocolate for everyone. With the teenagers tucked away in the game room, she and Frankie bundled up Lily and went out to the covered deck to wait for the snow. Frankie had asked Caleb to haul down one of the girls' old toddler chairs from the garage while he was gathering camping gear. Her daughters hadn't used them in more than a decade, but she was glad she'd kept them for moments like this. It felt good, almost bittersweet, to see child-sized furniture in the house again.

Seeing Lily on the chair, wrapped in a thick blanket, Frankie couldn't help but think of her own girls and their littleness. It was hard to believe that Rayna had been only a year older than Lily when Frankie finally stopped drinking. Not that it was a "finally," not necessarily. No one had put a gun to her head and told her it was time to stop. There were a lot of almosts when it came to her drinking. And still, in the end, she was never as bad as some of the other mothers had been these days during the PTA auctions for the girls' school. What was it with school functions and plying teachers, administration, and parents with copious amounts of alcohol? Was the idea that people would spend more money? Frankie was pretty sure there were ways to go about raising money while also keeping people's dignity intact.

Still, she sometimes ached for the years she'd blurred, when the girls were small and their needs came fast and loud. She hadn't meant to miss it. But in trying to quiet the noise, she'd dulled the joy too. When Mere got pregnant with Lily, Frankie had been secretly thrilled. It felt like a second chance, a way to relive the moments she'd lost through drinking. But Lily wasn't hers to hold on to. Access came in brief, careful windows, and so far, their relationship hadn't felt like a do-over at all.

"How do you ever get tired of this view?" Janey asked.

Janey had grown up just a few blocks from Frankie and Mere in Belmont. After Mere left for college, Frankie started sleeping at Janey's more often than she did at home with Ed. Janey had become the soft place she could always land, and her home was close enough that Frankie could slip over whenever things with Ed felt too sharp.

When it came time for college, Janey chose UC Blue Ridge—where Mere already was—and Frankie, determined to do something different, enrolled at UC Del Mar near Santa Barbara. She hadn't realized until she arrived that there was a deep rift between "NorCal," where she'd grown up, and "SoCal," where UC Del Mar was, but she soon learned that the divide was akin to a perpetual game of red rover. Every so often, NorCal would send someone across, only for SoCal's link to hold fast—because they'd rather break an arm than let *hella* into their vocabulary.

Frankie's start there quickly unraveled, in ways she never spoke about. Within a year she had transferred to UC Blue Ridge, and shortly after, she and Janey each started their families. For Frankie, home had never really been a place. It had always been Janey.

Frankie let out a long, pensive exhale. "I have to admit, when Caleb proposed we build on land, I wasn't thrilled about the idea of being removed from a neighborhood. Me being isolated away from people isn't necessarily good for my sobriety." Frankie stopped to look at Lily, curious how much of the conversation she was able to understand. But Lily was busy tipping her globe back and forth, watching the cars along the bridge, not paying any attention to Frankie. "But I don't know. I've just been feeling . . . itchy in my own life. Like I'm existing in a wool sweater I can't climb out of. Everyone needs something from me all the time—Caleb, the girls, even customers at the store who treat me like their therapist. I keep thinking if I could just get a little space, maybe I'd feel like myself again." Every day Frankie felt like the circus leader in the household and the lone performer responsible for retrieving all the fiery rings her family constantly tossed up in the air.

"But you love taking on other people's problems. That's kind of your whole thing," Janey said, turning her head to look at Frankie.

"I don't know how to interpret life advice from someone in the middle of what may or may not be a midlife crisis," Frankie said, scrunching her nose so Janey knew she wasn't entirely serious.

"I will walk out there and start hurling snowballs at you. Don't think I won't."

"Mom!" Chloe's voice sliced through the cold night air, sharp and panicked. She burst onto the deck, steps urgent, breath shallow. "They can't find Margaret's mom!"

The sound of her daughter's panic shot Frankie out of her chair like a cannon. The legs scraped hard against the wood.

"Margaret and her mom were supposed to go to San Francisco for her audiogram appointment this weekend. But Mrs. Hoover isn't answering her phone. Her family's freaking out."

Chloe's presence overtook the space as usual, all spark and static.

"I just saw Brie yesterday," Frankie offered, as if that would settle it.

Chloe stared blankly at Frankie.

"When's the last time anyone heard from her?" Frankie tried again.

Frankie had always admired her daughter's ability to read a room and then rewire its current. But right now, it felt like overkill.

Chloe frowned, exasperated. "Mom, you're not getting it. Mr. Hoover is about to call the police."

A slow chill ran through Frankie's arms. Brie hadn't responded to her text earlier during their driving lesson.

"They were supposed to leave a while ago. I've been texting Margaret all morning and she was totally ignoring me, but when I finally called, she said her mom's missing." Chloe's voice broke. "Like *gone*. Car's in the driveway, keys on the counter. And her phone's off."

Chloe looked at Frankie the way she had during the worst days of lockdown, like she should somehow know the unknowable. Frankie hated that look, but not as much as the newer one she'd been getting lately. The one that said, *Mom doesn't know anything at all.*

Frankie reached for the phone in her lap, fingers clumsy. "I'm sure she's okay," Frankie offered, but her voice betrayed her. "Give me a minute. I'll call around."

Chloe returned to her phone, violently texting as she slid the door closed behind her.

Frankie opened Instagram, hoping for the easy answer. A sign of life. Maybe the green dot next to Brie's name, but that would have been too easy. Across from her, Janey was doing the same, scrolling through their mutual friends online.

"When Chloe comes back out, ask who Brie's closest to. I don't really know who her friends are," Janey said, not looking up.

Frankie didn't know either. Brie never offered much beyond the margins of sobriety, and Frankie hadn't pushed. With Brie still clinging to the belief that she could control her drinking, not yet accepting her powerlessness over alcohol, every conversation between them as sponsee and sponsor felt like borrowed time—too fragile for small talk, too precious for anything but the truth.

"I remember when I couldn't get ahold of Jack for an entire day," Janey said, still scrolling through her contacts. "He was out hiking, no service. He warned me ahead of time, but after eight hours I was livid. Then he calls on his way home all casual, like, *Did you really leave me seven messages?* And I'm like, *Yes, we have children—what if something happened?*"

She shook her head, her fury at Jack so easy to conjure it almost made Frankie smile. That was Janey—always able to summon a storm at will. "The difference between the male and female brain, I swear," Janey continued. "Maybe Brie just went for a trail run and her phone died. I know last year she was always at my gym, training for a Spartan. Not lately, though." Janey paused. "But if her husband wants to involve the police . . ."

Frankie stayed quiet. Brie did hikes and trail runs; it wasn't out of the realm of possibility. And cell service was notoriously bad in those parts.

"Brie is sober, right? She goes to your meetings?" Janey asked, though it wasn't really a question. Frankie had told Janey when Brie first came—she couldn't help it. It had been the first time sobriety felt purposeful in a way that went beyond herself. Like Frankie's decision to speak out publicly about being a sober mom had reached someone. Helped someone. Janey knew they had been working together, but Frankie never shared anything further than that. Never anything that was discussed inside the meetings. That part of the program relied on anonymity and was sacred. Even Janey's status as the closest person to Frankie didn't warrant the breach of that trust.

"Yeah, she is," Frankie replied. It would have been so easy to unburden herself, to tell Janey about their last conversation at the arboretum, Brie's unswollen ankle, her weird declaration about wanting to flee the country. But Janey wasn't an alcoholic;

she wouldn't understand that sometimes Frankie didn't feel safe inside her own mind. That you just needed to share the darkest part of your thoughts, out loud, with another alcoholic so it wasn't rattling around up there all chaotic and dangerous. Janey didn't understand that Frankie's thoughts could become even more poisonous than the alcohol.

No, Frankie couldn't share their last conversation. As much as she hated to admit it, she didn't want Brie's past used against her. She didn't want Janey drawing a straight line between Brie's history and her disappearance, as if her addiction was the simple solution. Frankie felt fiercely protective of the idea that the two things weren't connected. That Brie's recovery was real and intact.

Plus, saying it out loud felt like tempting fate, like naming the fear might somehow make it true. She knew that thought wasn't rational, but she also knew she couldn't explain it. Not to someone who hadn't lived with addiction and recovery. Not even Janey.

As Janey continued to speculate and backtrack, Frankie stared out into the dark. The snow didn't fall so much as settle—slow, silent, each flake insistent on layering over the world until everything appeared calm, even as it was quietly being smothered.

"Lily, will you come sit on my lap?" Frankie opened her blanket, patting the empty space.

Lily hesitated, her almond-shaped eyes scanning Frankie's face, deciphering whether or not Frankie was someone she could trust.

"Come on, I'll give you squeezes." Mere had swung by Frankie's house after their dinner with Pearl, dropping off a binder so she'd have time to absorb the contents before Lily arrived. Inside was a meticulous guide—doctor's reports, PT and OT diagrams, Lily's routine—carefully curated by Mere for anyone entrusted with Lily's care.

Doesn't Dale need this? Frankie had joked.

I have a special one just for him. This is for other people.

Other people. It had landed like a slap.

Still, Lily moved slowly toward her, a little clumsy and off-kilter in her fleece blanket with her globe pressed firmly up to her chest. When she climbed into Frankie's lap, she didn't just sit; she leaned in, *hard*. All sharp elbows and stiff limbs. Despite the blankets and warm sweatshirt between them, she landed with a thump of pressure against Frankie's chest.

After Frankie caught her breath, she relaxed into the weight of having her niece in her arms. At Lily's age her girls had existed to her as an unrelenting vortex of wants and needs. Of seeking and touching. A conveyor belt of physical contact so endless that, by the time Caleb would reach for her at night, Frankie recoiled from the sensation of yet another person who needed something more from her body. Frankie inhaled the top of Lily's head, her sparse blond hair all wispy and elusive as her girls' had been.

Lily smelled like Mere, clean and freshly pressed with the faintest hint of a lavender and maybe honeysuckle shampoo. By the time Frankie had gotten sober, her girls' little-kid scent had already passed her by, one more regret in a blur of apologies and missed moments.

Frankie closed her eyes, anchoring herself. She wrapped the blanket around them both, taking her time in her tenderness, wanting to cloak them in a time machine and hold them there for as long as Lily would allow.

Stay here, stay in it. The voice inside her head always sounded like Pearl. But even with Lily pressed close, worry threaded through her like a spiderweb in the breeze, clinging where she didn't want it. And beneath it all, humming low in the corners of her mind, a question.

Where is Brie?

6

MERE

Saturday, March 16, 2024

The house felt cavernous without Lily and Dale. Silence pressed in, so complete that Mere could hear the creak of the floorboards, the hum of the refrigerator, even the faint catch of her own breath. She almost reached down to pat for Pancakes, who usually greeted her as urgently as if she were returning from war, even if she had been gone only five minutes. But Pancakes was with Lily this evening. For the first time in years, Mere was alone.

She moved slowly through the living room, fingertips grazing the back of the couch, the edge of the bookshelf, the sturdy red door to Dale's office. The one she had chosen. She could still see herself standing in the paint aisle at Home Depot, drawn to that particular swatch for its quiet strength. A deep, purposeful red. The office was right off the main living space, so the color had mattered. She hadn't known then how much she'd grow to resent that door.

During the pandemic, it became a boundary. Dale closed it so he could work. And Mere stayed on the other side. She taught school via Zoom with a baby strapped to her, juggling lesson plans and feedings. The door became a symbol of everything. Dale's ability to shut out the world while she stayed inside it, drowning.

She had majored in English with a concentration in creative writing. Teaching had always been the plan, but writing—that had been the dream. She'd even started a novel once, based on a short story she'd published years earlier called "One Red Wall." It followed a woman slowly unraveling after her boyfriend tried to convince her that the red wall in their home was actually black. That she was color-blind. That she was losing her mind.

She stopped writing because everything else took priority. And when Lily's milestones no longer matched what the books promised, Mere left her teaching job. Lily's needs were all-consuming. She could drain and revive Mere in the same breath, like a tide that never fully receded.

At first, Dale hadn't noticed anything unusual, but Mere's gut told her otherwise. At each pediatrician visit, she caught herself asking more questions. Lily was bright but unsocial, endlessly patient with tasks like spinning wheels or aligning objects, and her speech was delayed. Since starting therapy last fall, she'd made great strides. The sensory seeking, though, was still a concern. She flapped her hands when overstimulated, which was often, and sought pressure in ways that worried Mere. As a younger toddler, she would hurl herself into furniture, trying to feel something solid. Now, thanks to occupational therapy, those needs were met with weighted blankets and nightly massages before bed, when Mere would read silly books about a pigeon who was just as baffled by the world as they were.

Lily also struggled with sleep and had a deep aversion to textures. Anything "imy"—her word for slimy—like eggs, yogurt, or bananas was off-limits. So were "icky," or "sticky," foods like peanut butter, which made her pinch her fingers tightly together in distress.

Their days were filled with therapy: occupational therapy to help her tolerate sensations and learn basic motor skills like holding a crayon or brushing her teeth; physical therapy to build strength and coordination so she could climb stairs or run without stumbling. Caring for Lily was a full-time job, but it was one Mere accepted without question, a devotion born of her fierce wish for her daughter to flourish.

Upstairs, she stretched out diagonally across the bed, reveling in the sheer luxury of not having to share it, not having to consider others before herself. Caring for Lily had trained her to anticipate each need before it was spoken, to live in hyperalertness. It was a familiar posture, one she had learned long before she became a mother. Back then, the person she was managing wasn't her daughter—it was her own mother. The same vigilance that now kept weighted blankets washed and therapy appointments scheduled had once kept pill bottles organized and middle-of-the-night alarms set. And always, alongside the women she loved, there were the men who slipped responsibility through her fingers: Ed disappearing into smoke and excuses, Dale retreating behind a red door. Two women she would have given anything to keep whole, two men she could never rely on. Love had made her a caretaker; neglect had made her a custodian.

Now, with the duvet spread cool and smooth beneath her palms, the pillows a pile claimed all for herself, she found that the absence of responsibility left her thoughts unguarded, open to the memories she usually kept buried under routine. Her mind flashed an image of the charts she used to keep at sixteen—symptoms color coded by severity, morphine dosages penciled into margins, reminders of when to switch from antinausea meds to steroids. She ached for that younger version of herself, the one whose peers were going to football games and shopping for prom dresses while she was memorizing the subtle difference between her mother's "tired" and "incoherent," arguing with pharmacists about refills, and checking nightly to be sure her father hadn't left a joint smoldering in the ashtray.

She'd given up sleepovers and sleep itself, setting alarms for middle-of-the-night medications. She learned to change soiled bedding, to clean bedsores with baby wipes when the hospice nurse didn't come on weekends. Before she became a legal adult, she could insert a suppository without flinching, tell when dehydration meant an ER trip was coming, and recognize the quiet way someone died—not dramatic, like the movies depicted, but real and ordinary demise: appetite fading, skin cooling, the brightness behind their eyes dimming like a porch light unscrewing itself.

That was high school for her. Grief and caretaking, not dances or late-night drives.

But grief wasn't the only thing she'd folded away. There was Adrienne, her first real crush, a girl. Adrienne was electric, a live wire that reminded Mere there were parts of herself she longed to explore. Then her mom died, and with the loss came a decision: to close that door. To choose boys. To keep things simple. Agreeable. Safe.

She told herself it was just a phase, that she'd been too young to know anything for certain. Easier to follow the path already expected of her. Easier to pick the version of love that wouldn't invite more cruelty, more risk. She'd chosen Dale. And she loved him. But sometimes, in quiet moments like this, she wondered if she had also chosen him because he was steady enough to anchor her when she'd already weathered too much instability.

Now, years later, lying sprawled in the vastness of her bed, she was beginning to think her definition of fullness needed to shift. For so long she had equated fullness with stability: a marriage that looked steady, a home that stayed intact, a life that didn't invite risk. But staring up at the ceiling now, she felt the hollowness inside that steadiness. What good was safety if it left her lonely? What good was choosing simple if it meant carving out the parts of herself that once reached for more—for Adrienne, for joy, for a love that felt alive? Maybe fullness wasn't about anchoring herself against the chaos, but about letting herself want again, even if it came with instability.

That thought unsettled her, but it also reminded her of what she could hold on to in this moment. She picked up her phone and dialed Frankie, wanting to make sure it was a good time to get Lily.

"Hey, I don't want to worry you," Frankie offered, her voice low, "and we don't really know if this is anything yet, but . . . there's a mom from the girls' school. She's missing. Her name's Brie Hoover. No one's seen her since this morning. It's kind of freaking everyone out up here. But Lily's safe with me, I promise."

Mere heard the brush of a kiss, then Lily's familiar murmur, a low grunt of comfort rather than complaint.

"What do you mean, missing?" she asked. "Who is she?"

Frankie explained. Brie's daughter, Margaret, was Chloe's best friend. Mere realized she hadn't known that. She'd never thought much about the orbit of people who made up her sister's life—the other moms, the school friends, the daily exchanges Mere wasn't a part of. There was a whole rhythm to Frankie's world she had stopped trying to keep time with.

"But no one thinks it's serious?" Mere asked, trying to place the name, the face.

"We don't know," Frankie said.

When the call ended, Mere stayed in the silence a moment longer. She used to feel like more of a whole person. Or maybe just someone who believed that wholeness was possible. She closed her eyes, but her mind didn't settle.

Somewhere nearby, a woman was missing. Mere didn't know why that fact lingered the way it did. Only that it did.

She grabbed her keys from the counter. She was going to pick up Lily. The thought of her daughter's small body curled against her in the night felt like the only anchor she had. Still, as she stepped out into the cold, the hollowness remained in her chest, louder now in the quiet, demanding to be heard.

7

FRANKIE

Sunday, March 17, 2024

By the following day, there was still no word from Brie, and the sense of unease that had been simmering quietly erupted into full-blown panic across town. Volunteer search parties had been organized and dispatched to comb the nearby hiking trails, places Margaret and their other family members said her mother visited regularly.

After Mere picked up Lily at bedtime last night, another two feet of snow had fallen, blanketing the hills and woods, making the search more desperate with every passing hour. Cold like that wasn't just uncomfortable; it was dangerous. Brie's photo was everywhere now, circulating through neighborhood Facebook groups, Instagram stories, even the local news. Mostly family shots, centered by one main image from Christmas in front of a glowing tree. Brie looked small beside it, glassy-eyed but smiling.

Frankie had studied that photo, combed through every caption and comment, searching for any hint that her drinking might have been acknowledged. Nowhere did Brie's family mention her history of alcohol abuse. Frankie suspected Brie had done everything she could to shield her relapses from her kids, but it was hard to imagine she could have hidden them from her husband.

Frankie had even gone to the Sunday meeting that morning, hoping Brie might just show up, slip into the back row like nothing had happened. But she couldn't concentrate, not with Brie's face on every phone and the steady thrum of worry running through her.

Gossip had always been a problem for Frankie. Even in sobriety, she still felt the tug of secrets, the thrill of being the one who knew. It wasn't until her sponsor, Pearl, called her out a few years back that Frankie began to understand what was really driving it.

Her favorite target had always been Dale. His bumbling incompetence, once harmless, had started to feel dangerous after Mere had Lily. Frankie couldn't help but draw comparisons to their father. She'd confided in Janey that she was afraid Mere was stuck in the same pattern—that Dale was just a slightly more functional version of Ed, and that Mere would never get to stop being the responsible party.

Janey had jumped in, recognizing the same exhaustion in her own marriage—her husband's inability to multitask, his blindness to the mental load she carried. They fed off each other, their frustration gaining momentum, tossing around terms like *weaponized incompetence*. And maybe it was true. Especially with Janey's husband. And Dale.

After talking it through with Pearl, though, Frankie began to see how dangerous that kind of talk could be for her own marriage. How easy it was to get trapped in a feedback loop of resentment, a vacuum of male-hating toxicity that felt like solidarity but might actually be poison.

All of which was why, when the meeting ended today, she checked her motivation carefully to ensure she was being driven by genuine concern—and not gossip—as she stood and cleared her throat. Her voice came out louder than she meant it to. "I just want to let everyone know, in case you haven't heard already, that Brie Hoover hasn't been seen since yesterday morning. Her family's looking, and if anyone's been in contact with her, please reach out."

Back at home, after an hour of pacing the living room and refreshing her phone, Frankie finally called Janey. They were both starting to go stir-crazy. Frankie needed to move, needed to *do* something. So they decided to drive up to Hollow Ridge to try to find the guys, to intercept them and explain what was going on.

Hollow Ridge stretched for miles, its name taken from the scooped-out granite hollows left by glaciers thousands of years ago. Locals said the wind still carried through those bowls, bending sound in strange ways. In certain pockets, sounds came out sharp sometimes and muffled others, like the mountain couldn't decide whether to hold your secrets or give them away. With multiple entrances, it wasn't like the family-friendly campsites they usually visited with bathrooms and bear boxes. There was no way to know where the men had set up. This was wide-open wilderness, the kind Frankie had almost forgotten existed—too vast, too unchecked. At least in the arboretum, people and nature mingled close enough to look out for one another.

"There's no cell service out here," Janey said, confirming the futility of their search.

"Let's just get out and walk around. I can't sit in this car anymore." Frankie put her fingers up next to the heater for one final blast of warm air before venturing into the tundra.

It felt hopeless—there was nothing ahead but a blanket of white—but she was jittery, like she'd had too much coffee, even though she hadn't gone past her usual two cups. The *not doing something* made her feel complicit in a situation she didn't yet understand.

As they trudged through the snow, they didn't see the guys. They didn't see anyone. Or hardly anything.

"You like my hair though, right?" Janey asked.

She had a beanie pulled down tight, but Frankie still looked over like she could see it.

"I like that you did something for yourself. That's what I like most. You look gorgeous—truly," Frankie said.

She hadn't been sure at first. But after seeing her again, Frankie thought the cut had settled into Janey's face like it always belonged there.

"Jack hates it," Janey said, frowning.

"You already told me that." Frankie laughed a little. "And anyway, who cares what he thinks . . . right?"

"Right. You're right," Janey said, stopping mid-step. She grabbed hold of a nearby tree for balance, then dropped onto her back in the snow. She started moving her arms and legs back and forth, making a snow angel, just like their kids used to do after a fresh powder like this.

Frankie lay down beside her, her head just inches from Janey's, and mirrored her movements. Two snow angels, side by side. When they finished, they stayed there, staring up at the sky, their faces close, breath clouding between them.

When their kids were little, Janey used to come over with a bottle of wine. They'd curl up on Frankie's couch, watching the baby monitors, whispering—holding their breath anytime the green lights flickered toward red. Chloe was such a light sleeper, but all Frankie wanted was enough quiet to get through at least one bottle. At first, she told herself the wine brought them closer. That those hazy, late-night conversations were a kind of touchstone. Proof of how deep their friendship ran.

But Frankie always took it too far.

Over time, the bonds that held them together, those easy synchronicities that once defined them, started to dull. What had once been light and golden became muted. Frankie couldn't see it then, when she was in it, but the alcohol numbed out the good just as much as the bad.

"Hey, remember when our babies were babies and you'd come over and I'd drink too much? I swore that was the most fun we ever had back then," Frankie said.

"Well, that's just downright depressing." Janey's cheeks were bright red from being in the snow, but she turned her head so she could watch Frankie and wait for her explanation.

"No, I swore I was crushing it as a mom. That I figured out a way to cheat the system. Cure the monotony and tedium of diaper blowouts and colic. We had each other to do it with, and I wouldn't let myself feel sad that I didn't have a mom to be a grandma to my kids," Frankie said, her face starting to go numb, but she was working out her feelings in real time, so she wanted to keep going. "Then it was like I found how to have my cake and eat it too. I was encouraged to drink because motherhood was hard, and it was my free pass. Come August, the supermarket had a back-to-school-aisle sign hanging above the wines. I felt so vindicated. But then everyone else, like you and all the other moms, seemed to have the 'in moderation' thing down, and I was blacking out, leaving my kids in the bathtub basically unsupervised." Frankie was on a roll. "Not to mention the adventurous sex Caleb and I had when I was free from any inhibitions. Never mind that my body was stretched and jigglier because I'd birthed two kids—I felt sexy when I was wasted, and that made our love life more exciting."

Janey was sitting up now. They were both freezing, in at least a two-foot wall of snow, but Janey never rushed Frankie. She gave her exactly the amount of time Frankie needed to be understood.

"And then it all just stopped working," Frankie said, sitting up too.

Frankie had already made amends to Janey, who had really

made her work for it. Janey was always going to forgive Frankie, but not until Frankie promised to "bring back all the things inside her that drinking had stolen from her, all the things that made her magic"—Janey's phrasing, not Frankie's.

They both stood up, shaking off the snow. Frankie started jumping up and down to get the blood flowing back into her body. She'd be cranking up the heater when they returned to the car.

"I have a sinking, sick feeling about Brie," Frankie said. "I don't want to say anything aloud, and I refuse to believe this is because she struggles with alcohol. I'm scared it's something more sinister. But I can't just sit inside this feeling anymore. I'm going crazy."

"You have never been good with those uncomfy feelings." Janey turned her head away and looked up at the sky. The snow from the night before was no longer falling, but it had left behind thick drifts that made the trail uneven and hard to navigate. Each step back to the car sank deep, the crusted surface giving way beneath their boots. With every stride, Frankie felt her unease settle in a little further, as if the quiet around them had been replaced by something unspoken and pressing.

Once they reached her car, the cold still clinging to her clothes, her thoughts caught in the white silence they'd just weathered.

"Where is she?" Janey asked one more time before she opened the car door.

"*Brie!*" Frankie started calling out, her voice desperately trying to break through the wall of white. "*Brie!* Where are you?"

She waited and listened like Brie could call back and say, *Here I am. I'm right here.*

After stopping to search one of the wooded trails Margaret had mentioned to Chloe, Frankie dropped Janey off at the gym she owned and retreated to the one place Frankie knew she'd never have to be alone inside her own head: the bookstore she'd opened in the spring of 2019, right across the street from Janey's own successful business in the heart of downtown Big Sky.

It was nice to be consumed by something that was good for her, and in the bookstore, that usually meant a bustling business filled with strangers, family, friends, and hundreds of stories to get lost in. Most days, customers shuffled around, treating the store more like a personal library. But today there was a nervous hum, a constant circulation of heads looking around instead of down into their books.

Frankie checked her phone again and texted Chloe.

Any update?

The reply came almost instantly.

No.

She liked to make her daily bank run around this time, but since it was Sunday and the bank was closed, she'd brought change from the safe in her office instead. As she moved through the store, she caught sight of Professor Sam, a regular who taught at the university. Tall and lean, with a swimmer's build, he was easy to spot. Frankie knew he was waiting to say hello, probably with an extra coffee in hand—just like he had every day last week after his swims. Already her palms felt clammy. In the warmth of her store, she peeled off her snow-hiking layers, down to jeans and a thermal, then adjusted her bracelets and smoothed her hair, readying herself for their familiar, flirtatious exchange.

"Hey, Sam," Frankie said as he emerged from behind a display of greeting cards, hands empty. "What, no coffee today?" She liked that he smelled faintly of chlorine.

He smiled, a little apologetic. "Line was too long. Trying to squeeze in some work before I meet my niece for coffee while she studies on campus. She thinks her girlfriend is about to propose. I'm hoping to talk her out of it—she's way too young!"

Frankie gave him a look and said, "And what exactly would you know about marriage?"

Sam's shrug said, *Fair enough*. It was known all over town that Sam was a chronic bachelor and hot commodity. "Marriage wasn't really in the cards for me. Feels too . . . like what everyone does. No offense."

"Oh, none taken," Frankie said, genuinely unbothered. Even George Clooney eventually found Amal. But she recognized marriage wasn't for everyone. In her case, the idea of not marrying Caleb had never crossed her mind. Of course, back then, she didn't know what she didn't know about the true meaning of "in sickness and in health." In her case, it had looked like him accepting her alcoholism and loving her through it, and recently, she'd walked him through the death of his dad, whom Caleb had considered his best friend. Marriage wasn't all heart eyes and skipping on the beach, Frankie had explained to Pearl recently, complaining that she'd grown weary of their pecks that almost never included tongue. *You know*, Pearl said, *a quiet home isn't boredom—it's serenity.*

Frankie noticed the way Sam's eyes lingered as she typed her code into the register.

"That's an unusual ring," he said, nodding toward the counter where she had absentmindedly slipped off her peridot engagement band, the same color as her eyes.

Caleb had told her, when he proposed, that if eyes were the windows to the soul, he wanted to spend forever swimming in hers. She picked up the ring and slid it back onto her finger.

"Your husband is lucky," Sam added, with a small, deliberate smile.

She let her face flush as she blinked through her lashes.

Frankie had been doing this since she was a teenager, relishing the quiet power of attention, learning how to tilt it in her favor. Her mother had died right around the time Frankie realized the effect of a lingering glance, the subtle shift of her body, the way desire could be summoned and steered. And while she was powerless to stop her mom from dying or Mere from leaving her with their dad, she could make herself feel wanted. That was its own kind of high.

Now, at forty-one, she worried that power might be slipping. But sobriety had given her something else—something steadier, more real. And somehow, it still drew in men like Sam.

It was all harmless fun, she told herself.

Sam leaned against the counter, his quiet confidence settling into the space between them. He gave the impression of someone who didn't wake up each day with a list of people to answer to. Someone who had carved out a life on his own terms. Maybe that was what caught like envy in her chest—not just the flirtation but the idea of a life that wasn't constantly negotiated.

Frankie wasn't sure whether she craved that kind of freedom or just wanted to brush up against it for a moment. At meetings she'd admitted, if only vaguely, that Sam was a welcome distraction. Not a real threat. Just something to break up the rhythm.

Because Caleb, as steady and good as he was, didn't stir her like the idea of Sam did. It wasn't about love. She loved Caleb. That had never been the question. But the current between them, the low, steady charge that used to hum beneath everything, had quieted. Not gone out, just mellowed into something safe. Maybe that was what all marriages became eventually. Still, she missed the tension. The flicker of being seen in a way that made her stand taller without realizing it.

Time had only made Caleb more steadfast in his devotion, surer of their life together. He'd settled into their marriage like it was a destination, finding comfort in the certainty of it. He seemed to take actual pleasure in the "growing old" part of their vows. Frankie, on the other hand, felt herself tugging in the opposite direction. Not because she wanted to leave, but because she wanted to remember what it felt like to still be becoming.

Maybe that was why the smallest, stupidest things, like the laundry basket Caleb never put back or the trail of white T-shirts that always stopped short of the hamper, could spark something restless in her. It was never about the mess. It was about the nagging fear that this was it.

"Okay, fine," Sam said and laughed, raising his hands in mock surrender. "I'll stop shamelessly flirting. Can you point me toward short fiction? Looking for Carver or Flannery O'Connor."

He didn't need directions. He'd been in the store enough times to know where everything was. But Frankie told him anyway.

"Second aisle, left-hand side." Her voice came out slower than usual, like she wanted to make the moment last a second longer.

He smoothed his shirt and hesitated, just enough for her to register the shift in his expression. Disappointment, maybe. Or perhaps that was her own projection. She almost asked if he knew Brie Hoover was missing. She didn't think he had anything useful to add, but it would've been a reason to keep him there.

She felt guilty for the thought. Because here she was, distracted by the way his shirt hugged his arms, by the silver in his curls that reminded her of McDreamy from *Grey's Anatomy*. Whatever this was, it didn't exist outside the bookstore. And as long as it stayed contained, she could still call it harmless.

As she watched him walk toward the literature section, the idea of Sam felt like—what had Brie called it?—*the magic of sleepaway camp for grown-ups.* A break from real life, the illusion of freedom, just long enough to forget what you had to return to.

The quiet at home was unsettling. Like something could break it open at any moment. Before she and Caleb built their 3,800-square-foot dream house, they had lived in a cramped, single-story starter on the other side of town. It was where they carried their newborn daughters home, where they should have been wrapped in sweetness. Instead, Frankie remembered nights she'd rather forget—nights of pouring another glass of wine to dull the raw throbbing of early motherhood, when the relentlessness of it all only reminded her how motherless she was. She had wanted Donna to be there, to see Chloe and Rayna, to be the grandmother she never got to be. That ache was forever seeping through the walls of that first house.

It was permeating her when Mere hinted that things were getting serious with Dale. By then, Frankie already had Chloe and Rayna, so Janey offered to watch the girls and allow the four of them to go on a double date. It was their first and their last. Frankie had been trying, in her own way, to let Mere back in. She'd even asked her sister to stand beside Janey as co–maid of honor when she married Caleb. For a while, it almost worked. Phone calls. Little stitches of connection. But once Dale entered the picture, Mere slipped back to the periphery. Less a sister, more a recurring guest star.

Frankie still remembered that dinner. Dale's odd tangents had her and Caleb exchanging looks over their wineglasses, silently asking, *What is this guy even talking about?* But Mere seemed enchanted, and Frankie told herself her sister's happiness had to be enough. She didn't believe Dale was the one, not really, but when the courthouse wedding came, she smiled, raised her glass, and clinked in celebration. What she couldn't stop herself from wondering was why they had bothered with a wedding at all.

For years, Dale stayed mostly in the background, until the night Frankie spiraled in front of her daughters. That was when he surprised her, stepping in, pulling the kids out of the room, protecting them in a way she couldn't. At the time, she saw only red, humiliated. Later, after working it through with Pearl and in meetings, she admitted she was grateful. But gratitude didn't erase the sting. Even now, she preferred to keep Dale at a distance, regarding him in the same way she thought of that first house, which became a place she couldn't live inside anymore. Both were something tolerable in the moment, but ultimately temporary.

"I'm home!" Frankie called, dropping her keys on the kitchen island.

She received no response. Only the sound of her own voice bounced back off the high ceilings. The girls, she figured, must still be downtown passing out flyers about Brie, and Caleb would be home soon from camping. She stood in the entryway a beat longer, shoes still on, resisting the urge to rush forward into the stillness.

There had been a golden era once, before everything fractured. Back when their mom was still alive, when their dad was just their dad and not his illness, when Frankie and Mere were like two trees growing side by side, stretching toward the sun, their branches reaching upward into an enmeshed entanglement that made it almost impossible to know where one of them ended and the other began.

And then Mere went and ruined everything. Her decision to attend UC Blue Ridge, four hours north of where Frankie would be stuck home alone with their dad, who was steadily becoming more and more unstable, meant the end of Frankie's trust in her sister. She had Janey to pick up the pieces. Nothing catastrophic occurred when it was just Frankie and her dad—the fire didn't happen until Mere returned to help move him up to live with Aunt Gina—but it could have, and for Mere's betrayal, Frankie was perfectly capable of doling out punishment forever. Her ability to hold a grudge was a point of pride she wore like a badge of honor.

After Mere left for college, Frankie never knew what to expect when she came home from school and walked into the nine hundred square feet of cramped clutter that was their house in the Bay. Sometimes she was met with the distracted, chain-smoking man who watched *Jeopardy!* and told her to make dinner; other times it was the slurring, unpredictable one who mistook her for someone he could talk to like a friend, or worse, like an enemy. He was always in the living room screaming at the TV—at politicians, at commercials, at no one. Full volume, veins bulging in his neck, like the people on-screen could actually hear him.

Frankie would slip past the hallway without making a sound and duck into the laundry room, shutting the door behind her. She'd turn on the dryer, even if it was empty. The steady hum was the only thing that made the house feel bearable. The sound dulled everything else—his voice, her fear, the loneliness of a home that didn't know how to hold her.

That was the first time she learned how to disappear.

The second came during her first quarter at UC Del Mar, which was all she lasted there before following her sister and Janey up to UC Blue Ridge. Something had happened, something she still didn't have the right description for.

By then, she already knew how to listen for footsteps. How to read the mood in the air before she ever crossed the hallway. Survival had always depended on sensing the shift before it arrived.

Which was why even now, in a house she owned, in a life she built from scratch, silence made her skin crawl. She opened the fridge just to do something. The light cast a glow over rows of yogurt, berries, and leftover Thai.

When Frankie's phone rang, the sound made her jump. It was Pearl. For a moment, she thought about letting it go to voicemail—despite nearly ten years of proof that talking to Pearl was always good for her.

From the first time Frankie heard Pearl speak at a women's meeting, Pearl had made something click within her. Back then, in early recovery, she assumed sober women must all be dull. How could they laugh or carry any lightness when the only joy Frankie knew lived in those blissful sips? She didn't know how to live, let alone live without alcohol.

Pearl shattered that belief. Weathered and sharp, creative and funny, she could take down the most stoic man with a single line. Her face told the story of a hard life. There was a toughness in her eyes, the kind that came from years of squaring up against the world and refusing to flinch. Creases lined her mouth, pointing to her decades of chain-smoking, though she'd managed to quit for good, finally even giving up the nicotine gum. *Coffee's the one vice I'll never let go*, she liked to say, looking up at the sky as if addressing God herself directly. Not God *himself*, because in Pearl's world God was most definitely female—and she wouldn't hear another word about it.

She laughed often, a throaty smoker's cough woven through the sound, and every time Frankie heard it, she teased Pearl to get it checked. Pearl's humor and presence radiated exactly what Frankie had been desperate to find in sobriety: proof that hope was possible.

Pearl's story strengthened the argument. She was the child of two alcoholics, her twin brother had died of a heart attack on a Yosemite trail, and she herself had once lost twelve hard-earned sober years to a one-year relapse. She never had children, and only married for the first time in her late fifties. Yet here she was—back in the program, alive, unflinching, the sponsor Frankie hadn't known she needed until she found her.

"I just wanted to check in and see how you're handling everything," Pearl said lovingly into the phone.

"I've been super distracted. There's weird shit happening."

"All the more reason for you to call me, my dear," Pearl said, in a voice that made her sound like the Big Bad Wolf from "Little Red Riding Hood."

"You're totally right. I'm really worried with Brie missing," Frankie said, keeping her voice steady. She filled Pearl in on her exchange with Brie at the arboretum but left out the part about the gummies. She'd meant to give them to Pearl on Friday, but somehow hadn't. An honest mistake, she told herself—too much going on, too many moving parts. Pearl's stance on *substances other than alcohol* was absolute, but Frankie convinced herself she could hold on to them a little longer. They were still at the bottom of her bag, untouched. She could handle it. Pearl's protectiveness could be intense, even disproportionate. But Frankie had made it this far without a mother, and she guarded her autonomy fiercely. The problem wasn't that she didn't trust Pearl. It was that she knew what happened when she let herself need someone too much.

Pearl suggested they message the text chain with all the regulars from their meeting to help keep the line of communication about Brie open in case anyone missed Frankie's announcement. Pearl was surprisingly tech savvy, as she refused to be one of those "stubborn boomers" who couldn't get with the times simply because change felt overwhelming. *I'll be damned if I'm going to let an iPhone be the thing that takes me out in the end*, she had joked recently when she unpackaged a new phone because she wanted one with the best camera. She loved photography.

When they got off the call, Frankie's phone dinged with a text chain including thirty-two women from their phone list. She found it endearing that the last time they messaged was to say happy birthday to Sue, a retired English teacher who frequented Frankie's store and had recently celebrated thirty-two years of sobriety.

It was getting close to dusk, and Frankie felt a wave of relief when she heard the back door open and Caleb's boots hit the kitchen tile.

He looked awful—ashen, slumped, like he'd spent the weekend hauling boulders instead of camping with Jack and Dale.

"You look like shit," Frankie said, meeting him at the door.

He dropped the sleeping bags he was carrying with an audible grunt and wrapped his arms around her, burying his face in her damp hair.

"Mmm, you smell good," he murmured, voice muffled against her neck.

"You smell like campfire smoke and death," she said, wrinkling her nose. She tried to push him back, but his grip tightened.

"Just one more second." When he released her a moment later, he let out a sigh. "I'm not doing that again anytime soon."

He crossed the room, grabbed a glass from the cabinet, and filled it with tap water. "I need a shower. Maybe a juice cleanse. Do we have any spinach?"

As he made his way to the laundry room, peeling off his shirt mid-stride, he spoke as if the weekend required no further explanation. That was the thing with Caleb—his efficiency, usually helpful, could feel like a form of avoidance. He reduced things to bullet points. Moved through conversation the way he moved through to-do lists.

"How did Dale do?" she called after him.

"He didn't really hang out with us," Caleb called back over the sound of rummaging.

Frankie frowned, rinsing her hands at the sink. "Huh? How's that possible? Weren't you all in the same spot?"

"Yeah, but he mostly stayed at the site. We wanted to hike. We brought the shotguns, set up targets before the snow started."

"How'd that go in the snow?"

"It was gorgeous," he said. "This morning, we found all kinds of animal tracks."

Frankie dried her hands, her movements slow. Something felt off. Not dramatic. Just slanted. Caleb reappeared in the doorway, watching her from across the kitchen. His eyes were distant, like he was still somewhere else in his mind.

"What else happened?" she asked, keeping her voice soft. "I can tell there's more to the story."

He didn't answer right away. "I'm going to shower," he said finally. "Join me?" He started unbuttoning his jeans, eyebrow raised in an unsubtle invitation.

Frankie shook her head. "You go ahead—I just got clean," she said, stepping back. "Dinner is going to be leftover pizza from last night. We ordered too much. I think I'll bleach the house while you decontaminate."

He grinned faintly, but it didn't reach his eyes.

"Did you hear Margaret's mom, Brie, is missing?" She could have said her sponsee, Brie. Caleb knew the basic workings of AA, but she intentionally wanted to distance him from these kinds of nuances. She believed in the separation of church and state.

"We heard. Crazy. I hope she's okay." He grabbed the dish towel from her hands and wiped his face.

"We were out searching today. Janey and I even stopped by Hollow Ridge, but didn't see you guys. Which part were you at? Was it crowded?"

"Not crowded, exactly. But . . . yeah, there were some people around. I think the forecast kept most people away, but it wasn't storming so much as it was dumping snow. We were about a mile southeast of the main ridge." He hesitated just long enough for her to notice. His eyes dropped to the floor.

"I love how you say that like I have any idea what 'southeast' means," she said playfully. "Did you not get any sleep? What did you guys do all night? You look wrecked."

"Yeah. Just . . . dumb guy stuff. I've really got to take that shower now."

"What's 'dumb guy stuff'?" she called after him.

But he was already halfway up the stairs and didn't answer.

8

MERE

Sunday, March 17, 2024

Lily had fallen asleep in her car seat, her globe cradled against her chest, breath fogging a small circle on the window. Mere thought briefly about heading home on her way back from Avery's, but instead she kept driving. A nap in the car was too precious to waste, and if circling Big Sky's quiet streets meant Lily would sleep longer, she'd take it. Besides, she needed the motion. The solitude.

Driving had always been her escape hatch. She remembered the day she got her license—sixteen, jittery with nerves, the DMV examiner silent beside her as she white-knuckled the steering wheel through the test route. When she passed, her father handed over the keys to a used and battered "Taur-*ass*," as she and Frankie would come to call it, while he kept the minivan for himself. Their mom had cared for the minivan so diligently that it was still in good condition, and he figured the girls were bound to "get into some fender benders here and there," muttering something about responsibility before cracking open another beer. That first solo drive was intoxicating. Not because of speed or rebellion, but because of the quiet. Frankie had stood on the porch, eyes red from crying after yet another blowup with their dad, and Mere had left her there. The guilt pricked even then, but for a few hours she'd tasted freedom, the neighborhood streets unfolding like a promise.

Now, watching the wisps of clouds lap at the window, Mere thought of those long-ago car rides as moments of stolen peace, brief reprieves from a house ruled by her father's instability. Their mother, Donna, had tried to maintain order in her own distracted way, but after she died, it was Mere who ensured that bills were paid, that Frankie got to her appointments, that the chaos didn't swallow them whole. Mere had learned to navigate her father's moods, tiptoeing through the minefield of his good intentions gone awry. He could be loving one moment and terrifying the next, a whirlwind of unpredictability. By the time she left for college, Mere had been more than ready to hand the baton over to Frankie.

The day before she'd left for UC Blue Ridge, the three of them stood in the kitchen. Frankie, age sixteen, had sat at the table, picking at a yogurt while their dad rummaged through the fridge, muttering about making grilled cheese for dinner.

Frankie, you'll need to step up when I'm gone, Mere said, sliding a list of chores across the table. Frankie barely glanced at it, her jaw set in defiance.

I got it, she snapped, but Mere wasn't convinced. And moments later, when their dad accidentally sliced off part of his finger while cutting cheese, Frankie froze. Mere took over, rushing him to the ER while telling her sister to clean up the blood.

Once they pulled into the hospital parking lot, he tumbled out of the car, lying on the pavement, whimpering like a wounded animal left to suffer and die as roadkill. As he rocked from side to side, a broken bottle splintering beneath his back and drawing even more blood from new cuts, Mere recognized that he was too stoned to be able to feel anything. She crouched next to him, brushing his long hair out of his face as he howled in pitiful defeat, too exhausted to try to get him to stand. It was there, in that moment, Mere granted herself permission to leave for college. Up until then, both she and Frankie had figured she would never really go; she was too responsible to abandon them. But Mere was already the broken glass beneath her father's bloody body. If she didn't leave now, she never would.

No one stopped to help. Maybe they were too preoccupied with their own emergencies, or maybe they were simply afraid of the grown man wailing beneath a car. Either way, Mere felt an unsettling truth wash over her: She wasn't necessarily alone, but she had never felt lonelier.

Her father was right there, inches away, but his presence did nothing to anchor her, nothing to ease the crushing isolation of standing beside someone who couldn't meet her where she was. He needed her, but he wasn't with her. There was no reciprocity, no shared burden, only her, drowning in a role she had no choice but to play.

It was the first time she understood that loneliness wasn't always about being alone. The people you were with could make you feel it just as strongly. She thought of her mother and what it must have been like for her to raise children with a partner like their dad, how she managed to make it seem effortless. Had their mom felt this too? This bone-deep isolation masked as duty? Mere had always assumed that their mom was sustained by her daughters' love. But maybe she was just quietly surviving. The thought settled in her chest like sediment.

When Mere and their father finally returned home six hours later, Frankie was gone. The kitchen was still a disaster, blood dried on the counter, the trash overflowing. Mere scrubbed the counter clean, throwing out the block of now-sweating cheese. As she scraped at the congealed blood, she knew that leaving meant placing the full burden of their father's care onto Frankie's shoulders, that this might be the last time Mere was around to clean up the mess for her. She felt like the crushing ache of culpability was inescapable, knowing she was saddling her sister with a responsibility neither of them had ever been meant to carry. In that moment, she mourned Frankie's lost youth. She knew too well the pain of missing out on something that should have been. It was a different kind of heartache, one only a sister could understand.

After Mere left, Frankie managed their father alone, and whatever happened in those two years, they never really talked about it. The knowledge of her abandonment of Frankie sat in Mere's gut, solid and familiar. Guilt had become a constant companion, one she accepted as the cost of her freedom, as if it were just another expense tacked on to the price of her college tuition.

She hadn't thought about that day in years, the parking lot of the ER, the blood, the final straw, if there could ever be just one. There were hundreds. But now, with the road unspooling ahead and her daughter sound asleep in the back seat, the memory surfaced uninvited. The quiet tended to do that. Or maybe it was the guilt, always riding shotgun. She'd left Frankie behind, and in doing so she'd given herself a chance to build the life she currently had.

Mere couldn't help but consider what she'd actually built. A family, yes. But lately her homelife had started to feel like another role she was performing, another obligation disguised as love, because who was she if she wasn't Dale's wife and Lily's mother?

Except she loved being Lily's mother. She missed her daughter whenever they were apart, even if it was only for an hour or two. She wanted to believe it was because she couldn't bear the distance, but sometimes she wondered if it was also because she didn't fully trust Dale's ability to care for Lily on his own. Mere hadn't traveled anywhere alone since before Lily was born, and as a family they had never ventured farther south than San Francisco.

Last year, when Lily was two, Dale had insisted they walk across the Golden Gate Bridge. That was when they'd picked up the globe, the one Lily was currently clutching in her sleep—snowless with tiny cars that moved along the bridge when the orb tilted. It was meant to be a simple souvenir. But Lily had carried it with her ever since. To her it was an object that made sense and one she loved like a sibling. Mere couldn't remember whether Dale had first encouraged Lily to bring it everywhere or Lily had decided that on her own. Either way, they'd become a set. The sight of it, the devotion, the dependence, made Mere ache.

There would be no more children. She and Dale had decided together. Not just because Lily was more than they ever expected. Age, timing, logistics, practical reasons—they'd pulled all these and more from a carefully curated list Dale had once written on his whiteboard in the office. A list that had felt, at the time, like planning. Now it felt like closing a door Mere wasn't ready to close.

Maybe that was why it struck her sometimes, how similar Dale and Lily could be, both intense in their attachments, both prone to fixations that felt like gravity. His fascination with bridges had always been logical. He'd built a career on them. But it went deeper than that. They seemed to soothe him in the same way that deep pressure calmed Lily, regulating something in their nervous systems Mere couldn't quite access. Another child, maybe, would be more similar to Mere in her thinking. She watched the way Frankie's girls connected as friends, just as she and Frankie had when they were children, and Mere yearned to witness the same bond between two children of her own. It made her feel both guilty and hopeful. She didn't want to put her expectations of sisterhood onto Lily. Lily's interpretation of a sibling wouldn't be the same as Rayna's and Chloe's, and that thought alone made Mere hurt in ways she was scared to examine.

The state of the house could've qualified as a crime scene. Dale had been gone for only one night, but when he came home, he left a trail of chaos in his wake—boots abandoned by the door, sleeping bag unrolled halfway down the hall, gear spilling from his pack across the living room, and his clothes dropped like breadcrumbs all the way to their bedroom.

During her rare stretch of alone time, Mere had organized everything. Meals prepped for the week, clothes sorted into their labeled drawers, Lily's medical appointments updated, printed, and taped neatly to the fridge. Classic Mere. But she had hoped Dale would notice and appreciate her effort. She wanted him to understand that the real grind wasn't in the noise or the tantrums—it was in the constancy. The unending repetition of caregiving. The part Dale never seemed to grasp.

Lily had woken up as Mere lifted her from the car seat, and now she wriggled free, already on the move. She charged toward the dining table, tossing plastic play food across the floor and yanking books off shelves. Within seconds she'd managed to scatter the room in the way only Lily could—her play always left behind a wake, small explosions of chaos trailing her path. Pancakes trotted after her, stepping gingerly over the wreckage.

Mere dropped her bag on the counter, eyes sweeping. The trail of gear, the clutter, the thoughtless scatter of it all . . .

Dale was standing at the kitchen island, his hands braced on the counter as he stared listlessly into space.

"Unbelievable," Mere snapped. "I spent hours—*hours*—while you were gone getting this place together. Meals prepped, laundry folded, Lily's schedule organized and on the fridge, and it looks like I never even touched it. I finally get a break, a few precious hours to myself, and I used them to make things easier for you. For *us*. And now look at it." She gestured around them, hands shaking. "Back to chaos. Back to me feeling like nothing I do lasts."

Dale's head tilted. "What break?"

Her laugh was sharp, humorless. "Exactly. You wouldn't even know. While you were camping, Frankie took Lily so I could have some actual time alone. But instead of resting, I poured my energy back into this family. And now it's like it doesn't even matter."

Dale blinked back at her, genuinely baffled. "But . . . you wanted me to go camping."

Mere let out a sharp breath, half laugh, half exasperation. "Yes, Dale. I *wanted* you to go. I wanted you to have your thing, to see your friends, to take a break. But I wanted that for me too. That's the point—you don't even realize the difference.

You get to step away, and it's assumed someone else will hold it all together while you're gone. I step away, and I'm still holding it together. Even when I'm *off the clock*, I'm doing the work."

He ran a hand through his hair, still looking puzzled. "I don't understand. You're saying you didn't want me to go?"

"No!" She pressed her palms to the counter, leaning toward him. "I'm saying I wanted you to see me. To *notice* me. To realize that while you were out in the woods, I finally had a few hours to myself and I spent them making sure this house—*our* life—didn't collapse. And when you came back, instead of seeing that, you dumped a trail of mud and laundry from the door to the bedroom."

Dale shifted his weight, his expression still more lost than defensive. "I thought you liked things organized. I thought that's how you wanted things."

"What I want," she said, voice catching, "is to feel like I'm not the only one who cares whether this family runs smoothly or falls apart. What I want is for you to ask me how it felt to have time to myself. To wonder what I did with it. To notice that I'm *drowning* sometimes and try to throw me a rope instead of acting like everything is fine."

He opened his mouth, then closed it again, as if words were a foreign language he couldn't quite remember. His silence was louder than any argument.

Talking to Dale, she thought, was like trying to cross a river without a bridge—always building the planks herself, always hoping he'd pick up a hammer and join her. But he never did.

9

FRANKIE

Sunday, March 17, 2024

By the time Frankie crawled into bed, Caleb was already in his loud-snore position, flat on his back, head tipped just enough that his mouth hung open. She envied how effortlessly he could shut off his mind, as if the day didn't cling to him the way it did to her. He didn't lie there running through a list of everything still left undone—the groceries, the school forms, the management of their daughters' shifting moods. He didn't catalog their needs or try to outmaneuver tomorrow before it arrived. And that was all before her mind wandered into darker places: the late-night spirals about death, about outliving her children, about how love only made you more vulnerable to losing everything.

She hated that Brie was still missing for a second night in a row. She knew that the moment her head hit the pillow, she'd continue to battle with whether or not she needed to break Brie's anonymity.

She lay there for a moment, studying Caleb's face in the darkness. Even now, she could map out every line, every familiar feature. She was close enough that his breath brushed the tip of her nose. She lingered, tempted to wake him, but knew better. Caleb, like a toddler, was useless when overtired.

She turned over and grabbed her Kindle from the nightstand. At night, she allowed herself the convenience of e-books, even though she loved the sensation of a paperback in her hands. The soft glow of the screen quieted her thoughts in a way the rustle of paper never quite could. For a little while, she could slip into someone else's head instead of staying trapped in her own. She used to dread that window of time before sleep, when her mind would spin and darken, and back then she drank herself into oblivion just to outrun it. Reading became the healthier escape, the one she could return to night after night without fear. It was why she'd opened The Open Book—because stories had steadied her when nothing else could.

The vibration of Caleb's phone on his nightstand broke her concentration. It buzzed again, and again, and Frankie reached over to put it on mute. She read the screen as she went to silence it.

Jack had texted, *What did you tell Frankie?*

Tell me about what? A wave of liquid heat spread through her chest. She didn't unlock the phone, though her fingers twitched, wanting to scroll through the six unread messages waiting for Caleb. Jack wasn't usually so cryptic. And if *he* was texting Caleb like this, something was definitely off.

Frankie grabbed her own phone and crept downstairs to make tea. She turned on the electric kettle and sent a text to Janey.

J, you awake?

Her phone buzzed, Janey was calling.

"Hey." Janey's voice sounded scratchy.

"You sick?" Frankie asked.

"Did Caleb tell you about camping?"

"Not really. Why?"

Janey hesitated, a rare moment of silence from her. Frankie's irritation flared. Why did Janey know more than she did?

"They found a body," Janey said finally, her admission heavy. "Off the main path near the campsite."

Frankie's breath caught. "A body? Like a dead body?"

"They were too messed up to check. Jack said it looked like a pile of clothes, but by morning, it was gone. No sign of anything, but that's because of all the snow. I've been googling all night, trying to figure out if hallucinations like that are common on shrooms. They were all tripping so hard that they just left because Jack convinced them to check back in the morning. When they woke up and went back to the area, whatever it was . . . wasn't there anymore. They even drove up and down and still found nothing. I told him to go to the police immediately, but he's freaking out because of the drugs and swore to me that they'd been thorough in their search."

All the hairs on Frankie's arms stood to attention. Her body felt like it wasn't her own anymore.

"They did *shrooms*?" Frankie wasn't surprised Caleb had skipped that detail—it explained why he looked like hell. They had a marital understanding that Caleb kept his beer drinking to work events or the rare occasion that he went out with Jack. He was sensitive to her sobriety and careful not to be a bad influence on their girls. Frankie walked over to her purse hanging on the hook by the door. A chill swept over her, leaving a taut silence inside her chest, as if the air itself had shifted. As Janey continued to explain what Jack had said, Frankie found herself needing something to do with her hands. She rummaged through her bag in search of ChapStick. Instead, her fingers brushed against the tin that had belonged to Brie. She pulled it out and turned it over in her hand, studying it. "There has to be some sort of explanation," she managed to whisper.

"Besides that men are *idiots*?" Janey shot back. "Instead of bonding like normal humans, they act like they're in *The Hangover*. Heaven forbid they sit around and talk about their feelings! Frankie, this is so messed up."

"But Jack *told* you all this," Frankie pointed out, still clutching the container. "You guys are separated. Caleb, on the other hand, was acting cagey as hell and neglected to mention that he did drugs and may have come across a dead person." The kettle started to bubble, making Frankie jump.

"I *envy* you for not knowing. I've been sitting in it alone, and it sucks. Jack thinks I'm overreacting, which is just typical.

He shrugged when he told me, like that was a normal response. Accused me of being dramatic."

Frankie moved toward the counter to fix her tea, though her thirst for it was gone.

"Maybe it was someone resting, like, out in the snow? But still they should have checked—like, tried to shake them," Frankie said, trying to logic her way out of the fear. "Or maybe it was part of someone's encampment or something. I don't know how those drugs work. Maybe if one person sees a purple elephant, they *all* see a purple elephant?"

"I'm just pissed they didn't call it in immediately because they were on drugs," Janey nearly shouted. "Like, you guys are all *fathers*! That could've been someone's *child*. Grow up!" Frankie didn't miss the self-righteous note in Janey's voice. It was familiar. Janey loved capitalizing on any opportunity to showcase Jack's shortcomings.

"Caleb said they brought their shotguns. Were they using their guns while they were on drugs? I might actually kill Caleb."

"No, Jack told me they locked them up in the car an hour or so before, when it started snowing. But still," Janey said.

At least they'd thought to do that. She knew Caleb had never been reckless when it came to guns. Regardless, there was something infuriating about the way men seemed to think in packs. If women operated like a hive mind working toward the greater good, then when the guys got together, they became the exact opposite, some kind of collective stupidity vortex where logic went to die.

"Did they say if it looked like a man or a woman?" Frankie asked. She opened the lid on the tin of THC gummies and counted. There were nine, which meant Brie had taken only one. She studied the back, reading the suggested dosage as if it were Tylenol or Advil or something generic.

Neither of them had said Brie's name. They couldn't bring themselves to, even though Frankie knew they were both thinking of her. They had been saying things back and forth, but the only question Frankie really wanted to ask was: *Could it have been Brie? Is that who they saw in the snow?*

"He said it looked like a mound of coats or jackets or something," Janey replied, her tone quieter now. After a beat, she added, "I kind of want to drive back out there and look around." Frankie could almost see Janey up pacing, looking for her keys.

"That's one of your dumber ideas, J," Frankie said. "It's nighttime. It's freezing and dark. I'll go with you tomorrow."

The other end of the line went silent. Maybe thirty seconds passed.

"I'm going to call the police to go check it out," Janey said, like she was asking for Frankie's permission.

"Okay, yes. Call the police."

"You don't think there's something more to this, do you? Like . . . something they're intentionally leaving out because it's too horrible to say?" Janey whispered.

Frankie let the worry sit between them for a moment. Then, quietly, she said, "God, I hope not."

Frankie slept in fits and spurts. The next morning, well before either of their alarms was set to go off, when Caleb stirred beside her, she turned to study him. He looked haggard, hair matted, deep shadows under his eyes. He must have felt her watching him, because he started speaking even before opening his lids. "I can't get the taste out of my mouth," he muttered, scraping his teeth over his tongue. "I must've drank a gallon of dirty spigot water."

"Because of the *mushrooms*." Frankie had decided around two in the morning that she was just going to cut to the chase first thing. "I talked to Janey last night, and I'm very interested in hearing your version of events."

Caleb dragged a hand over his face. "Where to even start?" He reached for the water glass Frankie had thoughtfully placed on his nightstand and took a sip. "First off, Tom was acting like a total and complete lunatic. Dude cannot hold his liquor, so I'm not sure what he was thinking, but the drugs hit him hard. He swore he saw something in the sky, like a UFO or aliens." Frankie was already lost. She hadn't realized Tom, Avery's husband, had gone camping with them.

"Whoa, back up. I didn't know Tom was there," she said. Janey and Avery worked together at Janey's gym. They were friendly in a coworking sort of way, so maybe their husbands had hung out socially before. But Frankie couldn't think of an occasion where that would have been true.

"I thought I told you Tom would be there too. Tom and Dale already knew each other through your sister and Avery being friends, and since they're both kind of weird, Jack and I figured they could just be weird together."

"Like a bro date?" Frankie wanted to be playful with Caleb. They were always so good when they could be unserious together. But she couldn't afford to lose focus. "Where did you get the drugs from? Were they even safe?"

Frankie knew from their eighteen years of marriage that Caleb hated being peppered with so many questions at once, but she was too upset to follow their previously established rules of engagement.

"I'm alive, aren't I? So obviously they were safe," Caleb retorted.

Frankie shot him a warning look. He was in no position to be giving *her* any kind of attitude. When he continued speaking, his tone was much softer. "Tom brought 'em and got them from some guy at work, who I guess knows someone who owns a drug commune in Humboldt County. Everything was safe, in that it was natural." Caleb paused, shrugging his shoulders up to his ears, and gave her a look that asked, *Can I continue telling the story now?*

She remembered Jack had also shrugged in his explanation to Janey, and she wondered if she could strike a two-for-one deal with Janey's divorce attorney if—or maybe when—Janey finally decided to get one. Wearing a face that said *I really hate you right now*, Frankie gestured for Caleb to keep going.

"Dale was over it from the start. He crashed early, calling it a night after we went shooting and before the drugs. We didn't see him again until morning. He thought we were nuts for wanting to trip. Honestly, I'm jealous. I wish I hadn't done it. It started out fun, but then it got hard to tell what was real and what wasn't."

Frankie sighed, irritated that, of all four men, Dale was the only one with any sense.

"At first, Tom was just doing laps around the campsite, and I was seeing shapes and colors. Then Tom *took off*, and we let him. Jack was somewhere staring at a tree, I think." Caleb leaned against the headboard, closing his eyes, as if that would help conjure up the memories and bring everything back into focus. "Jack and I ended up walking the campsite. That's when we came across . . ." He paused, choosing his words carefully before continuing. ". . . whatever it was we saw. It looked like discarded clothes or like a mound or something. I dunno. But seriously, I mean bushes were little balls of atomic-looking gases, so whatever we were looking at, it didn't look like a person—not necessarily. Everything looked so strange."

"But you and Jack *both* saw something," Frankie said, pushing back.

"It looked like one of those donation piles that we see out here along our country road, where people ditch mattresses and old armchairs when they're too cheap and lazy to go to the dump." He paused. "Tom was missing his clothes when we found him. He was naked except for a fleece blanket. We figured that's what we'd seen. When we woke up the next morning, we went back, but there was nothing—no clothes, no person, nothing."

Frankie let out a long, audible sigh of relief. That made sense to her. If Tom was missing his clothes and they thought they saw clothes, then that's probably what it was. Still, she could feel her frustration begin to bubble up at their stupidity. "Tom was naked in the snow?"

"He got new clothes from his bag and we made him sit by the fire—close enough to stay warm, but not so close he'd burn himself. It felt like taking care of Chloe back when she was like three, stubborn as hell and convinced she could do everything herself."

She pinched the skin at the top of her nose. "So, instead of doing any sort of talking—I dunno, say, by asking each other about your marriages, or children, you know, communicating like adults—you all shot guns and did drugs, Tom almost got hypothermia, and you probably saw *laundry*?"

"I mean, it sounds terrible when you say it like that." He stretched his arms up over his head, a signal that he was ready to move on from the topic, but his nonchalance irritated her to the point that she was certain she was going to explode. "Really, it was all no big deal."

Men and their goddamn "no big deals." Janey had shared about a phone call with Jack where he went on and on about how he chased down the Amazon delivery driver who had thrown their packages in the bushes, and they'd almost had it out in the middle of the street, before Jack even bothered to mention that he was currently in the waiting room of the ER because their son had potentially broken his wrist jumping off the couch. And now Caleb was shrugging off . . . whatever *this* was.

"Who first said the word 'body'?"

Caleb paused to consider her question. He opened his mouth, then immediately closed it, only to open it again. "Dale asked if it could have been, like, an unhoused person when we were explaining our walkabout to him the next morning."

"Dale as the Dude Voice of Reason is extremely unsettling."

Caleb chuckled a little, and Frankie felt better. It was easier to make Dale their common enemy instead of continuing to be angry with Caleb. She didn't have the bandwidth to stay mad at her husband, not when she knew from endlessly checking her phone that Brie was still missing.

"Well, I'm glad you went back and checked it out. I'm even more glad it was nothing and that nobody got hurt during your psychedelic vision quest."

"No harm, no foul." Caleb stood, giving one final stretch overhead, ready to start the day as if everything were perfectly normal.

On the way to their businesses that morning, Frankie grabbed Janey. They detoured past Hollow Ridge, sure they'd find the place swarming with cops. But the lot was deserted.

"I'm not gonna lie," Frankie said, scanning the stillness. "I thought we'd roll up and it would look like a scene straight out of *Dateline*."

"I left a message on the tip line but didn't actually talk to a person last night. Do you think they've already come out here?"

Janey looked concerned as she reached for her phone. "Should I call again?"

"Let's walk around a bit and then decide," Frankie offered, as if she'd had any experience with such matters. They'd each called in to be sure the gym and the bookstore were covered, freeing them to spend the morning at the campground, driving up and down the main road. Frankie even borrowed one of Caleb's compasses to go southeast as he had said. They searched for anything—*anything*—that might bring them some peace of mind.

Frankie hadn't told Caleb that they were heading back to Hollow Ridge. When she was upset with him, it was all too easy to slip into old habits, like leaving out details she'd decided were "unimportant," the same way he had casually dismissed the specifics of their trip when he got home. She knew, especially in recovery, that it was a slippery slope. *Secrets keep you sick*, as Pearl would say. But she couldn't help feeling a bit vindicated. After all, Caleb had reopened that door when he conveniently forgot to mention the magic mushrooms.

The campsite was buried under snow, any potential clues lost beneath the drifts. After about an hour of fruitless searching, they couldn't delay their workdays any longer.

"I don't feel any better," Janey said as they pulled into the parking lot downtown. Frankie thought looking would help, but what was she expecting? To find Brie just standing there like, *Hey, guys, just finished a marathon hike*?

"I know. This whole thing is deeply unsettling." Frankie hesitated, the words bottling up in her throat before she finally let out a long breath. “I saw Brie on Friday,” she said slowly, “and she said something strange. About disappearing . . . or wanting to disappear.”

The admission hung between them, heavier than she expected. For a beat she regretted saying it aloud. But then, almost immediately, relief swept through her. At least she wasn’t the only one carrying it anymore.

Janey’s eyes went wide. “What? How are you just saying this now? You have to tell the police.”

Frankie bristled at the idea. “Do I? What if they take it the wrong way? What if they assume she just ran off and they stop looking, when really, something horrible could have happened?” She’d listened to enough true crime podcasts to know missing women only got attention if they fit a certain mold: white, first and foremost. Innocent, respectable, easy to root for. But women like Brie? The ones who were sensitive, or struggled, or needed too much? They weren’t seen as victims. They were seen as problems. In a man’s world, a woman like Brie didn’t go missing. She abandoned her family. Neat. Tidy. Easy. Especially if they knew about her drinking.

“How could you just be mentioning this to me now?” Janey asked again, her expression wounded.

Frankie’s irritation flared. Why was Janey making this about her? If it had been Mere, Frankie might’ve snapped and told her to get out right then and there. That was the difference between Frankie’s chosen sister and her biological one. With Mere, Frankie’s patience had thinned to a thread years ago.

“I guess I thought that if I shared it with you or anyone . . .

I dunno. It was some superstitious-type shit. Irrational. I didn't want to say it aloud and make it come true." Frankie conceded then and described their meetup at the arboretum, recounting it beat for beat in case some overlooked detail might help piece together where Brie had gone.

When she finished, the car fell quiet. Finally Janey said, "It sounds like one of three things happened." She paused.

Frankie stiffened. "And? What are those three things?" She already knew, but she needed to hear Janey say them out loud.

Janey's jaw tightened. "She intentionally left. Like, checked out. Or she relapsed. And—"

"And what?" Frankie snapped, sharper than she meant to. Her chest constricted. The only reason Janey even understood the nuances of addiction was because Frankie had let her in—shared her own story, her own shame. She hated when anyone, even Janey, spoke like they had lived it. "Either of those suggest it's somehow Brie's fault she's missing."

"I didn't say that." Janey's voice stayed steady, though her brows pulled tight. "What's going on with you? It feels like you're coming for me pretty hard, and we both want the same thing."

Pause when agitated.

It was one of those overused recovery slogans Frankie kept in her back pocket. She rarely remembered it when she needed it most, but now it surfaced.

"You're right." Frankie let out a shaky breath. "I'm sorry. I just hate the idea that maybe if I'd said something different, she'd have stuck around for the Sunday morning meeting and—" Her voice broke.

Janey reached across the console, threading her fingers through Frankie's. The gesture said everything neither of them could.

They didn't speak again. Just sat there in silence, watching their small town in motion—students trudging past with backpacks, a mother balancing a baby on her chest while steering a stroller.

"I thought for sure she would have turned up by now," Frankie said finally, shaking her head. "What's the third thing? You said one of three."

Janey's eyes widened. Her lips parted slowly. "Maybe someone has done something to her."

10

MERE

Monday, March 18, 2024

The night after Mere's outburst at Dale, she was propped up in bed, Lily asleep beside her with Pancakes curled into her body, their breathing syncing in a slow rhythm. Across the room, Dale sat in a chair, in a hooded sweatshirt and sweats. Even after two showers in twenty-four hours, he still carried a faint trace of campfire smoke into their bedroom.

They hadn't talked much since the argument. Mere had slipped back into her thoughts, alone in the way she so often was even with Dale in the house. Determined to connect rather than spend any more time shut away in her own mind, Mere asked, "So . . . what happened on the camping trip?" When he only glanced up briefly before lowering his eyes back to the e-book he was reading, she narrowed the scope. "Are you glad you went?"

Dale shook his head. "No. Honestly, it would've been easier

staying home with Lily. Just a bunch of grown men acting like it was some bachelor weekend."

"What do you mean?" Mere deflated. She had hoped, maybe naively, that Dale and Caleb would find some common ground. They were so fundamentally different, like her and Frankie, but without blood to link them, there had never been a reason for the men to really try. Connection during holidays and birthdays was only ever at the women's insistence.

"I tried shooting with them. It's kind of like archery, which I was always good at, so that part was fine. But once the guns were put away, they lit a fire and started drinking. Then the snow really started to come down, and it was just better for me to read alone in the tent." He paused, and his leg finally stilled. "I was exhausted, so I went to bed early. I came out a few times to add kindling to the fire."

Dale went back to reading, his Kindle propped on the table beside him, hands tucked into the front pocket of his sweatshirt. Mere had bought the e-reader for him after he'd complained one too many times about the tiny print in paperbacks, knowing how much he loved to read.

Mere stayed still, stroking Lily's hair as Pancakes sprawled heavy across her legs. Bedtime always stirred the same pang—how she wished Lily had a sister. Someone to make nights feel like one long, perpetual sleepover, the way Mere had once felt with Frankie. But even what she craved for Lily no longer existed between her and Frankie. It had lived only in that brief period after their mom died, and then it was gone.

Losing her had awakened a new kind of vulnerability that

bloomed between Mere and Frankie, but it came with a time limit. Mere hadn't realized then that the window would close and never reopen. Each day, they took turns falling apart while the other acted as the lighthouse, tall and steady, keeping watch in case their father started to storm. At night, they shared a bed again, something they hadn't done since childhood. Frankie was a volatile sleeper, kicking and flailing the way she always had. But instead of abandoning her for a good night's sleep, Mere would build a pillow barrier between them, close enough to still listen for the rhythm of her sister's breath.

Mere told Frankie about her crush on Adrienne. About how soft a girl's lips could be, how much better they smelled. How their bodies became like paper accordions folding into each other. And even though Mere took the lion's share of the responsibilities—she was older, after all—Frankie stepped up in other ways. She loved so big that sometimes it almost filled the hole their mother had left. So when it came time to apply for college, it wasn't a complete leap that Mere pulled Frankie aside for her blessing.

I can't handle him on my own! Frankie had protested. At first, Mere assumed she'd come around. But Frankie could hold a grudge. She treated Mere's plan to leave like a hypothetical. Even as Mere packed her boxes, Frankie kept saying things like, *Let's get matching haircuts this fall*, knowing damn well she'd be starting her junior year of high school while Mere would be hundreds of miles away in Big Sky, a college freshman.

The morning Mere left for UC Blue Ridge, Frankie let her feelings of betrayal rise like a barricade. All the ground they'd gained after losing their mom—their tender nights, their whispered confessions—slipped away. Mere had let herself believe their connection was the gift their mother left behind. But she learned the hard way: When you remove the glue in a relationship, either it finds something else to hold it together or it dissolves completely.

And then there was the fire.

After that, Frankie found drinking.

Mere had read up on what it meant to love someone who was an alcoholic. She'd learned that bitterness was the chief culprit for those who struggled with drinking, the way they clung to every wound. Frankie was no different; she held tight to Mere's abandonment and wore it like armor. On the last night of Frankie's drinking, when she wasn't safe to be around her girls, Dale and Mere had stepped in at Caleb's request. They came to take the girls for the night so Frankie could sleep it off.

Frankie had been vicious in her rage, spitting venom about how they didn't understand what it was like to be a parent, how easy it must be for them, childless. Then she said the thing that would haunt Mere on her darkest days:

I hope you never have Dale's kids. Those little weirdos wouldn't stand a chance.

From that moment on, it was Mere who couldn't let go of her resentment.

Yet here was the contradiction that lived inside her. Frankie could say the cruelest, most scathing thing and Mere would still need her. She'd still need to know that despite everything, she was alive, here, beneath the same sky. That was sisterhood too: the impossibility of love and hate existing in equal measure, neither ever fully eclipsing the other.

"Did they ever find that woman who was missing? Frankie told me about it Saturday night—it sounds troubling," she said.

Dale crossed the room to where Pancakes was curled into Lily's sleeping body. He shrugged. "I haven't heard."

She had just seen her sister over the weekend, but the need to get to Frankie pressed in on her now.

"Can you stay here with Lily while she sleeps? I need to go out for a little while." She hesitated, then added, "If she stirs, just keep your hand on her back. The steady pressure helps—don't try to talk her through it." Dale nodded without complaint. He always took direction well when she spelled things out for him, and in Mere's mind, that was the closest thing they had to teamwork.

By the time she pulled into Frankie's driveway, the urgency had settled into her chest like a weight. She sat for a moment, staring at the house her sister had built, marveling at the life she had created. It struck her that she couldn't take a full breath until she was standing right in front of Frankie, touching her, making sure she was real. Frankie was okay. She was sober. She had a family. Whatever damage Mere had done in the past by leaving—surely it wasn't beyond repair.

She walked to the front door and rang the bell. Frankie appeared wearing an oversized gray men's undershirt, the kind she used to steal from their dad, though this one was far too big to be Caleb's. Mere felt a pang of nostalgia—her sister clinging to comfort in stubborn, familiar ways.

"Nice shirt," Mere said, tipping her chin toward it.

"Thanks. Men's 4XL." Frankie smirked. "Got them when I was pregnant and just never stopped. I like to look hot for my hubby. We keep it spicy."

"Well, he's a lucky guy." Mere smiled, relief hitting hard. It was them. There they were.

"What are you doing here?" Frankie asked, more curious than irritated.

"I just . . . I needed to see you," Mere admitted, her eyes dropping. "Any word on Brie Hoover? This has to be so scary for her family."

Frankie shook her head, tugging at the hem of her shirt. "No."

"You're close with her, right?" Mere pressed gently. She could sense something taut in her sister, as if Frankie was wound too tight. "Have you been in touch with Pearl?"

"Our girls are close. And yes—I talked to Pearl yesterday," Frankie said.

The answer should have reassured her, but the unease still sat heavy.

"So, yeah." Mere exhaled. "It's silly, I just . . . I felt like I had to come by, to see you. Make sure."

Frankie didn't hesitate. She stepped forward and wrapped her arms around her sister, holding her close until that familiar scent rose between them—the same one that always conjured their mother. For a moment, it was as if she were standing there with them, holding them both.

11

FRANKIE

Tuesday, March 19, 2024

"You're really pretty." Caleb had finally gotten his infected tooth extracted by the oral surgeon. He was so loopy coming down off the anesthesia that Frankie had to treat him like one of the kids.

"Okay there, cowboy. One last stop before beddy-bye." Frankie eased the car into the drive-through lane of the South Lake pharmacy, pulling up behind a sedan with Idaho plates. Caleb was slumped low in the passenger seat, eyes closed, mouth slack. She rolled down the window and he nudged his head toward the fresh air like the lovable puppy he was, soaking in the cool breeze. His curls fluttered against his forehead.

The car line moved slowly. Frankie passed the time scrolling on her phone. Social media was flooded with posts about Brie. That same Christmas family photo shared again and again.

Even if Frankie hadn't known for a fact that Brie wasn't sober in the photo, she could see it in her lifeless, vacant stare. Christmas, and the holidays in general, could be brutal for mothers in recovery. So much of the magic landed squarely on their shoulders. Brie had confided in Frankie during one of their one-on-one meetings that her husband, a youth minister, was always overwhelmed with church duties that time of year, leaving her to hold everything together at home. But the truth was, Brie could barely string together a few sober days leading up to Christmas and New Year's. The photo Frankie was staring at had been taken after a fight. Brie had begged her husband for just one picture in front of the tree to use for a holiday card she never ended up sending. He told her he had to get to church early to coordinate the live nativity. She just wanted one moment to look like they had it all under control.

Frankie stared at the image. That's how it always was with mothers, memorialized in moments they had carefully curated to represent something that was never an authentic snapshot of what it took to get them all there, standing and smiling.

When it was finally her turn, Frankie pulled up to the intercom station, and a pharmacist leaned forward and said flatly through a microphone, "Go ahead with the name."

"Caleb Marino. There should be an antibiotic and a painkiller," she replied.

"Spell the last name?"

"*M-a-r-i-n-o.* Sent in by Dr. Johnson, oral surgeon."

There was a long pause, the sound of a keyboard clacking behind the glass. "Found it."

More typing. "Give us five minutes and pull up to the second window."

Frankie let the car idle forward. Caleb was still half asleep, head tilted back, lips parted. She opened her Notes app and stared at the script she had typed up last night when she couldn't sleep. She had rehearsed it already and used the number from the tip line on social media.

She put her phone up to her ear. "Hi, yes, I'm calling in a tip about Brie Hoover. I don't know if this matters or if you already know, but she's struggled with substance abuse in the past. I had a troubling encounter with her on the afternoon of Friday, March 15, around four o'clock."

The police line routed her to a volunteer, who began typing as Frankie recited what she knew. She repeated the time and location. Brie's offhand comment about leaving the country. "I'm sorry I didn't report it sooner," Frankie rushed to say. They were already past the forty-eight-hour mark, and every crime junkie knew that was when a missing person's case started to shift into something darker. "We have a code of anonymity in our program—hence the *Anonymous* part—and I didn't want to betray that. But I also want to do whatever I can to help."

The woman on the other end offered no real response. Frankie chose not to leave her name. She told herself it was about protecting anonymity, about honoring the rules of the program that had returned her life to her. And maybe that was true. Still, it felt like she was breaking something sacred, like she'd stepped outside the circle of trust people built their sobriety on.

But as she hung up, she felt something else—something harder to pin down. Like she'd sidestepped being pulled into something messier than she could handle. Like naming herself might've opened a door she wasn't ready to walk through. She didn't let herself dwell on it. Just set the phone down on the console and stared out at the car ahead, unsure whether she'd done the right thing—or simply the easiest thing for herself.

By the time she rolled forward to the second window, a different pharmacist appeared, passing off a small yet bulky brown paper bag with practiced detachment. Frankie took it with both hands, the weight of it feeling heavier than it should, and muttered her thanks.

"I can go over these with you, if you'd like," the woman in a white lab coat said.

Frankie checked the label. Oxycodone. Twenty pills. Stronger than anything she'd been prescribed after Chloe's vaginal delivery—or even after Rayna's C-section, with a split abdomen and stitched-up uterus. Apparently, a man's bad tooth merited more relief than a woman's battered body bringing life into the world. But twenty was excessive. This had to be a mistake. She debated whether it was worth saying anything to the pharmacist, but instead simply replied, "No thanks, we're good," and slipped the bag onto the floor of the back seat. As she shifted, she glanced over at Caleb and let out a startled yip.

Caleb had pulled himself out through the waistband of his boxers, pants still on. He held his penis loosely in his hand, the gesture oddly vacant—like a child fascinated by a body part he hadn't yet learned to claim as his own.

Frankie glanced back at the pharmacist, who was watching with an unreadable expression, then tugged her sweater over Caleb, shielding him.

"I wish I could say this was the first time I've seen that at this spot," the pharmacist said, her voice flat enough that Frankie couldn't tell if it was a joke or not.

"Caleb, honey. Let's put that away now," she said gently.

He didn't respond. He was still reclined, still half outside the window, still humming something tuneless under his breath. The wind fluttered his hair. His hand remained where it was. This wasn't arousal. This wasn't intentional. It was his body acting without him. Caleb, who never even took Tylenol for a headache. The anesthesia had jumbled something.

As she pulled the car forward, he began to stir. His eyes blinked open and he looked down, removing the sweater with one hand to find the other still positioned there.

"Oh no," he whispered, as if only now surfacing. He scrambled to tuck himself back in, fumbling clumsily with his boxers and pants.

"It's okay, my love," Frankie said softly, sliding the car into Park and leaning over to help him. Her hands steadied the fabric, zipping his fly, adjusting his seat belt.

"Where are we?" His eyes flicked over the dashboard like it might hold an answer, then he pressed his palm against the window as if testing whether it was real. His confusion was sharp, like he'd been dropped onto the moon. All the while, he watched her with the uneasy look of a man who no longer trusted his own body, like she was the only anchor left tethering him.

"We got what we needed. Let's go home and get you to bed." The words came out calm, but inside, she felt herself lifting out of her body—the string of her kite unraveling, drifting higher, farther away from the car. Every nerve screamed to run. The moment was too familiar, too haunting, being trapped in a parked car with a man who had exposed himself. A glitch in the system. Only this time, the man wasn't a predator. It was Caleb, her golden retriever of a husband, bewildered and harmless, the one she had chosen precisely because he wasn't capable of that kind of harm. She had picked him for his goodness, for the promise that her body and heart would be safe.

"Yeah," Caleb grunted, still lost. "Where are Chloe and Ray?"

"Home," Frankie said gently. "Where we're headed."

Once they made it out of the car in their driveway, Frankie linked arms with Caleb, struggling to maintain balance and carry the handleless bag filled with an encyclopedia's worth of warnings and side effects.

When they entered the house, Chloe was sitting on the stairs waiting for them. "Can I talk to you?" she asked, her expression laced with something Frankie couldn't quite pinpoint.

"Is there an update on Brie?"

Chloe shook her head. "No. No news."

"Let me just get your father tucked into the guest bedroom. But before I do, take a long, hard look at him. Don't do drugs, kids." Rayna was sitting at the kitchen island nearby, eating a bag of pretzels. Frankie tried to make her words sound lighthearted, but she hadn't shared them for the sake of her daughters. She was hoping to grind down the edges, the way she always did—to make light of what had just felt ugly and awful so it appeared softer. Perhaps then the parallels of her husband's exposure could be put to bed along with him. The moment was an uncanny coincidence and nothing deeper, she told herself.

Chloe lifted a single eyebrow, as if to say she remained skeptical that the dopey look on her father's face was anything other than endearing. "Can we not turn this into one of your teachable moments, please?"

"Fine, fine," Frankie said, shooing them aside so she could help Caleb into bed. They made it to the guest room next to his office, with Chloe trailing behind. Caleb collapsed onto the mattress, all deadweight. Frankie knelt at his feet and began unlacing his shoes.

"If he falls asleep with his shoes on, we get to mess with him," Chloe said, her voice light with mischief.

That old prank had been a rite of passage in her own college days. Funny, in a harmless kind of way. But as she heard it now and surveyed Caleb lying dulled and lifeless on the bed, it landed differently.

"I think your father's been messed with enough today," she said softly, pressing her palm to his swollen, purpling cheek. She crouched to tug off the heavy steel-toed work boot he still wore out of habit, even though it had been years since he was regularly on job sites. "Help me get the other one off."

Caleb stirred and sat up, suddenly sharp, just like that brief lucid moment in the car. His eyes locked on the corner of the room, where a stack of folded quilts sat on the lounge chair.

His grandmother had been a quilter, and this was the most Frankie could do with them. Hanging them on the walls wasn't her style, so she kept them here, contained but present.

"Like that. Blankets. Nothing but a human-shaped blanket," Caleb said. His voice was clear, too clear, as if he'd stepped out of the fog just long enough to say something that made Frankie's skin go cold.

She froze. Her mouth filled with that thick, sour saliva that comes right before nausea.

Chloe, unfazed, finished pulling off his shoe and then crept up beside him to kiss his cheek. Caleb grinned, loopy and sweet, and just like that, the tension dissolved, at least on the surface. To Chloe, the comment was nothing more than her dad being weird on meds.

But to Frankie, it was something else. A protectiveness surged up so fierce it bordered on panic. She wanted to curl her body around her daughter, to shield her from whatever invisible danger had crept into the room with his utterance. She couldn't name the threat exactly, but the instinct came all the same, sudden, primal, and impossible to shake.

"I want to tell you something, but I don't want to freak you out and I don't want you to tell Auntie Janey," Chloe said, avoiding Frankie's eyes. Janey had long ago reached honorary aunt status—even without blood ties—and so the girls called her Auntie Janey, while Mere was simply Aunt Mere. "I'm just going to say it and I don't want you to react." She stopped and transferred her voice into a whisper. "Wait, Dad is asleep, right? Let's go in his office." Frankie went to the corner and pulled one of the extra quilts up over her husband, wanting to trap him inside his memory so he'd come to and recognize whatever it was that felt familiar moments earlier.

In the office, Chloe sat atop her father's desk, ignoring the papers she was disturbing beneath her as she did. Frankie decided to sit down in his office chair. Whatever her daughter had to say, she wanted to give her the floor.

Chloe's face wasn't her own. "We did it."

"Okay," Frankie managed, her voice barely above a whisper. Her chest hammered so loudly she was sure Chloe could hear it. She forced herself to meet her daughter's eyes, green like sea glass left out in the sun. When she was little, Chloe used to boast that green was the rarest eye color, proudly reciting how less than five percent of the population had that trait, like it made her rare too.

"Patrick and I." Chloe's face flushed, and Frankie knew immediately there was so much Chloe wasn't saying. A mother always knows her daughter's heart. *It*, she repeated in her head so she understood. She struggled to reconcile her daughter in this sixteen-year-old body when it felt like only yesterday she'd been guiding her out of her own.

"How are you feeling?" Frankie asked, forcing her voice to remain steady. She wanted to immediately ask about birth control, ensure they were being safe, but Chloe had always been a sea anemone, quick to shut down if pressed too hard.

Chloe hesitated, then said, "I thought, maybe if I gave him that part of me, it'd make us closer." Her voice was low, uncertain. "But now I think that's all he wants. And I don't know,

I guess I thought we were more than that. Like, real friends too. Did I just mess it all up?"

Chloe's phone lit up on the desk beside her.

"Should you get that—if it's about Margaret's mom?" Frankie asked.

"It's not. Just Patrick," Chloe said.

Frankie pictured the string of notifications waiting, each message another thread pulling Chloe further away from this rare moment of honesty. How she longed for the days before cell phones and social media, when teenage walls weren't reinforced by glowing screens and endless feeds. Then, as if by some small miracle, Chloe flipped the phone face down and looked back at her expectantly.

Frankie tried to keep her expression neutral. The dreams she and Janey once had about their kids growing up together, and maybe even falling in love, felt idealistic and naive now. Chloe was no longer just Chloe. Part of her would forever be tethered to Patrick, her identity indelibly intertwined with his.

"He's pressuring you? I'm not going to ask if you're being safe, because I trust you," Frankie said carefully. "Thank you for telling me." She hoped Chloe would roll her eyes, brush it off, and say she was overreacting. That of course she wasn't pregnant because they'd watched *Teen Mom* together, and no part of those girls' lives seemed remotely appealing.

"Uh, yes, Mom, we are being safe." She kept her gaze on the yellow floral phone case, her fingers tracing its edges. "But tell me I'm not stupid for thinking it would make us closer," she said quietly.

"You're not stupid," Frankie said, leaning forward. "It makes sense you'd want it to bring you closer. Look, this might sound gross, but—"

Chloe groaned, her cheeks already turning pinker.

"The difference for women and men when they engage in sex is that women let someone into their bodies. It's intimate in the truest sense—"

"Please stop. I want to die now," Chloe muttered, burying her face in her hands.

"I warned you," Frankie said, undeterred. "If you're old enough to have sex, you're old enough to talk about it. Deep breaths, everyone. They're just words." Frankie positioned her hands out flat in front of her, as if steadying herself, too, before continuing. "Of course you wanted it to mean something. He has become a part of you in a way that is different for girls than it is for guys. Have you talked to him about it?"

"Yeah," Chloe said, lifting her head. "And he's acting like everything's fine, which just makes me madder. Please don't tell Auntie Janey. Seriously, Mom. Swear you won't. I'd usually talk to Margaret, but I can't. You know, because of her mom." Her voice caught, and Frankie's stomach twisted. Sixteen was far too young to carry so much, and all she wanted was to shield her daughter from life's unnecessary cruelties—the ones that showed up too early and stayed too long. The ripple effect of Brie's disappearance had made its way downstream to Chloe, and Frankie hated the thought that it might have influenced such a monumental decision in Chloe's life.

"Is that why you decided to have sex? Because of Brie?"

Chloe hesitated, her fingers fidgeting again with her phone case.

"We'd talked about it for a while now. I always knew it would be him. I've loved him since I was fourteen, when he wrote me a poem about the dead bird during that joint family trip to Monterey. After I made us have a funeral for it, he said I cared for everything with my whole heart." She sniffed and looked away. "But then with Mrs. Hoover missing . . . What if life is short? It just felt like, what's the point in waiting?"

Frankie bit back the urge to remind her it had been only three days since Brie disappeared. Could that really be enough time for Chloe and Patrick to make such a choice, and then for it to have already soured into something that left Chloe doubting his motives?

"I just don't know." Chloe shrugged.

The casualness of that gesture made Frankie's chest ache. She wanted to lift her daughter upright, make her stand tall, remind her to treat herself like something sacred. Her girls were Frankie's finest creation, built from all her best parts. Inviting a man to share your body didn't warrant a shrug.

But it was already done. "I'll make you an appointment with Dr. Linda to talk about birth control."

Chloe's cheeks flushed again. "I already did."

Frankie was both surprised and not at all surprised. Chloe was responsible in all the ways a parent could ever want. She'd stopped needing reminders to brush her teeth twice a day starting in kindergarten. She even remembered to floss in the evenings.

"Did you go see Dr. Linda?" When Chloe nodded, gaze still averted, Frankie said, "I'm glad you are safe, and I'm impressed you took care of this all on your own." Her daughter's profile—those sharp cheekbones—reminded Frankie of pictures of her mom at that age. It was a reflection in a genealogical rearview mirror, distorted by time.

"Thanks for not freaking out," Chloe said softly.

Frankie let out a sigh. "Thank you for telling me," she said again.

They sat in silence for a moment, Chloe staring at the pattern of the couch across the room while Frankie tried to pinch at some of the office chair's irregular stitches that had come loose over time. Caleb didn't care about having nice furniture in his office, so this was a chair brought over from their old place, their old life.

"Some of my friends are on IUDs, but I went with the pill," Chloe said, her voice breaking the silence. "Dr. Linda helped me figure out what was best for me." Her words were careful and measured. Frankie felt a flicker of relief that they weren't done talking after all.

"But Patrick still wore a condom? Don't let him try to convince you otherwise. The guy always says they don't need to once you go on birth control, but he still should. The whole *It doesn't feel as good for the guy with a condom* argument is manipulation. You know what else doesn't feel good? Pushing out a baby before you're ready." Frankie could no longer stop herself from sounding like a worried mom.

"Ugh, yes." Chloe rolled her eyes. "He still is!"

Frankie knew she was on the verge of losing her. So she stood and sat down next to Chloe on the desk, gently bumping her shoulder, a small gesture of reassurance.

"Do you feel . . ." She paused to make sure her next question wasn't overly intrusive but still hit the mark, since she might not get another chance to ask. "Do you feel respected by Patrick?"

"Mom! Come on. It was my decision completely. I love him."

Frankie smiled sincerely. "First loves are special."

"I can't help but think of him as my first and last love." Chloe's eyes gleamed, catching the light in a way that made it seem as though they were keeping a secret too big for this world. As if she were the first one to discover how the connection of her body with his could alter a woman's brain chemistry forever.

Later, Frankie lay alone in her and Caleb's bed, staring at the ceiling. She hoped the timing of Chloe and Patrick's decision to have sex had come from a place of closeness, not confusion. But she couldn't shake the worry that Patrick had taken advantage of Chloe's rawness, her sensitivity around her best friend's mom going missing. Frankie didn't want to believe he was capable of that. That Janey, a lifelong friend, could raise a son who would exploit someone else's pain, even subconsciously. But he was a teenage boy. And Frankie knew how narrow that mindset could be, how one-track and impulsive, especially when it came to sex.

Even her own husband, long past his teenage years, had

regressed to something primal in the car that day, half conscious, pants down, hand instinctively wrapped around himself like it was the only thing he knew how to do. The thought rippled through her, cold and unwelcome, like someone else's fingers tracing the knobs of her spine, vertebra by vertebra.

She thought back to when she was just a little older than Chloe. Choosing UC Del Mar hadn't really been a choice at all—it was a reaction. Mere had gone north, so Frankie had staked her claim in the south. It felt less like independence than severing, a way to prove she could exist apart from her sister.

Janey's decision to attend UC Blue Ridge gutted her. Frankie pretended she didn't care, but the truth was she'd barely looked into Del Mar. She hadn't toured it, hadn't compared programs. She'd only seen the beach photo on their website and decided that was enough. The school had the UC name, yes, but everyone knew its reputation rested on sand, parties, and excess—and that drew her in.

She signed up for a dorm with a pool, only to arrive and find it was a converted off-campus hotel. The vending machines hummed in the fluorescent hallways, casting shadows that made it feel more like an abandoned asylum than student housing. Her roommate was kind but insecure, and neither of them had the tools to navigate the upheaval of a new life. Frankie wanted connection badly enough to throw herself into the chaos, and soon their room became a revolving door of social distractions.

Her first weekend, before classes even started, a care package arrived from her high school boyfriend up at UC Blue Ridge. Inside were snacks, a handwritten note, and a handle of Smirnoff Raspberry vodka. Frankie could still remember unscrewing the cap, the sharp scent hitting her throat before the liquid ever did. Even now, anything with artificial raspberry flavoring turned her stomach.

The bottle didn't last the weekend. They passed it around like a rite of passage, one that initiated her into an illusion of belonging. By the next night, Frankie needed more, and she aimed to use her newfound freedom to get it. She didn't yet understand that freedom wasn't the same as safety, lacking both the life experience and fully formed frontal lobe she needed to tell the difference.

So that night, wanting to keep the warmth of the buzz going, she said yes when a guy—just visiting the dorms—offered her a ride. She didn't ask his name. Couldn't remember his face now, wouldn't be able to pick him out of a lineup. But he had a car and a fake ID, and he'd been nice. At the time, that felt like enough to let her guard down.

No one had ever taught her that niceness wasn't proof of decency. Her mom had died before she could have those important mother-daughter conversations—not just about sex or heartbreak, but about that quiet gut instinct that Frankie, like all women, would get when something felt off. How it wasn't anxiety or drama, but survival. And how girls were often trained to ignore it for the sake of being polite. To smile through. Stay agreeable.

Choose flattery over fear in the face of a danger hidden in plain sight.

No one had taught her to trust that flicker in between, the part that whispered, *This might not be okay.*

If her mom had lived long enough to teach her, if Mere hadn't left her alone with their unstable father, if someone—anyone—had shown her what to do with that unease, she never would've gotten in that car.

If only, if only, if only.

As a mother, especially a sober one, Frankie had spent years having open conversations with her daughters about their bodies and their decisions. She had tried her very best to create the kind of home where nothing had to be hidden. And now, Chloe had handled everything, made the appointment, even shared the news without flinching. Frankie had done everything she said she would do as a mom. So why did it feel like something inside her had slipped out of place?

She couldn't shake the unease. Something about Caleb's actions in the car and then the way he'd fixated on the blankets. And now Chloe, her oldest, was no longer a virgin. The dominoes toppled one by one, and for a brief moment, Frankie let herself feel envious of the mothers who could take the edge off with a single glass of wine. Who could mute the noise without unraveling.

But then came the familiar recoil. She'd always hated that narrative, the subtle misogyny that framed mothers as too fragile to bear the weight of their own lives without a crutch. Still, beneath that resistance was the creeping dread about Brie, who might've been reaching out to Frankie just hours before she disappeared. In sobriety, Frankie had come to understand that drinking was modeled as a solution in her childhood home after their mother died. Her dad used booze the way other people used sleep or prayer. Intoxication was what coping looked like.

Frankie knew she couldn't drink, but she did have something natural and supposedly safe she could try. She'd brought her purse upstairs earlier and put it on the nightstand, opening herself up to the possibility without really thinking about it. Like she'd been in the same half-in, half-out daze her husband was in earlier. Some primal, unconscious part of her knew she'd need something to reach for. And so she did. She pulled out the tin. Even though she'd already memorized the fine print, she read it again: *1–2 gummies for desired effect.*

Her desired effect was simple: She wanted relief. An exit ramp, however brief. Not to disappear, but to dim.

Her phone buzzed. Caleb was texting her from the guest bedroom where they had left him.

Caleb: *I got up to pee but now I'm going back to bed down here.*

The image of Caleb, uninvited in her mind, blurred into the memory of him in the car. She popped two gummies in her mouth and waited for the relief to come.

12

MERE

Tuesday, March 19, 2024

"Hey, this is weird," Mere said, phone in her hand. "Adrienne—my crush from high school—just shared the post about how Brie's missing. How would they even know each other?" She and Avery sat on the back patio while their kids played nearby, the weekend's snow now thinned to a manageable layer. It was late afternoon, that gray stretch around four thirty when the day sagged toward dinner and bedtime, and Mere and Avery had fallen into their familiar cadence, each instinctively knowing where to step in.

"I've seen that too. My aunt in Portland reshared my post. Hey, what does she look like?" Avery asked inquisitively, tilting her head toward Mere's phone. "Do you still think she's hot?"

"Yes, I mean she's beautiful," Mere confessed, warmth creeping up her neck. "I follow her on Instagram and usually see her stories. She's married now, to a woman, with two kids."

Secretly, she was enjoying their exchange since these types of moments never really happened for her in high school.

"Is she more beautiful than me?" Avery stuck her lips into a pout. The question came out teasing, but something else lingered on Avery's face that Mere couldn't quite place. Mere had long suspected there was more to Avery and Tom's marriage than met the eye. They had yet to fully delve into the intricacies of it, but she knew Avery would get there whenever she was ready.

"Well now, no one is more beautiful than you," Mere offered, watching Avery closely. There was a flicker here that felt electric. A tension behind the joke. Was it jealousy? Mere couldn't pin it down, but it curled in her stomach like a question she didn't know how to ask.

Avery grinned, grabbed Noah's hands, and spun with him through what was left of the snow until they collapsed in a breathless, dizzy heap. Noah darted over to join Lily a few feet away, picking up where they'd left off with their snow activity. Avery returned to standing beside Mere. She tugged her coat tighter, shoving her hands inside the front pouch to keep warm.

"Last night," Mere said suddenly, as she examined Avery's coat, "Dale was in the reading chair in our room. He was hunched over in that hoodie he always wears . . . with his hands shoved inside like that." She nodded toward Avery, then looked away abruptly, blinking hard to try to clear her mind. "It sparked this memory I haven't thought about in years. And now I can't get it out of my head."

Avery angled toward her, waiting.

"There was this boy in high school—Jason Hyde. He sat next to me in Mr. Pierce's World History class. I loved that class. The first day, Mr. Pierce said, 'Does anyone know why we learn about history?' I raised my hand and said, 'So we don't repeat the mistakes of our past.' I became Mr. Pierce's favorite after that." Mere's smile faded as the memory turned darker.

"So Jason Hyde sat one seat over from me, in the row directly beside mine. He wasn't exactly popular, but he wasn't an outcast either, just one of those kids who hovered in the middle. Every day he wore an oversized hoodie, with his hands buried deep in the front pocket, just like Dale's were last night in our bedroom. But unlike Dale, Jason never sat still. His legs bounced constantly, and something inside that sweatshirt was always twitching, jittery, like he was plugged into a low-voltage current. He'd rest his head on the desk, and all the girls would give each other the signal, like little looks or nudges. It became a routine of its own, watching and waiting for the moment when he'd put his head down and start twitching."

"Like he was having a seizure?" Avery asked, genuinely puzzled. Which made sense. The scene had been equally as confusing to witness.

Mere shook her head. "Not a seizure. One day Jason finally pulled his hands out of the pocket. There was a gelatinous, whitish goo webbed between his fingers. Then he stood up, walked to the sink, and rinsed his hands clean. The girls never signaled each other after that."

Avery's eyes widened.

Mere pressed her lips together. Even now, it felt almost

humiliating to say. "I didn't understand what I was looking at until Frankie—God, Frankie was younger than me—said it straight. He was jacking off. In class. Right beside me."

Noah whooped as he threw a pine cone into the "soup," splattering snow across his mittens.

"I couldn't stop showering after that," Mere whispered. "Like my skin knew before my head caught up. And when I saw Dale sitting like that last night . . . I felt it all over again. Like I'll never be clean."

"I'm really sorry that happened, Mere. That's not okay." Avery wrapped her arm around Mere's shoulder and drew her in.

"Is Jason Hyde on Instagram?" Avery asked.

"I have no idea. I haven't checked."

"Do you think anyone ever confronted him about what he did?"

"No way," Mere exclaimed. "What would they have even said to him?"

"That witnessing someone masturbate without your consent is a violation. A form of lewd conduct and he could be charged with a crime." Avery was suddenly all business.

"Of course he wouldn't be charged with a crime. Rape isn't even a criminal offense anymore. You can still be president," Mere grumbled, then threw in, "Plus I never really saw anything, only the aftermath."

Avery stayed firm. "You're allowed to feel defiled if that's how it felt."

Mere thought back to her excessive showers, how even

boiling-hot water hadn't been enough to make her feel clean.

"You know, that was my first image of male ejaculation."

Mere lifted her head off Avery's shoulder, and Avery regarded Mere with such compassion that she didn't want to look away. She felt seen—really seen.

Over the years they had fallen into an unspoken choreography of friendship. If one of them had eyes on the kids, the other managed snacks and cleanup, switching without ever needing to ask. It was easy, efficient, comforting. Intimate in its own quiet way. Earlier that winter, Mere had discovered that Lily loved sitting outside in the snow, especially when it was fresh and untouched. The four of them had made a habit of it, spending nearly every afternoon bundled up in that makeshift winter routine, a rhythm that felt like its own kind of survival.

The snow was slushy today, perfect for Noah's "snow soup" project. He stirred with enthusiasm while Lily gathered leaves and twigs, handing them off so he could toss them into the pot. Technically, it was still considered parallel play, Lily mimicking the activity beside him rather than diving into his world of imagination, but Mere counted it as a win. To be fair to Lily and her developmental milestones, sometimes Mere felt like everyone was just living side by side, eyes fixed on their own paths, only looking up when they needed someone else for survival. *Oh hey, you're there too.* Or maybe that was just her experience with Dale. Some days, Mere wanted to throw open the red door and shout, *Connect with me, please.*

"Do you ever think certain people show up in our lives exactly when we need them most?" Avery asked.

Mere glanced sideways at her, surprised. "I do. Sometimes I think about my mom that way. Did I ever tell you I had a dream about her the night we found out I was pregnant with Lily? It was so unexpected, after years of trying and giving up, but in the dream, my mom whispered in my ear and put her hand on my belly. I woke up and took a test in the middle of the night. Positive. It made me believe she was still looking out for me. It's why, no matter how hard things get, I never worry too much about Lily. I feel like Mom has her."

Avery's expression softened, snow light reflecting in her dark eyes. "Mmm, that's so lovely."

Mere's words tumbled out before she could stop them. "I think I want another baby. But I'm so scared."

Avery didn't rush to fill the silence, didn't start rattling off reasons it was a bad idea, like Frankie would have. She just asked, quietly, "What scares you most?"

Mere's throat tightened. "Dale barely manages with one. We're not young anymore. By the time Lily's in elementary school, people might mistake him for her grandfather. And then . . ." She paused, searching for breath. "What if another child is also neurodivergent? I don't know if I could handle that. I don't know if Dale could."

Avery reached over, squeezing her wrist through the thick wool of her sweater. "You don't have to know all the answers right now. You just have to know what your heart is asking for."

Mere nodded, though her mind caught on the same snag as always. *If we were to have another baby, he'd have to change. He'd need to learn how to be more intuitive about our children's needs. He'd need to meet me halfway.*

Noah crouched by a square of fresh snow, scooping fistfuls into a dented mixing bowl he'd carried out from the play kitchen, announcing the soup was almost ready for everyone. Lily sat beside him, not exactly helping but not apart either—lining up sticks along the rim of the bowl, tapping each one three times before setting it in place.

Neither of them spoke as they watched the children. Mere found herself noticing Avery's beauty again, not in her features, but in the knowing she carried, the way only a woman could, the same kind of knowing Adrienne had possessed back in high school. That fundamental understanding made her all the more appealing.

"Wanting Adrienne back then felt as impossible as wanting another baby now," Mere whispered just loud enough for Avery to hear, but not so loud that it warranted a response, because both longings collapsed under the weight of what she was already carrying.

"You know, I can totally see the appeal of women-run communes, the ones up in the mountains exclusively for women and children," Avery said, brushing ice off her pants.

"What, like a cult?" Mere laughed.

"No, not like a cult. A community. Gah, think of the efficiency. I imagine they'd run like a well-oiled machine."

Mere lowered her gaze in agreement, trying to envision the lightness she'd feel if all forms of labor were divided equally. If that were the case, if Mere were to run away and take Lily to a women-run community, she knew without a doubt she'd want another child. But that was crazy. Of course she would never do that, and yet strangely, she could envision a life in which it was her and Avery and their children, churning butter, tending to goats like her father up in Washington. A simple, stripped-down life with no Dale but two children. She could want something like that and still be happy in the life she currently had, right? She was allowed to have those thoughts at the same time.

"I'm hoping, praying, that Brie just snuck off to a place like that," Avery said, her voice soft but tight with emotion. "An intentional space. Somewhere she could slip away on purpose. Her husband is a youth minister, so I can't help but think she was trying to hide from something."

Mere shrugged, but she didn't speak. Mere hadn't known Brie. They didn't have children the same ages, so they only managed to be connected through Janey, and of course Frankie. But it was enough of a connection that Mere's social media had been swallowed whole by the algorithm's obsession with the story.

Every time she opened Instagram, there it was again: *The Vanishing Mom of Big Sky.* Clickbait, dressed in tragedy. The captions were all variations on the same sick melody: *How could a woman just vanish? Why didn't anyone notice she was struggling? Was it foul play—or a mother pushed too far?*

"I hope she went someplace safe. I hope she's safe," Mere echoed twice, for good measure, her voice catching a little. Saying it aloud felt like a talisman, like maybe if she repeated it enough times, it would be true. "There is no way she'd just leave her kids behind. That doesn't seem plausible. The more I think about it, the more I believe something awful must have happened."

"I know," Avery said quietly. "I worry about the exact same thing."

Lately there had been a few good days in a row with Lily. Her therapy sessions had gone well, and she'd started requesting sensory input before moments that might have overwhelmed her. In those manageable stretches, Mere couldn't tell if what she felt was a longing for another baby or a fear of disrupting the fragile progress they were finally making.

"I've been writing," Mere said, ready to move the subject away from Brie.

"That's great, Mere. Like what? A book?"

"No, not a book." Mere shook her head. "Lily, don't put the brown snow in your mouth please, yuck." Lily made a face of disgust and wiped at her tongue with her bare, reddened fingers. But those, too, were dirty. "Right now it's just kind of a collection of thoughts, I guess, like a journal. But it feels really good. Like a way to connect myself back to . . . myself." Mere laughed. "If that makes any sense."

"That makes perfect sense." Avery's smile lit up her face as she said, "Look at you coming home to yourself."

Mere gripped the shopping cart handle with one hand, balancing a small basket against her hip with the other. Just a quick trip—milk, apples, something for dinner. In and out. That's what she had told herself.

Lily rode inside the cart, her legs dangling through the holes, buckled in with the little red strap. She clutched her blue silicone chew necklace against her lips, the globe secured beside her in a quilted purse. Mere had engineered it like a toddler-safe version of the high school egg drop project she'd once won: an insulated lunch box with padded sides, layered with fleece scraps, cotton balls, and the sleeves of an old baby sleep sack she hadn't been able to throw away. Nestled in the center, cushioned and contained, was Lily's globe. It had become her most beloved of the "softs"—her word for anything that brought comfort, even if it was made of glass.

Mere had secured the whole thing with a tangle of Velcro straps and added a crossbody belt so Lily could carry it like a purse. It bounced gently at her hip when she walked, the buffered lining muffling the clink of glass. Dale had suggested 3D printing something "more efficient," but Mere had waved him off. This wasn't about efficiency. It was about comfort—the assurance that she could keep Lily's most treasured object safe, even if it was, at its core, just a giant sphere of fragile glass. Dale hadn't thought much beyond the novelty when he gave it to her. Neither of them could have predicted Lily would imprint on it so completely. The tiny cars circling inside soothed her, a little world she could control, and Mere wasn't about to take that away.

As they muddled toward the milk, Lily began making guttural sounds, the kind that signaled she was edging toward overload. The noises came again and again, raw and pained, and Mere couldn't ignore the way shoppers stiffened at the edges of the aisle, as if the sound itself carried something unhinged. Their faces flickered with concern, then hardened into suspicion, as though she might be hurting her own child. Mere could feel the weight of their glances pressing against her back, the unspoken question hanging in the air: Should someone step in? She wanted to tell them she understood; even she could remember, in the beginning, how those unfamiliar noises had spiked her pulse.

They turned into the dairy aisle just as a baby wailed from a few carts over. A sudden crash followed, the sharp explosion of a jar somewhere shattering on tile. Mere felt it before she saw it. The tension running through Lily's small frame, the quick, jerky movements, her breathing going shallow. She went rigid. Her noises stopped.

Mere braced herself. For all the progress they'd made in therapy, there was no way to prepare for the sudden sounds beyond their bubble. Lily couldn't ask for sensory input when she didn't know what was coming. It was all so spectacularly unfair.

The scream began as a vibration, barely a sound at all, just a tremble behind her teeth, before it sharpened into a single, slicing note that could split glass. Lily threw her arms out wildly, kicking as if an invisible monster were pressing down against her, limbs rigid, like a toy solider that was never meant to see combat. From a nearby aisle, a customer grabbed a bottle of juice, sending a second one tumbling from the shelf and rolling across the floor. Then there was more shattering and screams from across the store, and Mere wished she could tuck them both safely inside the egg drop basket and furl her body around Lily, hold her and protect her until the storm had passed. Even if there was only room for Lily, Mere would be just outside, standing guard.

Mere hunched over, reaching for her inside the cart, but Lily recoiled as if she were being scalded by hot pokers. Her hands flew to her ears, eyes screwed shut, body rocking violently against the seat.

The stares started immediately. A woman near the yogurt case sucked her teeth, shaking her head. A man in a fleece vest muttered something under his breath. Even if he had spoken loud enough for Mere to hear, she'd trained herself to mute other people's cruelty whenever this happened. Mere had no point of reference to compare, but it felt like as Lily got older, these kinds of episodes were getting more volatile, and the bigger she got, the harder it was to settle her down. A teenage boy near the self-checkout actually laughed. To onlookers it must have seemed like nothing more than a toddler in a tantrum. But she saw it in their eyes too—that flicker of unease, the way a sound so sharp and body so rigid made them wonder if Lily could be dangerous. Fear disguised as judgment.

Lily flailed, her face growing blotchy with panic.

"Lily, it's okay. You're okay." But she wasn't. And Mere couldn't fix it.

Lily let out another piercing wail, twisting in the cart, trying to free herself—not from the red belt across her lap, it seemed, but from the confines of her own skin. Sometimes

Mere imagined her daughter as one raw, exposed nerve ending. And Mere had to be losing it completely to think another baby might be the right thing for their family. Her eyes stung. If someone walked by and saw her now, they'd assume she was crying because Lily was too much, when really it was the guilt that undid her. Was it selfish to long for a child who wouldn't get overstimulated in the middle of a grocery store? Were mothers even allowed to think like this—to wish, secretly, for someone easier—she wondered, as Lily's wails cut through her chest.

Control your child. Was it coming from her own mind, or was she picking up on everyone else's silent communication?

The strangers' wide eyes churned something older in her too. A memory of Dale, years ago, waking her in the middle of the night when they were first dating. He had driven her out to a dark field to look at the stars, gentle, almost boyish in his excitement. And yet, in those first seconds, jolted from sleep and led into the shadows, she had felt a prickle of fear. She never suspected he would hurt her. But does anyone harbor suspicion, until they do?

After what had to be Lily's third piercing screech, one that, to an untrained ear, might've signaled she was in need of outside help or intervention, Mere made the call to abandon ship. She emptied the cart right there, refrigerated items and all, dumping them in the nearest pantry aisle. It killed her to break the rules, but she needed the stroller-sized support to get Lily safely back to the car.

Mere hoped the rush of cold air when they made it outside

would help soothe Lily. She wanted to unbuckle her, but her daughter was still thrashing, a sob choking in her throat, little hands clawing at everything in sight. Mere gently held her arms away, doing her best to keep Lily from getting hurt. People passed. They stared. No one stopped.

As Lily shrieked—wanting to be held for pressure but unable to bear touch—Mere's mind spiraled back to the version of Frankie who had arrived in Big Sky. Her sister had been the same, craving closeness yet recoiling from it, receiving tenderness like a blow. From then on, touch seemed to mean something different to Frankie, though Mere never knew exactly what had bent her that way. Was it whatever she'd been through before she came, or just the years Mere hadn't been there to shield her? All Mere knew was that Frankie had learned to brace herself against love, even as she longed for it.

A mother with two school-aged kids passed in the parking lot and caught Mere's eye. Her children darted from the cart, weaving between slow-moving cars, and she corralled them with quiet urgency. She loaded them into the car, pausing for a moment to glance back at Mere. Just two mothers, side by side, each straining to do right by their children. Neither could help the other, but the acknowledgment was oddly comforting.

Lily kept stimming, her small body taut with restlessness, until Mere shifted her stance so her daughter could press her forehead against her shoulder blade. The firm contact offered Lily a kind of anchor.

Then, as the other mother lifted a brown paper bag from her cart, the handle tore. Groceries spilled onto the pavement.

Mere bent automatically, picking up the cantaloupe that had likely caused the collapse. Lily stirred, stretching toward it, and Mere let her take the fruit. The rough rind drew Lily in; her fingers traced the ridges as if they were tiny tracks, and her body began to quiet.

Mere started toward the woman's trunk to return it, but Lily protested.

"You keep it," the woman said. Mere nearly waved off the gesture, nearly folded it into the pile of everyday kindnesses that slipped away unnoticed. But this one lingered.

Lily continued her quiet exploration, breathing slower now, steadier.

The woman pressed the button on her key fob to close the trunk, then—before leaving—reached toward Lily and ran her own fingers across the cantaloupe's patterned skin, mirroring Lily's small, curious touch. When she looked up, she gave Mere a soft, knowing smile, the kind exchanged in the universal language of motherhood, where no words are needed, only the quiet recognition of what it means to love a child so fiercely it aches.

That night, back at home, she texted Frankie, wanting to hear if she had any update on Brie.

Still no word.

Mere pictured her sister at home with her two girls, doing ordinary things, maybe even grocery shopping, and thought of how different their experiences had become. After college, she had believed that as they stumbled forward, got married, and started families, their parallel paths would finally converge. When she became pregnant with Lily, Mere was certain it would be the bridge between them, the one language they could both speak fluently: motherhood.

But their experiences were too different, the gap too wide. It wasn't resentment Mere felt, not exactly, when she looked at Frankie's two healthy, neurotypical daughters. To call it envy implied she wasn't grateful for her sweet Lily. She was. But she did envy the simplicity. The ease of their early years. Even now, her jaw tightened at the thought of how, in those precious and irretrievable days, Frankie had been too drunk to notice what she had—the sort of days Mere would have given anything to experience with Lily.

Mere got a text from Avery checking in.

You good?

Mere almost said yes but instead typed and deleted a dozen messages. She wanted to tell Avery that a woman in the supermarket parking lot made her feel more seen in a few minutes than Dale had since he got home from camping. But instead she said, *Today was hard.*

Come over. I'll make tea. You can just sit.

Mere paused, staring at her phone. She knew she wouldn't go. Knew she wanted to. She set down the phone and curled her body around Lily's in their bed, syncing with her breath while her mind still tugged toward the warmth on the other side of town.

13

FRANKIE

Tuesday, March 19, 2024

Somewhere in the haze, Frankie found Brie's pink '80s-themed sweatshirt from chaperoning the school dance and pulled it on, despite the lingering sour scent of vomit. She pretended not to notice, tried to convince herself it was just a different detergent, another woman's natural musk. Frankie had told Brie she'd wash it and bring it back, but Brie, embarrassed, asked her to keep it—said she didn't need a physical reminder of her humiliation when it already lived rent-free in her mind, playing on a loop.

Where are you, Brie?

She stared at herself in the full-length mirror Caleb had hung after they built the walk-in closet. She pulled up her hair, folding it in half the way she and Mere used to do in the pool when it was wet and moldable, shaping it short to match Brie's blunt bob. She squatted, lowering her center of gravity. Brie was such a tiny woman. *She* is *a tiny woman*, Frankie corrected herself immediately.

She hated that she hadn't pushed harder for Brie to attend their women's meeting. *As her sponsor, wasn't I responsible for looking out for Brie?* Why had she not taken her message in the arboretum as a warning? The last time they spoke, Brie had been cagey about her recovery. *It is my job to guide her.* Frankie also hated that the THC wasn't dulling the gnawing sense of dread bubbling up inside her, and her mind latched onto the promise of another option.

Sometime between taking the gummies and whatever time it was now, she had made it down to the guest room to check on Caleb. He was awake and on his phone. She asked about his pain level, offering his prescription pain meds along with his antibiotics, and he waved her off. "Nah, frow dose out. I'm goo' wif Advil," he mumbled, his response thick with gauze and numbness. His face was puffy, and she could tell he was still frozen by the way he fished around for the words like they were hiding somewhere inside his swollen cheeks.

She hadn't responded to his request, so it wasn't a lie, necessarily, that she'd left the orange bottle of oxycodone prescribed to Caleb in the medicine cabinet. It was more a withholding of certain information, just as he had withheld details about taking mushrooms on his camping trip. Now, Frankie made her way there. Before she could overthink it, thankfully dulled by the gummies, she shook two pills into her hand and swallowed them, bending to drink straight from the faucet on Caleb's side of the sink. Then she tucked the bottle deep inside her makeup bag, out of sight.

Frankie told herself that if Caleb had been up front about taking drugs with the guys—and about how confused he still was about what he'd seen that night—then she would have dumped the pills. But in some twisted way, keeping them felt like a middle finger. A petty tit-for-tat move that should have been far beneath her after so many years of marriage. The gummies blurred out the voice of reason she'd managed to cling to for the past decade. And what did it matter? She wasn't drinking. It was fine to leave her body for a while.

Then there was the thing that happened in the car, something she couldn't even begin to think about bringing up with Caleb. That would invite questions, and he'd want to make sure she was okay. Sometimes their marriage felt like an echo chamber, the same concerns bouncing between them until Frankie wanted to stick her head out the window just to interrupt the noise.

Caleb thrived on routine. He took pride in being steady, a pillar of financial security and stability. But mundanity made Frankie restless. Her instinct was to burn it all down, a truth she had come to understand in recovery. Her alcoholic brain wasn't wired for peace; it was wired to keep her sick, to whisper that chaos was comfort, and to do whatever it took to stoke the flames.

Caleb had always been her touchstone. Her constant, even when she wavered. For so long, she had prided herself on being a fiercely independent feminist who didn't need a man. But Caleb had confronted her in therapy once, saying, "You make it sound like needing someone is a bad thing." She had fought so hard after everything that happened in Santa Barbara. Had trauma-dumped in her first AA meeting, rattling off every excruciating detail of the night that had left her physically and mentally shattered. She had convinced herself that she needed a horrific event in order to qualify as an alcoholic. That she wasn't allowed to be just another privileged white woman who had everything and still drank too much pinot.

It didn't feel safe to need people. Look what had happened when she needed her mother, who died, or when she had tried to connect with her father, whose mental illness made any real dependency on him impossible. Her sister? She left.

The warmth of the pills settled into her, tucking her thoughts neatly onto shelves, placing them just out of reach. Thanks to the combination of gummies and pills, she no longer had access to any of those worries. And the truly glorious part was that she no longer cared. She floated around the room, amused at how the concoction somehow made worrying about Brie bearable. She'd discovered the secret passageway that could best mirror the relief alcohol once gave her. She grabbed her phone and did a quick Google search. It was disturbingly easy to buy oxy online. Wanting to be selective about when she took the pills, she downed two more of the gummies for good measure.

Back in the closet she found her reflection, surprising herself that she was still in Brie's sweatshirt. That night at the high school dance when Brie was wasted, Frankie had, thankfully, parked in the staff lot after hours, figuring she was permitted as a chaperone. She had led Brie out the side entrance, and none of the administration or students caught on to what was happening. Brie slept it off in Frankie's truck while Frankie went back and forth between the gymnasium and the parking lot, between chaperoning students and caretaking for another mom. When the dance ended and Frankie returned to her truck, Brie was awake and sipping the water Frankie had left next to her in the cup holder.

I jus'—I don' get it, okay?

Get what? Frankie asked, settling into the back seat beside her, holding out the water bottle and gently encouraging her to take another sip.

Like, how do those moms drink their . . . their White Claws at soccer games like it's no big deal, and then go home and—what—cook dinner? Do bedtime? Be there and not need more. I mean . . . why can't I just have a glass of wine at book club without it being a thing, huh? When did I become a clichéd character from The White Lotus*? When did I become invisible to everyone?* Brie was slurring, her delivery landing thick and bitter with resentment. It was the way she shared at the group level, never reaching the point of complete and total surrender. Frankie understood. She'd resented her alcoholism for years before she made peace with the fact that she could never drink like other people, and it was easier to quit completely than continue trying and failing to moderate her drinking. The early 2000s were littered with her attempts.

Frankie knew in the back of the truck that nothing she could have said to Brie would sink in. Brie likely wouldn't remember what they'd talked about at all, but still Frankie wanted to give her some kind of message of hope.

I promise it is so much easier once you let go absolutely and stop fighting it.

Brie must have remembered what she said after all, because the next day she reached out and asked Frankie to be her sponsor. And look at all the good that had done.

Nope. She cut short her toxic thoughts, wanting to halt the negativity before it took root. No point in wasting the THC and oxy, which had her wrapped in dopey sleepiness, the kind that made her want to put on Stevie Nicks and sway in her underwear, not drain a bottle of vodka. She wasn't worried. She was chill.

She scrolled through Spotify and found an old playlist she hadn't listened to since the girls were little.

"You get it, Stevie," she said aloud, as if Ms. Nicks herself had floated down using one of her capes as a parachute right there in Frankie's closet.

Frankie made her way to the bed and curled up, letting the high settle over her, hoping to sink into the sensation like diving into a cloud. Even as a kid, she'd tucked cough drops into her backpack and sucked them in class, thrilled by the small rebellion, convinced they held more power than they did. When her daughters were toddlers, she'd over-ordered children's Motrin, stashing bottles in the car and bathroom cabinet, comforted by the thought that she could soothe any fever, any pain. She'd seen for herself the transformation lithium worked on their dad once he went to live with Aunt Gina in Washington—how she got him stabilized in a way the sisters never could, how most days he passed as fully functional. Maybe drugs weren't the enemy at all. Maybe they were the magic.

Instead of the comfort she'd expected, her skin began to itch as her breathing turned shallow. Panic slithered into her thoughts, and suddenly she felt it—that terrifying sense that the simple act of keeping her blood moving was now up to her. She clenched her fists, convinced that was the only way to force it to circulate. But the harder she tried to control it, the more her breathing fractured into short, splintered bursts—nowhere near enough to keep her alive.

Whoa. Am I being erased? She felt as if her fingertips could separate from her hands, no longer part of her at all. The thought only made the sensation intensify, as though her own body were conspiring against her, as if some outside force were peeling her apart. It was like trying to shove a nightmare back once it had already broken loose.

Her phone was buried somewhere in the folds of the comforter, and she clawed through the blankets until she finally dragged it free. She tapped Janey's contact, her thumb hovering over the call button as her focus caught on the photo of them at the state fair, perched on the Ferris wheel. Janey had insisted they go up, even knowing how much Frankie hated heights. Yet somehow, with Janey beside her, she'd felt safe—even in her fear. She wished she'd never gone to Santa Barbara. She wished she'd come straight to Big Sky instead.

No one ever died from weed, she reminded herself.

"Hello?" Janey's voice came through, distant and muffled.

"Can you come over?" Frankie whispered. She didn't wait for a response, ending the call and flipping her phone face down.

Time became elastic. Whether ten minutes had passed or four hours, she couldn't tell. Then, suddenly, Janey was standing over her, her face inches away. Relief bloomed in Frankie's chest, knowing Janey would take over and fix whatever was happening to her. But then Frankie remembered she was responsible for her heart beating, and for that to happen she needed to open and close her fists to pump her own blood. "I crossed over," she whispered, voice trembling. "I need to sleep for a thousand years."

"Jesus Christ," Janey muttered, snapping her fingers in front of Frankie's face.

"I'm too high," Frankie admitted. "This is so scary. I fucked up. I want off the Ferris wheel." Her voice escaped as a raw and jagged edge, unrecognizable even to herself, while Janey maneuvered around her, propping her pillows higher so she could be upright in the bed.

"What did you take?" Janey demanded, her voice slipping into that maternal tone Frankie recognized—the one she used when she was scared for her boys. When Patrick was twelve he broke his leg snowboarding. Frankie met them at the hospital, and Janey was sheet white, clutching Patrick's hand as he sobbed in the wheelchair they'd put him in while they waited to be admitted.

The snow is just a death trap disguised as one big fluffy pillow, Janey had said, shaking her head like she couldn't trust anything anymore, not even the softest parts of the world, to keep her child safe.

As Janey fussed around her in bed, Frankie noticed she was wearing an old pair of her jeans. They'd always been about the same size, even during their pregnancies, and had treated each other's closets like a shared wardrobe since they were kids.

"I love that episode of *Friends*, the one where Monica accuses the housekeeper of stealing her jeans. Poor Matthew Perry."

"Frankie, are you drunk?"

Janey should've known she wasn't drunk. Obviously, she wasn't drunk, so Frankie plowed ahead to finish her thought. "I read his memoir. Remember when I texted you immediately after I finished reading and predicted his death? He hadn't surrendered completely. He claimed the 'big, terrible thing' was his addiction. I mean, I get it. But that meant he hadn't truly accepted his disease. And now he's dead. All he wanted was an end to his suffering, a tiny taste of euphoria to carry him higher."

They are all dead, Frankie thought, and before she could resist the implications of that one intrusive thought, there it went. *People like me.*

"What have I done?" Frankie squeezed her fists over and over in an effort to keep herself alive and her blood pumping. She stared at the veins in her wrist to see if they were bulging enough. "Help me."

"Come on, let's get you in the shower," Janey said, tugging on Frankie's arm and pulling her upright.

The bathroom swam into view, the world still tilting as if

she were horizontal. Movement was strange to Frankie. She had to put all her body weight into Janey, who didn't seem to have any issues holding her upright.

"Have you been working out?" Frankie tried to joke, but nothing felt funny, only sad and bleak, like the day Frankie read the headlines that Matthew Perry was dead and the articles that went on to list celebrities like River Phoenix and Heath Ledger, who had succumbed to similar fates.

"You even lift, bro?" she tried again. She was certain Janey had spent that morning at her gym teaching a class. Even though they were both tall women—Janey was five nine and Frankie five ten—while Frankie could beat Janey in a cardio challenge, Janey could bench Frankie's body weight. Maybe they could forget this whole thing, forget that her husband's exposure in the car was exactly the beginnings of how Frankie had been assaulted. Forget how she was pulling off a sweatshirt of a woman who'd gone missing.

Inside the bathroom, Janey sat Frankie on the ledge of the bathtub. "Remember when we used to put all four kids in the tub together?" Frankie laughed for the first time that night. "They'd be just a stew of limbs." She mimed stirring an imaginary pot, like Strega Nona with her endless pasta.

Janey leaned over the shower, twisting the knobs until steam began to fog up the mirror, the air thick with leftover jasmine. Frankie had done one of those bubble bath setups for Caleb recently—roses, candles, the whole deal—and the scent still lingered like a memory that couldn't read the room.

"To be young and in love," Frankie mumbled.

Janey helped peel off the remainder of Frankie's clothes, guiding her toward the water.

"They're having sex, you know," she spat out, like it was somehow Janey's fault. "*S-e-x*."

"It will be okay now. I've got you," Janey cooed. She always knew when to be tough and when to be delicate. It was how she mothered her children, and Frankie envied her ability to parent with such authority.

"Sex," Frankie repeated. "Our children. But you know who I'd love to try sex with? Professor Sam. He's sexy." Frankie closed her eyes and pictured Professor Sam naked behind her in the shower, licking the water droplets off her bare back.

"How many of these did you take?" Janey held up the tin of gummies, but Frankie had stepped into the shower, allowing the water to pound against her skin. She hoped the pressure would help push her blood through her veins so she could finally be relieved of the duty. The spray from the shower blurred Frankie's vision, forcing her to close her eyes.

"Nobody ever died from weed," Frankie mumbled, resuming her mantra from earlier, but the word *died* clanged in her head, ricocheting off the tiles like a curse.

"How many of these did you take?" Janey repeated.

Even in her deep state of fatigue, Frankie decided not to mention the oxy. She wanted to hold on to it, her singular secret that could belong only to her. The blurriest corners of her mind still knew that if she let it go, she'd also have to let go of the fog—the one thing making it possible not to think about the demons rattling around in her brain. And letting go of the promise of that relief felt far more terrifying than whatever version of hell she'd landed in.

After Janey had helped her shower and dress, she tucked Frankie into bed. Frankie had never felt more excited to sleep. But before she drifted off, a singular, hideous thought clawed its way to the surface, flapping around like a ripped flag in the wind.

What had Brie wanted? To disappear? To dull the pain? In the arboretum, Brie carried a caginess that hadn't been there before—subtle, evasive. She looked altered, like someone who'd been cracked open and was trying to hold the pieces in place before anyone could see. Why hadn't Frankie looked harder at Brie? Why was she only thinking of it now?

But the pull of sleep was too powerful.

14

MERE

Tuesday, March 19, 2024

Mere was wiping the counter when the nighttime silence caught her attention. Not the alarming kind, but the gentle kind—a gift that feels almost too fragile to unwrap when you're the parent of a child with a disability. She peeked into Lily's room and found her asleep, a dozen stuffed animals scattered around her head like a halo.

Mere stepped closer. Lily hadn't fallen asleep in her own bed—let alone put herself to sleep—in longer than she could remember. As Mere reached to feel her daughter's forehead for a fever, Pancakes lifted her head from Lily's back but settled again almost immediately. Relieved to find no trace of heat, Mere stroked one of the dog's long, silky ears and whispered, "Good girl, Pancakes," before tiptoeing out and leaving the door cracked a sliver.

Mere was happy to be alone with Dale in their bedroom.

She stepped closer, running her hand along his arm before looping her wrists behind his neck. They fit together so neatly she only had to tilt her head a fraction to meet his gaze. Dale looked at her then, holding it—an intentional kind of intimacy. She leaned in and kissed him softly. He kissed her back, and she let out a quiet hum, welcoming the closeness.

Dale had always been different from the men who came before, not that there had been many. Mere had been drawn to the ones who burned too brightly, men of grand gestures and quick apologies, who pulled her close only to push her away again, blaming the pull for their inability to stay. That turbulence felt like love because it mimicked what she'd grown up with: the unpredictable cadence of a father who swung from charm to chaos, and a mother whose harboring presence had been taken too soon. Even into her late twenties, she mistook intensity for intimacy, mood swings for connection. One boyfriend, Damien, claimed two years of sobriety, but he wasn't sober. She'd picked him up from jail after a DUI on a night he swore he was at a meeting. Sometimes Mere wondered what might have happened if she'd allowed herself to explore relationships with women—women more fluent in emotion. If she had never met Dale.

Their first date had been at the arboretum on the UC Blue Ridge campus. Dale had graduated eight years before her with a degree in civil engineering and was commuting daily to South Lake for work. When the pandemic hit, his firm, like many others, discovered engineers were often more productive from home. Dale wasn't a people person. He thrived on routine and predictability.

For their date, he took Mere to the Sky Bridge, which students had started calling the Lock Bridge, thanks to a new senior tradition of attaching padlocks to the metal fencing. The locks were meant to symbolize wishes, or luck, or maybe love. Mere had never known which, only that once the lock was snapped shut, the idea was meant to stay sealed there permanently. They walked the path around the pond, a loop just over three miles, and ended at the bridge.

Mere hadn't been out there in ages. She noticed the way students and longtime residents shared the path, moving side by side without speaking.

I did a project on this bridge my senior year, Dale said. *I haven't been back since I turned it in.* His pace quickened, as if he was eager to get there.

Dale had been handsome in an unconventional way. A little nerdy, with dark square-framed glasses that matched his hair, which he always wore the same way, neatly parted, like he had made a quiet decision long ago about who he was and never felt the need to revisit it.

As they approached the bridge, his steps slowed until he came to a stop.

What? Mere had looked around, confused.

The locks, Dale said, shaking his head. His brow furrowed in that way Mere would later recognize—something she first noticed when they learned of Lily's diagnosis. It wasn't just concentration; it was a quiet kind of grieving.

Do they think people are trying to steal the bridge? Dale had asked. Mere had laughed, but the stoicism in Dale's expression made it clear he was interpreting the situation differently. The theory behind the locks seemed sweet to most people, symbolic even. But to Dale, they were a slow form of sabotage. He explained how they were collectively destroying the bridge, how the weight added up over time. Dale couldn't understand why people felt the need to ruin a perfectly sound structure for the sake of sentiment. To him, the structural integrity of the bridge mattered more than some made-up gesture of love.

Mere didn't fully understand Dale's discomfort—why the locks unsettled him enough that he'd started fidgeting, rubbing his hands together as if to warm them by a fire. She reached for one of his hands and kissed the inside of his palm, the way their mother had done for her and Frankie as kids. It would likely seem strange to Dale, but she hoped he felt the comfort in it, this simple ritual her mother had treated as a one-size-fits-all Band-Aid. Mere had received a kiss on the palm when she fell off her bike, when she and Frankie fought, when they learned her cancer diagnosis had gone from stage 4 to incurable.

Inside their bedroom, Mere kissed Dale with more urgency than she had in years—maybe since before Lily was born. Mere and Dale had missed their standing Saturday night appointment to have sex, since he'd gone camping. She doubted Avery and Tom or Frankie and her husband had to schedule their intimacy. Not that she wanted to imagine her sister's sex life, but Frankie had always been a fly-by-the-seat-of-her-pants person, even as a teenager. Mere didn't know what it meant to go with the flow, only that it made her nervous. She preferred to put sex on the calendar, color coded, with plenty of notice. Her window of ovulation was happening right now, and Mere wondered if she should mention it to Dale.

It took him a moment to respond, like his mouth had forgotten the choreography. But then he found the rhythm, and they kept kissing, slow and searching, like they used to when sex wasn't assumed but imagined. It felt good, their bodies remembering something they hadn't touched in ages, something separate from sleep schedules and therapy appointments and who was going to do the dishes. She tried to keep them connected as she moved toward the bed, guiding him down beside her, still kissing, as if momentum could carry them the rest of the way.

"Lately I'm not sure. I feel like we should have another baby," Mere whispered in Dale's ear. "I know there are many reasons not to, but sometimes things don't have to be reasonable." They weren't actively trying not to get pregnant; it was assumed that they couldn't. That it had been difficult enough for them to have Lily, and with Mere being in her forties, perimenopausal, it likely just wouldn't happen. Mere kissed him back again with intention. Dale pressed into her. She could feel his want and she wanted him back. Wanted to connect with him in the way they had when they'd made Lily together. The best pieces of her and the best pieces of him, regardless of what anyone else had to say on the matter. It was true in her heart.

15

FRANKIE

Wednesday, March 20, 2024

"Is it you?" Janey asked as if Frankie had transformed into something else entirely. A wolf in sheep's clothing. Her face hovered just inches above Frankie's. She must have spent the night. "What the hell was that?"

Frankie reached for the water on the nightstand, using it as a much-needed pause button. A glance around the room told her that Janey had cleaned while she was asleep—or passed out, whichever had occurred. Janey placed a hand atop Frankie's forehead, checking her temperature. Frankie checked the clock. It was a little before seven in the morning, and she'd need to get the girls up within the next ten minutes if they were going to make it to school on time.

"I feel like such an idiot," Frankie offered, which was the easiest apology she could make of the many she knew she needed to.

"What the hell was that?" Janey repeated.

Despite the water, Frankie's throat still felt coated with something thick and earthy. She swallowed, but it stayed. Heavy. Unmoving.

She wanted to bolt for the bathroom, rinse it out, drown it with mouthwash. But Janey was there. Watching. Frankie knew she wouldn't be allowed to slip away without a reason.

Her mind lagged, struggling to line up the pieces. The "right" thing floated somewhere out of reach. *Tell the truth. Admit it.* But old instincts crept in faster than her clarity could.

Lie.

Say it was a fluke.

Onetime thing.

Too much by accident.

Next time she'd be careful. Next time she'd pace it. Just a little here, a little there. Manageable.

Then she looked at Janey—her furrowed brow, the crease of concern etched straight down her forehead—and Frankie felt the lie collapse before it could even reach her lips. She knew, with the same certainty she carried about never safely taking another sip of alcohol, that this secret would rot her from the inside if she tried to keep it. Yet some stubborn part of her still wanted to hold on.

"We are not leaving the bed until you come clean and tell me what happened." Frankie felt herself flinch at the word "clean."

"I thought I was doing so well. I mean, I was. I haven't had a drink in a decade. And I didn't drink, I promise." Frankie stopped short. The truth lodged somewhere between thought and speech, refusing to surface. She turned her head so her gaze locked with Janey's. "I took too many gummies, and it messed me up. I had a bad reaction. Don't worry, J. I won't be doing that again," Frankie said, offering it like an apology. She couldn't bring up the oxy. The mix of the pills and the gummies—before she'd gone too far—had been too good. She wanted to guard it the way she once protected her drinking, as fiercely and instinctively as she'd protect her own children.

"I'm embarrassed, and I'm sorry. I don't want to get into this right now. Please."

Frankie didn't know if Janey would let her off the hook, but before she could find out, Chloe came crashing in, still dressed in her pj's. Her panic filled the room like a sudden draft, sharp and undeniable.

"The police found something," Chloe said, breathless, phone clutched tight in her hand. "Margaret just texted. Her dad's on his way to the station. What if she's dead?" Panic radiated off Chloe, her whole body taut with fear.

Frankie's heart thudded in her chest. She couldn't tell if the fuzziness was from the pills last night or the sudden jolt of dread—dread she hadn't felt this sharply since she'd learned her mom's cancer was terminal. Even then, her teenage understanding of death was padded with denial. "Forever" felt theoretical. Now wasn't so different. Some part of Frankie still refused to believe death was final.

Sometimes she let herself hope—just a flicker—that her mother's reflection might appear in the bathroom mirror while

Frankie stood brushing her teeth in that worn 4XL T-shirt. But so far, she'd only ever seen her in dreams, and those dreams she could count on one hand.

"Come here." Frankie waved Chloe into bed, and she crawled on all fours between Frankie and Janey. Chloe curled on her side, clutching her phone as if it alone carried Brie's fate. Frankie ran her fingers though Chloe's hair, long golden strands that were silky with youth, resisting the urge to kiss her on the forehead in case Frankie's breath might somehow give her away.

"What else do you know?"

"Nothing, literally nothing." Chloe held up her phone a quarter inch from her face and checked it again for good measure.

"Okay, then there's nothing you can do but wait. Just be there for Margaret until we know more. Hopefully it's good news," Frankie said. "You can be late to school until we know more. I'll write you a pass."

Janey sat up straighter, pressing her back against the headboard. She had always slipped into the role of aunt with Frankie's girls in a way Mere never had—especially with Chloe. The two of them would sometimes sneak out for ice cream or coffee, little rituals of one-on-one bonding that grew even stronger during the years when Frankie was drinking.

Now, Janey placed a hand on Chloe's back and rubbed slow, gentle circles, just like she used to when Chloe had colic as a baby. Back then, Janey would show up every evening from five to six o'clock to give Frankie a one-hour break, even with her own newborn to care for. She'd wear Patrick in the front pack, where he'd stay fast asleep. Frankie used to joke that he could sleep through a Mack truck barreling through the living room, while Chloe cried and cried and was inconsolable.

"Can we talk about literally anything else?" Chloe asked. "I don't want to think about what could be happening."

There was a beat of silence.

"So, sex, huh?" Janey said.

Frankie bolted upright, horror flashing across her face as she shot Janey a look that screamed, *That was a secret!*

"Mo-om! You told her!" Chloe shot out of the bed as if the down comforter had caught fire, standing to face both of them with a look of total and utter betrayal.

Frankie scrambled to recall how she must have let it slip. She knew she mentioned it before she fell asleep, but she was certain she told Janey *not* to bring it up.

"No, it's okay. I'm not trying to embarrass you. I want to make sure Patrick is being safe and respectful," Janey said, putting her hands out in front of her as a peace offering.

Frankie was fairly confident she hadn't shared any of the private details about how Chloe felt. Janey must've meant to show support, but in doing so she'd just handed Frankie a one-way ticket off the island of trust. What was she thinking?

"I seriously cannot believe you, Mom! I'm never telling you anything again."

"No, lovie, I didn't say anything, I swear."

Frankie pushed to stand, but the blood drained from her head and the room tilted. She steadied herself, but it was too late—Chloe had already bolted, her door slamming at the far end of the hallway hard enough to rattle Frankie's bedroom walls.

Frankie swung back to Janey, who was still perched on the bed as if nothing had happened. "Are you kidding me? Why would you bring that up?" Her voice cut sharp, edged with fury. Was this Janey's way of punishing her for last night? Some twisted attempt to even the score?

"Okay, maybe my timing was off," Janey said, hands raised slightly, "but I want her to know I'm here for her. This is a big deal. We're not just going to ignore it." She said it like she was talking about something else entirely.

"I was handling it. And now you can go handle it with your son. Tell him to keep his dick in his pants and not to take advantage when my daughter is at her most vulnerable!" Even as the words left her mouth, Frankie wished she could take them back. This wasn't who they were. Attacking each other's children had never been part of their friendship. But it was too late, and she was too angry to backpedal now.

"Who even are you right now?" Janey said, her face straining like she might pop a vein in her forehead.

"Thank you for coming over last night, but I think you should go," Frankie said, turning and walking out of the bedroom.

All the gratitude she'd felt for Janey's support the night before had drained away. Her daughter needed to be able to trust her. Frankie had shared that with Janey in confidence. And even if she hadn't said it out loud, she'd been foggy and half asleep, and Janey should have known better.

She had never kicked Janey out of her house before. During her drinking days, sure, she'd picked petty fights, but recovery had brought apologies, amends, and a bond she believed was stronger for it. Or so she'd thought.

Tragedy has a texture, a way of filtering out the ambient noise of life, pushing everything else to the margins. Chloe's anger had melted away, replaced by sobs that broke against Frankie's chest. Even before her daughter spoke, Frankie could feel the layers about to unravel. She realized then that she had been waiting, waiting for someone to finally say aloud what her gut had already known to be true.

"They found her. Mrs. Hoover—she's dead."

"God. Oh god. What happened?" Frankie's own voice sounded far away.

"They found her in the snow out by Hollow Ridge. She was wrapped up in a blanket, frozen to death. They don't know anything else yet."

"I can't believe it," Frankie whispered.

Chloe crumpled against her. Frankie held her, rocking her gently, murmuring useless comforts until the sobs wore Chloe down to a state of trembling exhaustion. She guided her daughter upstairs, pulled the covers around her, and smoothed her damp hair away from her face. There would be no school today. Chloe was wrung out, grief drained, already half asleep as Frankie whispered she'd be right downstairs.

Frankie made her way to the guest room, where Caleb sat propped up in bed, phone in hand. From the look on his face, she could tell he already knew.

"She was there. Less than a quarter mile from where we were camping at Hollow Ridge." His voice was raw and unsteady, scraped thin as if he'd been repeating the words to himself before saying them out loud.

"So that was her?" Frankie didn't want to say it, but the words pressed out anyway. Her throat closed around the phrasing as she whispered, "That's what you saw?"

Caleb sucked in a sharp breath, as if pained by the accusation, internalizing it for the first time.

"She must have been buried beneath the snow when we went back in the morning," he finally said. "But yeah, Frankie. We definitely saw her. It was Brie."

They sat side by side on the guest bed, not touching, not speaking. There wasn't anything left to say.

Frankie no longer wanted to exist in her body. She was transported to her childhood, to a younger version of herself. The news of Brie's death knocked Frankie sideways, and what came rushing back wasn't Brie at all but the backyard. Weeds had taken over, dry rot chewing at the deck boards, ivy climbing the pergola like it was trying to choke the place out. Once, their mother had cared for it with quiet patience, pruning and planting, her garden gloves soft with dirt. Now it was nothing but ruin.

Frankie remembered the weight of the box in her arms, how her wrists ached from carrying too many alone. Mere had just come back from college, swooping in like the responsible one, like the hero. But Frankie had been here the whole time. She was the one who'd sat through the worst of it, who'd watched their father roll joints of marijuana and heard them crackle as he lit one after another, who'd witnessed him sinking deeper into grief—only for Mere to show up and bark instructions, steering the whole operation as if Frankie hadn't been surviving in the wreckage.

Their dad had wrapped his leather belt around himself and the beam in the living room, tugging it tight like a lifeline, tethering himself as if it were a permanent solution to his being forced to leave.

The spirit of your mother lives here. How will she find me if I leave? His voice broke on the words.

Mere had looked at Frankie then, eyes begging for help. Frankie felt something hot coil in her chest—resentment, sharp and sour. *See what you left me with?* she said.

Frankie tried not to remember what came next, but the memory rose anyway—billows of smoke, so dense she could taste it. She couldn't recall if it was her or Mere who noticed first as they loaded the boxes for Washington into the car, only that they froze mid-step by the half-packed car, something primal sparking between them as the sharp scent of fire cut through the day.

They ran together, instinct more than choice, fingers brushing as they pushed through the house and out into the yard. Their father sat calmly in the middle of it all, flames curling around him like he'd wanted to become the king of ashes. For one sickening moment, Frankie thought he meant to stay there, to burn with the ivy and the pergola. Somehow they dragged him out. No major burns. Just the singe of something neither of them could name.

The police were told it was an accident, a cigarette butt left smoldering, and that they'd caught it just in time to keep the flames contained to only their backyard. The simplicity of the lie was so much easier than the truth, than whatever had really happened. *What* had *really happened?*

That same obscure, out-of-body terror gripped her now. The image of Brie frozen to death, right where they'd all been looking. Had Brie been alive while they searched? Suffering while they mistook her shape for a mound of snow? Why had Caleb been there?

There was a foregone conclusion to it all, a marble run with two parallel tracks and only one that led to relief. A straight shot, a guaranteed absolution from worry. Frankie had found it once with alcohol, and now again with the careful cocktail of gummies and pills. She'd just overdone it last night, too quick on the trigger, but this time she'd recalibrate. The risk of that panicky edge was worth it if it meant escaping the suffocating darkness of her thoughts. This time, she'd get the dose right. This time, it would feel better. In her mind Frankie was already making her way up the stairs where she'd swallow two oxy and two gummies in tandem. If ever there was a moment to detach from reality, this was it.

16

MERE

Wednesday, March 20, 2024

Normally Mere walked Pancakes with Lily once in the morning and again in the evening, but ever since Brie went missing, she made sure to get the second walk in before dark. Not that she truly believed something nefarious had happened. Mere was practical by nature, but maybe that was only because she had never experienced anything firsthand the way Frankie had at UC Del Mar.

Lately Lily didn't want to be in the stroller, so Mere had to manage holding her hand and the dog leash at the same time. Not that Pancakes really needed one. She never wandered more than a few feet ahead. Mere was pretty sure Pancakes was some sort of novelty dog, and she counted her lucky stars that the sweet pup had found her way into their family.

She and Frankie had bunnies growing up, but they had always begged for a dog. They almost got one from the pound, but then with their mom, Mere couldn't imagine taking care of anything else.

Maybe Pancakes was a gift from their mother, from wherever she was now. The perfect companion for Lily. A sibling of sorts. The thought made Mere smile just as her phone rang and her sister's name lit up the screen.

"Mere?" Frankie said, as if anyone else would have answered Mere's phone.

"Yeah . . ."

"They found Brie's body. She's dead. She was at the campsite the guys were at." Frankie's intonation was chilled. Mere shivered despite the sun being out and the snow almost completely thawed.

Mere stopped walking and immediately Pancakes sat down and waited for direction, but Lily tugged on her mom's hand.

"I don't understand." Or, perhaps more accurately, she wanted so badly to misunderstand. But she feared she knew exactly what Frankie was saying.

"The guys were there that night . . . I'm not suggesting it's related or anything," Frankie said, stumbling over her story. She sounded unmoored, like she was using echolocation, sending out incomplete thoughts the way whales sent sound, just to hear what bounced back and might help her make sense of it all.

"Of course it's not related," Mere said quickly. How could she even imply that? "Oh god, how horrible. I can't believe she's dead. What happened?"

"We don't know. I only know because Margaret told Chloe.

They'll be announcing it to the press soon. Can you meet Avery, Janey, and me at my store in about two hours?"

In the five years since The Open Book had existed, the only time Frankie ever invited Mere to stay after hours was for open mic night.

"Can you come get me?" Frankie asked.

That caught Mere off guard. Frankie's house was out of her way. But maybe, like Mere had felt after Brie's initial disappearance, Frankie wanted eyes on her sister as soon as possible. This was her way of reaching for connection in the middle of tragedy. Mere couldn't help but feel the faintest flicker of hope.

"Yeah, of course. Let me just check with Dale to make sure he can be with Lily," Mere said.

She paused, half expecting Frankie to make a snide comment about Dale "babysitting" his own child. But Frankie stayed silent.

Frankie was pacing on the porch when Mere pulled up to the house. It was cold, so seeing her outside felt strange. She wasn't bundled up, just moving in tight, agitated loops. When she slid into the passenger's seat, Mere instinctively reached over and touched her arm, grounding her in place.

"Your girls are safe?" Mere asked. She had the sudden urge to go door-to-door, counting her most important people in Big Sky.

"Yes. You guys?" Frankie flicked a glance her way but didn't hold it, already looking past her again, as if just now realizing that to get to the bookstore she'd have to leave the house at all.

"Safe," Mere said softly. She hesitated with her hand on the gearshift. "You good?"

Frankie scoffed. "Brie was my sponsee in the program. And now she's dead. So no." She had a way of shutting down conversations with as few words as possible.

They drove the rest of the way in silence. Mere's mind crowded with questions—specifically whether Brie's drinking might have played a role in her death. But she knew her sister too well. One wrong word and Frankie would bristle, shut down, and turn combative for the rest of the night. They couldn't afford that. They needed to stay aligned, focused on piecing together what had really happened during the men's camping trip. So she said nothing. The only sound in the car was the heater, humming through the vents as Frankie held her hands in front of them like a fire.

When they reached The Open Book, Frankie fumbled with her keys, dropping them on the pavement. She bent to retrieve them, but her bag slipped off her shoulder and threw her off balance. Mere stepped beside her, using the flashlight on her phone to help guide the key into the lock.

Mere hadn't been surprised when Frankie opened the store in 2019. Once Frankie found a spark, she burned with it. The place was a charming nod to Central Perk, the fictional coffee shop in *Friends*, complete with a giant orange couch, mismatched green armchairs, and a low coffee table stacked with handpicked books. Signs in whimsical lettering marked each section, adding to the cozy, lived-in feel. When their mom was alive, the three of them would snuggle up to watch the show as it aired, their mugs of her world-famous hot chocolate—more marshmallows than milk—warming their hands. After she was gone, Frankie and Mere carried the tradition forward. When Mere realized Frankie had found a way to memorialize that slim portion of their childhood, her heart ached and broke in equal measure.

While they waited for Avery and Janey to arrive, Mere suggested they do the weekly check-in with their dad. Usually they took turns, but now they sat close together on the orange couch so the speakerphone could pick up both voices.

The phone rang twice before their dad answered, his voice gravelly and slurred. "Yeah?"

"Hey, Dad, it's Mere," she said, pushing false brightness into her tone.

"I'm here too," Frankie added, arms crossed, her voice flat.

"Oh," he said, as if weighing whether that was good or bad. "What's going on?"

"Not much," Mere lied. They both knew the drill: Pretend everything was fine, keep their voices steady, don't risk stirring him up.

There was a pause, then they heard the faint clink of ice against glass.

"I had a dream about your mother last night," he said. His voice seesawed low, slipping sideways into memory.

"What kind of dream?" Mere asked carefully. Frankie sat rigid beside her.

"She was standing at the end of my bed. Her hair was wet, dripping all over the floor. She looked wrong. Not like herself. Her face was pale. Her eyes weren't hers. She just stood there. Wouldn't speak. I kept asking what she wanted. Then finally she said it."

Mere swallowed. "Said what?"

"She said I let her down. Blamed me. For everything. For her life. For her death. Said I ruined it all."

Frankie let out a sharp, disbelieving laugh. "What the hell is that supposed to mean?"

"She blamed me," he repeated. "She was right there. That wasn't a dream. That was her. A visitation."

"Dad," Mere said gently, gripping the phone tighter. "You've been drinking. You told us the meds are messing with your sleep."

"I had a couple," he snapped. "Don't start with that now. You think I don't know the difference between a dream and someone standing in my room with wet hair and hate in their eyes?"

Frankie lunged forward, snatching the phone. "Okay, stop. You're spiraling. Take a breath."

"You weren't there," he hissed. "You didn't see her."

"And she's not here now," Frankie shot back. "So maybe sit down, drink some water, and stop dumping this on us." She shoved the phone back at Mere like it was toxic.

Mere pressed it to her ear, voice smoothing automatically. "Dad, we'll call you tomorrow, okay?"

"Yeah, sure," he muttered. "If you want. Doesn't matter."

"It does," she said softly, though it felt like breath on glass. "Just get some rest. We love you."

The line went dead.

Mere set the phone down, staring at it.

"Should we check in with Aunt Gina?" Frankie asked finally. "He's definitely drinking." She exhaled hard. "He always finds a way to make something awful worse."

The bell above the front door jingled, breaking the tension. Avery stepped inside, her hair piled into a top bun that pulled her face taut, brightening her features. Mere stood to hug her, holding on tightly. Their bodies said what words couldn't. *How lucky are we to be alive?* Death had a way of making the living grateful.

Janey arrived moments later and wrapped her arms around both women, beckoning Frankie in with a wave. Mere wasn't sure she would join—this kind of affection wasn't part of their usual rhythm. But then again, nothing about this was usual.

It felt like the thing you were supposed to do. When their mom died, everyone had clung to each other, hugging as if to check for pulses, as if touch could guarantee permanence.

Frankie stepped in at last, her head resting against Janey's for a fleeting moment. When they let go, the four women were left standing together in silence.

"Should we sit?" Avery asked.

They drifted back toward the couch and chairs, settling in quietly. No one wanted to be the first to name what they were all afraid of.

"Let's recap what we know," Janey said finally.

"We know she was found less than a quarter mile from the guys' campsite," Avery said. "That's all."

Frankie added, "I saw her just before she disappeared. She said some things that worried me. I should have followed up. I should have made her come with me to a meeting."

"This isn't your fault, Frankie," Janey said quickly.

"You're not responsible for someone else's recovery," Mere said, trying to draw wisdom from the handful of Al-Anon meetings she'd attended. She hoped it would bring Frankie even a sliver of comfort.

"But the guys," Avery said. "What do we know about what they know?"

Janey leaned forward, elbows on her knees. "Jack told me they saw her—or thought they did. It was early, still snowing. She was under some blankets. They didn't know what they were looking at." She rubbed her hands together like she was trying to scrub something invisible off her skin. "Jack keeps repeating what the cops said, that it wasn't foul play. That it was just . . . a tragic accident."

"She didn't just accidentally die alone in the woods," Frankie said, her voice low. "She wouldn't have done that. Not to her girls. Not to herself." She sounded like she was trying to convince herself as much as the rest of them.

Mere studied her sister. There was a tightness in her voice, something off in her coloring, and her pupils were slightly too large. Frankie didn't seem right.

"They didn't hurt her," Janey said softly. "But they didn't help her either."

"That's the part that keeps looping in my head," Mere murmured. "The question of culpability. If someone's being mugged on the street, don't we, as a society, have an obligation to step in?"

"But it's not like they saw her dying and walked away," Avery said. "They didn't know. If they had, they would have helped."

No one responded.

After a moment, Avery reached into her bag and pulled out a small notebook, placing it on the coffee table.

"These are the times Tom mentioned. When they left their tents. He doesn't know I wrote it all down. I just . . . needed to see it. To line it up."

Mere stared at the scribbled notes.

Avery inquired, "But, Janey, Jack told you right away that they saw something? See, Tom was so out of it, he said he thought his clothes had caught fire, which is why he took them off."

"Why didn't Caleb immediately come home and say something to me about it?" Frankie was biting on the skin around her fingernails. Mere wanted to do the same.

"Because they're men," Janey said flatly. "And they think silence protects them."

"Or maybe they think silence protects us," Frankie whispered.

That quieted the room.

Avery glanced between them. "So what do we do now?"

"They were high," Frankie said. "They panicked. I'm not saying it's right. I'm just saying maybe that's why they're acting like it didn't happen."

Janey looked up. "They left her there. Whether they meant to or not."

The words sat there like a weight on the table.

Frankie glanced around the room, her voice low but steady. "And now we all have to live with that."

17

FRANKIE

Wednesday, March 20, 2024

Frankie was all alone in her bookstore. The women had left. She'd just gotten off the phone with Caleb, who went to the police station with their lawyer, which wound up being unnecessary—they already had his statement, but he wanted to be overly compliant because that's who he was.

It was lonely in the store with the other women gone. She wished she had taken Janey up on the offer to drive her home. Instead, she'd lied, said she needed to finish up some billing she'd fallen behind on. The truth was, she wanted to be alone. For the time being she and Janey were sweeping their argument from this morning under the rug. It all seemed impossibly stupid now, fighting over their kids having sex. Yes, it was big news, but in the shadow of Brie's death, their petty problems felt small and childish.

She curled her legs beneath her in the oversized armchair

in the corner of her store. There was movement outside, the college students out for the night, probably heading to The Tavern nearby. Frankie checked her phone. She had a missed call from Pearl. The voicemail was simple—just checking in, asking how she was holding up now that the news about Brie was everywhere. She scrolled social media while she listened to the message. It was all over the local stations and in everyone's feeds. Brie Hoover: a beautiful white mother of two, wife of a youth minister, with one daughter who was deaf. And now she was dead, and foul play wasn't off the table.

It was too salacious for the public to resist. They were like a pack of rabid dogs lured by the promise of flesh. Except Brie wasn't a headline. She was a real person. No one should be stripped down like that and sold for parts.

Pearl had ended the message the way she always did, pointing Frankie toward what she thought was best: *Come to the Alley Oops Group, noon at Tammy's tomorrow. I'll see you there.* She said it like the matter was settled, like Frankie's attendance was inevitable.

But Frankie had ten years sober. She didn't need to chase meetings the way she had in the beginning, when one a day felt like the only way to keep her footing. Now she stuck to her home group, which she liked best because it was for women only. She didn't bother with mixed meetings anymore. Too much posturing. She'd only kept showing up to the Sunday women's meeting because it was progressive, the kind of room where she didn't feel like she had to shrink to fit.

Pearl meant well, sure, but she hadn't been there in the

arboretum, hadn't had the chance to maybe save her while Brie piled excuse on excuse, hadn't felt that shift where the truth was right there and still out of reach. Frankie was the one who was supposed to keep Brie tethered. And now Brie was dead. If a sponsor was supposed to guide you out of the dark, what did it mean that Frankie's sponsee never quite reached the light?

Frankie reached for her bag and pulled out the tin she hadn't let out of her sight since Brie first went missing. It felt like a safety net, a cloak of invisibility she could wrap around herself, something that let her slip out of this world and into the warm, quiet one waiting for her inside the hush it promised. She'd combined the remaining pills and the last three gummies into the tin, tossing the orange prescription bottle into a milk carton before sealing it and burying it deep in the trash. Now she took three pills and one gummy, swallowing without hesitation. She didn't have her car—Mere had driven them to the store—but that was the least of her concerns. What she wanted now was to forget what worry even felt like.

When she looked up, Sam was standing in the doorway, tapping gently on the glass. She crossed the room and unlocked the door. He didn't step in right away. Maybe he'd only stopped because he saw her through the window and planned to chat from the sidewalk.

"Hey," she said.

"Hey. I was walking by and saw your light on. I wasn't sure what kind of book magic happens after hours, but I wanted to check on you. I read about Brie Hoover . . . It's just awful. Did you know her?"

"Yes," Frankie said, stepping aside to let him in. They drifted toward the couch and sat, knees angled close but not touching. "Our older daughters are extremely close. We went to AA meetings together." The words slipped out before she could catch them. It was gossipy. Also, she didn't know if anonymity was something you still protected after someone died. She'd have to ask Pearl.

"I'm so sorry. Such a tragedy. Do you know anything more than what they're sharing?" Sam asked.

Frankie bristled. Why did tragedy turn everyone into detectives? When her mom died, the questions had been the same: What happened? How old was she? But beneath it was always something else: *Could it happen to me?* Death made people selfish, reminding them their own ending was inevitable.

"I don't have any of the details," she said quickly, eager to move on. "What are you doing downtown?"

"I came from campus, just walking home." He nodded toward the door, and she remembered he lived nearby. No wonder their paths crossed so often.

When he smiled he was so handsome it irritated her. If this were a TV show, he'd be Kyle Chandler—Coach from *Friday Night Lights*—handsome in that haunting, morally ambiguous way. The kind of man who could press his hand to the back of her neck, weave his fingers through her hair, and claim her mouth like it already belonged to him. If she let him.

Frankie's cheeks warmed. She shot up, pretending to straighten the books on the coffee table. The motion sent a head rush barreling through her, nearly knocking her back down.

Sam reached out instinctively, his hand catching at her waist. The heat of it jolted her, a dangerous pulse of want. She stepped forward, fast, putting space between them before her body could betray her again.

In her head, Frankie loved the idea of blending flirtation with her current feeling of euphoria. Layer upon layer, building higher every time. First the gummies, then the pills, and maybe, if she let herself, sex with Sam could be the hat trick. Of course she wanted him. He was gorgeous, and she was certain he wouldn't refuse if she made the first move. But her desire wasn't really about him. It was about drowning out the guilt pressing on her chest, the guilt over Brie. What she wanted, more than Sam, was the relief of not having to feel anything else.

The closest she'd ever come to slipping up in her marriage was during her drinking days, when she'd lie about book club and sneak into The Tavern instead. Sometimes she'd flirt without meaning to, just to feel alive. Once, a couple of guys followed her into the parking lot, and her gut told her something was wrong. She went back inside and called Janey, who showed up without hesitation, drove her home, and lectured her the whole way. Frankie never set foot in The Tavern again.

"I should get back home and be with my family. I was here finishing up some work," Frankie said.

"You okay to drive? You seem a bit . . ." He paused, and Frankie wouldn't let him finish that sentence.

"Yep, totally good. I've been sober for a decade, you know. I don't drink," she said, assuring him as much as she was assuring herself.

"Right, yeah. Still, I can go grab my car and bring you home. It's no trouble."

Why was he asking her that? Was he flirting? Wanting her to go home with him?

"I'm fine. I'm going to get an Uber or something," she insisted.

"No, no, I'll be right back. Don't go anywhere, okay? Seriously, it will take me two minutes. I'll honk when I'm out front," Sam said. Before she could tell him no, he was already making his way toward the door.

That would be fine. She'd get a ride home with Sam. She knew Sam more than she knew some random Uber driver. It would be fine.

She liked the butterflies Sam gave her; the wistfulness reminded her of the early days in her relationship with Caleb. She hadn't had butterflies in so long. That was the thing about being married for almost twenty years; you forfeited your right to any prospects of future butterflies with cute guys who looked like Coach from *Friday Night Lights*.

Frankie wasn't sure how long she'd been standing there, lost in her rom-com-like fantasy of her and Coach on the orange couch, when a car horn snapped her out of it. She made sure to lock up, then checked the handle again, one hard shake to be certain. The last thing she needed was to have to file another insurance claim. Early last year, a dumb college kid had thrown a rock through the front window on what looked like a drunken dare. The security footage caught the whole thing. Nothing was stolen, and insurance covered the repairs, but still, it felt like a personal violation of something she'd built that was entirely hers.

"This really isn't necessary, but I appreciate it. Thank you, Sam," Frankie said, pressing her lips together and realizing—belatedly—that she must have put on lip gloss while she waited for him to pull up.

She glanced around the car, taking inventory. It all seemed to line up with the picture she'd already drawn of him: textbooks stacked neatly in the back seat, an old coffee cup in the console, a dented reusable water bottle covered in stickers. One was an ally flag—probably for the niece he'd mentioned, the one whose girlfriend was about to propose. The other simply declared *Banned Books* in a fading typewriter font, half peeled at the edges, like it had been riding around with him for years.

"My pleasure. Happy to help." He smiled, adjusting her seat back. Whoever had ridden shotgun before her clearly hadn't needed the legroom. "Where do you live?"

She typed her home address into his GPS, a gesture that felt like a betrayal to Caleb. What was she doing? Except Caleb had gone off into the woods, taken mushrooms, and left a woman for dead in the snow. And now Frankie was high, clinging to the thought that she'd try to sort all of it out in the morning.

Sam kept talking, but Frankie couldn't focus on the context. She just hoped he wasn't expecting a response. He seemed mid-story, gesturing animatedly with one hand while the other stayed on the wheel. She glanced over just to check—his pants were on. Nothing had happened. Everything was fine. Sam was one of the good ones. He was doing her a favor, going out of his way to get her home safely.

She smiled at him, suddenly feeling overcome with a bone-deep kind of fatigue, the same kind she'd experienced the minute she arrived in Big Sky, far away from Santa Barbara.

"Do you mind if I just close my eyes for a moment? It's been such a hard day, and I think I need to rest," Frankie said.

She shouldn't be falling asleep in Sam the Hot Professor's car. What if Caleb was in the driveway when they got there? How would she explain this? He would be home with the girls. He'd see a car he didn't recognize and come outside—of course he would. He hated when people came onto their property uninvited. That was part of why they'd moved out there in the first place. Caleb didn't like her open-door policy. She warned him when they moved out there that she would want to host people because, unlike him, she was social. And so was Sam. He was just being friendly.

She didn't need to explain it any further than that.

"You know my husband and his friends were at the campsite where Brie died. Same night. Wha' do you think of that?" Frankie's words came out a little slurred, but she didn't care. *They* were the ones who got high on mushrooms.

Suddenly, they were in her driveway. Caleb opened the passenger door. The men were talking, one on either side of the car, but Frankie couldn't tell who was who. Their voices blurred together.

Oh good. The men are coming to save me.

18

MERE

Wednesday, March 20, 2024

Mere lay in bed, staring into the dark, the soft hiss of the white noise machine failing to do its job. Lily and Pancakes were back in their spot squished toward her side of the bed, but Dale's side remained empty. He hadn't come out of his office when she got home. Mere felt wrung out, the kind of fatigue that came not from lack of sleep but from memories looping in her head that refused to settle.

Frankie had been off the entire time they were at the bookstore—jumpy, cagey, like she was made of glass and guilt. Which made sense. Mere knew she was carrying the weight of responsibility as Brie's sponsor. No wonder Frankie looked haunted.

It reminded Mere of the time she'd driven down to their home in Belmont after nearly two years without seeing Frankie, the night of the fire. The front door had creaked open, and there she was, a fragile version of her sister, all shadows and sharp bones.

Mere blinked up at the ceiling. The image wouldn't leave her.

She remembered standing in the kitchen that day, two barely grown girls, each holding the pieces of a shared history that didn't quite fit anymore. And how, even then, her mind drifted to their "restaurant" days, when they'd played waitress with toast and cereal, serving their mom like she was the Queen of England. Their mother would sit at the table with a tired smile, humoring them, praising their soggy toast like it was caviar. There was still so much love in that house.

Mere turned on her side, the sheets too warm and twisted around her legs.

She reached for her phone on the bedside table and typed out a text to Frankie:

Can we talk?

The three dots appeared.

Vanished.

Then nothing.

She thought about texting Avery for her take on how Frankie had seemed, or maybe Janey, though they didn't usually text. She even considered talking to Dale. But this kind of knot, made of shame and sisterhood, wasn't something Dale would know how to walk her through.

Then again, maybe that wasn't entirely true.

On Frankie's last night of drinking, Mere and Dale had sat at the kitchen table while Frankie's girls slept upstairs in the guest room for the first time.

Are you okay? Dale asked, his voice quiet and careful in a way that made Mere want to fold in on herself.

Mere hadn't known how to explain the fear that had taken hold of her. That terrible, sinking sense that Frankie was following in their father's footsteps. That soon, Mere would be either picking up the pieces or watching it all fall apart.

No, I'm not okay. And neither is Frankie, she'd said, her voice catching. *I left her alone with Dad and now she's turning into him. It's my fault. I was so selfish.*

Dale had moved his chair a little closer but didn't touch her. *None of this is your fault*, he said. *Alcoholism is genetic. You're blaming yourself for her DNA?*

He had a scientist's logic, but Dale was an only child. He didn't understand that sisterhood wasn't just biology—it was a kind of emotional custody. You didn't just *have* a sister, you *held* one. You carried her bruises. You felt responsible for her joy because the power of your opinion alone shaped who she became far more than anyone else's ever could.

I will always feel responsible for her, Mere had tried to explain.

And she did. But what Frankie truly needed was something Mere could never give her: their mother. Mere turned to stare at the ceiling again, trying to find more room without disturbing Lily. Dale's immoveable weighted blankets made it so that Lily and Pancakes overtook more than their share of Mere's side of the bed. Mere's memory drifted back to her mother's bedroom, where hospice had set her up in the end, machines humming softly in a space heavy with grief, her mother's breath shallow and rattling.

Did you both eat? her mother had asked, her voice soft but insistent.

Mom. Mere coughed on her tears, a watery laugh escaping. *You're dying and you're worried about lunch?*

Yes, her mother said plainly. *I want to mother you as long as I possibly can.* That had gutted Mere, but before she could linger on the sentiment, Donna added, *Frankie too. That girl runs on caffeine and nerves.* She spoke about Frankie as if she wasn't a few feet away, curled into the chair, arms tight around her knees, trying to fade into the background.

Their mother had tried to shift in bed, but couldn't keep from wincing. Frankie stood and came to where Mere was standing. Mere reached for the morphine pump but was stopped by a paper-thin hand.

Not yet. I need to say this. Donna's message came slowly, deliberately. *Mere . . . you take care of everyone but yourself. Frankie . . . you'll go until you collapse. You both think strength means never asking for help.* She paused, gathering breath. Then came the plea, softer, urgent. *Promise me you'll look out for each other. Even when you don't want to.*

It was then that their mother took each of their hands, her grip trembling with effort as she brought them up to her lips. Both girls knew to keep their palms open wide, like the poor begging for food. In perfect unison, as if they were one, she pressed a single kiss into the center of each hand, equally measured, as only a mother could do.

They'd promised. What else could they do?

Mere swallowed the lump in her throat and gently got out of

bed. In the living room, dominoes lined every available surface. Her OT had suggested toys designed for lining up as a way to support Lily's need for order, an appropriate outlet, they'd said. Still, Mere couldn't shake the question: Was guiding Lily to fit safely within the lines of their world the right call, or just the easiest one?

She stepped outside Dale's red office door and tapped lightly with her fingertips. He opened it looking rumpled, not quite himself. When she tried to peek in, he shifted forward, blocking the view, positioning himself in the narrow slice of space between her and the room.

"I've been wanting to talk to you more about camping," he started right in, while he was standing there in the doorframe.

"Okay? Are we going to stand here?" Mere asked, thrown off.

He shut the door behind him. Apparently yes, they were. "The parts I liked about camping were the shooting, because it reminded me of archery, which I'm good at, and sitting around the campfire. I liked the heat it provided in the snow."

If Frankie and Caleb had been there, they would've rolled their eyes. Mere knew they thought Dale was odd, and yes, statements like that could sound offbeat. But she recognized it for what it was—his way of reaching for connection. And that was exactly what she wanted from him right now.

"You didn't tell me you liked the campfire," she said gently, coaxing, the way she might with Lily. "What did you guys talk about?"

"We didn't, not really. I just liked being in the snow with a fire going. Something about sitting in a circle. I got tired early and wanted to unzip the top of my tent so I could watch the stars while I read, but of course I couldn't because of the snow."

The mention of stars pulled a smile out of her. "You know, that reminds me—remember the time you woke me up at four in the morning and drove me out to that field in a rental truck?"

Dale tilted his head, considering. "With the telescope."

"Yes." Mere's smile softened. "Coffee, a blanket, just us watching shooting stars. You didn't think about snacks or a bathroom, but you thought of me. That was . . . that was something I loved about you."

It had been unexpectedly sentimental, sparking within Mere a flicker of hope for the life they were building. Years later, in the loneliest parts of their marriage, she'd twist that memory into something else. Even the fact that she was momentarily afraid, because she'd allowed her sister's interpretation of Dale as quirky to cloud her judgment. She'd focus on what was missing—no food, no foresight—and let it sour. When she got stuck in that mindset, it poisoned everything. All she could see were the ways Dale fell short, instead of the many quiet ways he showed up.

"Can I say something?" she asked, leaning her back against the hallway wall. "When Frankie mentioned that the dads were going camping, I hoped it would be . . . I don't know, something good. A chance to connect. I have this friendship with Avery, and I thought maybe you'd find that, too, with the guys. That fatherhood might be enough to create some kind of common ground."

Dale shook his head. "It wasn't that," he said matter-of-factly.

Mere exhaled. "I get that I might not have had a realistic expectation. But . . ." She glanced around at the dominoes lining their house. "When I see Lily struggle to connect, or even just to exist in all the noise and chaos around her, I feel it in my chest. I see you struggle, too, and I don't want you both to miss out."

Dale looked genuinely puzzled. "Miss out on what? Why would I want to take mushrooms and wander around a campsite in the middle of a snowstorm? Jack thought he saw aliens, Caleb kept going on about colorful shapes, and Tom stripped off his clothes and nearly froze to death. They weren't even having the same experience. I was in my tent, reading. Honestly, I think I got more out of it than they did."

Mere had imagined the men sitting around the campfire, swapping dad stories and bonding over the shared demands of parenthood, but that had been her fantasy, not their reality.

"You're right. You're so right," she said, shaking her head. "It's just that sometimes I worry. The world is hard enough to understand as it is. I just think about Lily trying to make sense of it . . ." She paused, wanting to tread so carefully now. "I wonder if maybe some of what Lily's up against might not be unfamiliar to you. It breaks me open a little. Not because either of you are broken but because I don't want people to be cruel to you."

He stood still, adopting a quiet, pensive look, as if he were constructing all she'd said into his own formula in his head. A mathematical equation that translated her maternal worry into something he understood.

"I don't categorize people that way. I don't experience anything as missing. Other people don't give me what they seem to give you," he said simply. "It'll probably be the same for Lily."

She saw then that the reason her expectations hadn't been met was due to her own shortcoming, not his. She was the one who sometimes felt left out, even among the people she loved most. She had placed expectations on Dale he'd never agreed to carry. He went camping to camp. That was enough for him. It didn't have to mean the same thing to both of them. And maybe that was okay. Maybe they could still share a life, still be happy, even if they found meaning in different things.

She liked that Dale had always seen things a little differently. She had known that from the beginning. It was one of the things she loved most about Lily too. Lily's interpretation of reality didn't have to mirror her own. In fact, Mere felt lucky to be invited in, to tuck herself into the hidden corridors of their minds, to map the places where things clicked, where emotions translated into something only Mere could understand. Because some people weren't meant to be solved.

The door creaked open and Dale began to speak, his voice pulling her back into the moment. She realized she hadn't been in his office since before the camping trip.

"Come in," Dale called. "I've been trying to understand what happened."

Mere stepped into his office. On the wall, he'd pinned index cards to the whiteboard, each one scribbled with his narrow handwriting, Brie's name circled in bold block letters at the center. It looked like something out of *A Beautiful Mind*, timelines, guesses, notes all orbiting her name.

"I heard something outside the tent," he admitted. "Sounds. Footsteps. But I didn't come out."

Mere's stomach twisted. "You heard her?"

"I don't know. I don't think so," Dale said quickly. "I was half asleep. I assumed it was the guys coming back; maybe Tom was looking for something. But there was a voice, moving near the firepit. I was exhausted, so I just rolled over and went back to sleep."

She knew this version of Dale too well: the one who met feelings with logic, who tensed at crying, who tried to reason his way through things that required softness, not solutions. It wasn't unkindness. It was the way he operated. Still, the gap between what she needed from him and what he was capable of giving cracked open again, wide and familiar.

Her voice was tight. "And you didn't think to tell the police everything?"

"I did," Dale said, sharper now. "I told them exactly what I just told you."

She glanced back at the whiteboard. All those notecards, arranged like an equation, his attempt to make sense of something senseless. She stepped closer, fingers brushing the corner of Brie's name. *Brie.* And yet, what if it had been Dale's name there? Or Lily's?

It didn't seem to matter how careful you were, how faithful or flawed, how much you loved or prayed or hoped. Brie was a mother, like her. Married to a man of God. Raising a daughter who, like Lily, had needs that didn't fit into neat, easy boxes. Brie had been in recovery, just like Frankie. And sometimes Mere's father. Maybe no one was ever truly safe.

And if Mere saw herself as the protector of her family, how could she ever do enough with stakes like these? How could she even think of bringing another child into a world like this, where everything felt rigged from the start?

"Why wouldn't you tell me this sooner?" Her voice was soft, but the hurt pulsed underneath. "It makes me feel like you're hiding something."

"Hiding what?" Dale looked genuinely perplexed.

"I don't know. I know you would never hurt someone. I know that."

If he were anyone else, this would have been the part where he said it outright—with anger, even horror—*Of course I would never hurt anyone.*

But instead, his face stayed neutral. "I don't understand what you think I could be hiding. If I thought it mattered, I would've said it earlier. I would never hurt anyone. That feels obvious to me, so I didn't say it."

The words were right, but the delivery was wrong—so flat it left her stomach uneasy. As if he were reading lines without grasping their weight. As if the absence of emotion mattered more than the content.

He wasn't wounded by her suspicion. He wasn't anything, really.

Mere exhaled. He truly didn't see it. There it was again—that fundamental divide. His version of reality and hers. The frustration drained from her, replaced by something heavier and quieter. Not grief. Not even anger. Just the bone-deep exhaustion of trying, over and over, to translate her world into his. And yet, a thought she hated herself for crept in: If she, who loved him, could feel unnerved in moments like this, how easy would it be for others to believe the worst?

19

FRANKIE

Thursday, March 21, 2024

Frankie woke up in the guest room downstairs, still in her clothes, alone in the bed. The other side was untouched. It used to be her litmus test for how bad her drinking had gotten the night before. On the nights she blacked out and couldn't remember putting herself or the kids to bed, waking up alone meant Caleb had slept on the couch. It meant she'd taken it too far, again, even though she never meant to. She only ever wanted a brief reprieve, from the smoke in the air, from the internalized feeling of being trapped, the way she had been in the car in Santa Barbara.

Caleb appeared in the doorway holding a cup of coffee she hoped was for her. She didn't feel sick, not like she used to when she'd been drinking, when she had to throw up just to make it through the day with the girls at home.

He stood there unmoving, so she motioned for him to

come closer and hand her the coffee. When he didn't, she knew she was in trouble. It all rushed back, the slow drip of dread, the way her stomach turned like she'd been summoned to the principal's office. She'd humiliated herself in front of Sam and Caleb, and now everything she'd been keeping separate had blurred into one messy scene. She hadn't been thinking clearly, but she was lucid enough to realize how bad it looked: Professor Sam driving her home after she told Caleb she'd be at the store with her sister and friends.

And if the roles were reversed, if Caleb had pulled into the driveway with Connie Britton, the actress who played Coach's stunning wife in *Friday Night Lights*, he wouldn't have made it to the front door without an interrogation. And he sure as hell wouldn't have slept in their bed.

"I'm so sorry about last night," she started. It was always best to start with an apology. To make amends and do so sincerely. "I promise nothing happened with Sam. He walked by the store, and it was late, so he offered me a ride home. I was finishing up some work and Mere had dropped me off earlier."

"Were you drinking?" Caleb said, sucking in his breath like he was preparing for the impact of her answer.

"God no. I'm sober. I swear to you," she said, knowing she'd have to give him something. "I started taking these weed gummies, and they messed me up. I needed to take the edge off. With Brie and you guys being there, I haven't been in a good headspace." Frankie paused, wading out into the water. It felt easier to blame him and make this somehow his fault, because he *had* been there. In fact, he had been at the police station last night. "What did the police say?"

"Oh no you don't." Caleb held up the hand that wasn't holding the coffee mug, halting her redirection. "We aren't done talking about *you* yet. So you started doing drugs? How does Pearl feel about that?" Caleb adored Pearl. She could get him talking in a way no one else could.

"Says the guy who did shrooms and stumbled onto a crime scene." The words spilled out before she had a chance to swallow them back. "I didn't mean that," she said quickly. "I just—god, I feel so guilty. I was her sponsor. I should have done something. I'm sorry." There it was again. That word. She felt like she was back in the worst days of her drinking, tripping over apologies, bruising people with her wreckage and then offering up, *I'm sorry, I'm sorry, I'm sorry*, like a broken record.

Caleb looked like she'd slapped him.

"You think I'm not beating myself up?" he said, his voice tight. "You think I don't feel responsible? Why do you think I brought our lawyer to the police station? If I'd had something to confess, I would have said it. What I can't forgive is that I didn't check under that mound of blankets. If I had, maybe . . ." His voice trailed off with a quiver on the end that made her want to wrap her arms around his neck and pull him into her. "If I hadn't been high, maybe we could've helped her. We would've seen her. Really seen her. And then . . ." His voice cracked, and he didn't continue. For a second, she thought he might cry. She stood to reach for him, instinct kicking in, but he stepped back.

"Don't," he said.

Now Frankie was the one to hold up her hands. Why had she done this? Her husband was a good man, the very best one, which was why she'd chosen him, and then somehow their daughters had chosen them. And she'd gone and accused him of what, exactly? On the morning after she got dropped off by a man Frankie knew had a crush on her. She wanted to reach out and kiss the inside of his palm. It was a universal anecdote, one whose meaning Frankie only came to understand long into adulthood. It was their mother's way of saying without saying, *The world is cruel and I'm so sorry it has to hurt you sometimes. Right now, with this kiss, just let my love for you be enough.*

But instead, Caleb turned and walked out of the room.

Chloe had a follow-up appointment after school with Dr. Linda. They had yet to address Frankie's betrayal of her confidence with Janey, but after the news about Brie, the breach had quietly dissolved, if only temporarily. Frankie had insisted Chloe go to school to maintain some sort of normalcy, but at drop-off Chloe seemed almost afraid to let her mom out of her sight. She asked Frankie to come with her to the appointment.

"Did you want to reschedule?" Frankie asked as they made their way toward Dr. Linda's office.

"No," Chloe said, shaking her head. "I'm having breakthrough spotting between periods, and I want to talk to her about switching my birth control."

Frankie couldn't imagine doing anything like this with her own mother—let alone uttering the words "breakthrough spotting" without dying of embarrassment. Her relationship with her mother had never felt surface level, but it existed within the unspoken boundaries of a 1990s childhood. Which, Frankie was learning in real time, was an entirely different universe than raising kids in the 2020s.

Despite whatever criticisms people had about this next generation, her daughters' openness, their willingness to speak honestly, had allowed her to form real friendships with each of them. Relationships that bloomed into something deeper, that seeped into the quiet, untapped corners of her own womanhood.

In the office Frankie was surprised Chloe wasn't on her phone. Instead, she was looking around, watching people walk by.

"It feels really weird to, like, go to school and be at the doctor, all when what? We can just suddenly die?"

Frankie looked over at her, feeling her heart swell with tenderness. Chloe was Frankie's daughter in every way imaginable.

"Chloe Marino," the PA called from the doorway. Frankie and Chloe both stood.

"We'll just take Chloe back for now," the PA said, holding up a hand to stop Frankie from following.

"I'm good, Mom. I'll see you afterward," Chloe assured her, all calm and grown. Like their roles had reversed. The door closed behind her with a dismissive click. They hadn't discussed that part, and Frankie had let herself imagine she'd stroke Chloe's hair while Dr. Linda explained the options. But Frankie had never been great at managing her expectations.

She sat back and watched the hallway. Aged patients shuffled by in masks, trailed by adult children helping them to appointments. She thought of her dad and decided she should check on him after the strained call last night. He shouldn't be drinking on his meds.

He answered on the first ring.

"Hey, Dad."

"Hey, kiddo."

She could instantly tell he was sober, which was an enormous relief. "How are Birdie and the goats?" Birdie was his herding dog, and their dad liked to pretend he was a full-time goatherd while Aunt Gina actually did the work, turning the milk into cheese and soaps. Strangely, the setup suited them both.

"All fine. All fine." Frankie knew her father wouldn't inquire about her or his grandchildren. Not because he didn't care—they simply weren't in his immediate orbit the way Birdie and the goats were.

"Aunt Gina? She still doing well?"

"She's cooking lasagna tonight. That woman makes a mean lasagna. She won't tell me, but I swear she doubles the cheese recipe or something. When she lifts it off the plate, the mozzarella could stretch out for a literal mile."

"Imagine that." Frankie smiled into the phone. She could picture Aunt Gina and their father sitting at the breakfast nook, Birdie curled beneath the table, hopeful for a slice of garlic bread to fall. It was a cozy, contented image—one she and her dad had never quite managed to create in the two years they'd lived together, just the two of them, trying and mostly failing to feel like a family.

"My orgasms are back on track," he said, as if she'd asked.

"Uhhh . . . that's great, Dad. Sorry to hear they got off track." Frankie rubbed her forehead, trying to wipe the image from her mind. Why was he telling her this?

That was the thing about living with him—what those two years had taught her. Mental illness, like cancer, could hollow a person out from the inside, leaving behind pieces you didn't recognize. There were flashes from their childhood when things had felt normal, even joyful. Like the day they picked out bunnies from the neighbor's house. Hers was a warm chocolate brown, which she named Cookie. Mere had chosen a white one and named it Snowball. The matches were perfect. Mere took meticulous care of her rabbit, wiping its paws daily to keep them clean. Frankie was grateful she hadn't chosen a white one. Cookie's fur never would have stayed that pristine.

Still, those sweet memories didn't stick the way the painful ones did. Just like the parts of Santa Barbara that lingered were not the beach days or sunshine. Instead, waking up alone in the hospital was the memory that stayed.

"Birdie's barking. I need to see what that's about. Love you, honey."

"Love you too, Dad."

For years, Frankie blamed herself for the second part of her assault. She could have so easily avoided the second half, the physical part, if when he had exposed himself and tried to get her to touch his penis in the car, she had just exited the car and gone back to the store to call for a cab.

Frankie remembered how expectant the boy had been. They met, drove to the store, exchanged only a few words, picked up the booze, and in the parking lot he had taken out his dick as if that were the next logical step. He reached over and tried to guide her head down, as confident that she would happily put her mouth around it as if it were a flesh-colored Otter Pop.

Frankie's whole body shook as she remembered. She reached inside her purse and pulled out the tin. She'd learned her lesson with dosage and found that if she did a one-to-one ratio during the day it muddled all the worry about Brie, their husbands, and her fight with Janey. She'd be sure to have Chloe drive home.

In the car, Frankie had frozen. Her body felt far away, like it belonged to someone else. She couldn't move except to jerk her head aside. She remembered hearing the sound of her own voice, thin and unfamiliar, saying, *The fuck do you think you're doing?*

From that angle, the cavernous pock marks on his face had looked magnified and strange.

Come on. Just a little BJ. I'll go quick, he said, as if that were a selling point.

She recoiled, or maybe she only thought she did. Her limbs became heavy, useless. If she could just sink deeper into the upholstery, she thought, blur into the fabric, maybe she'd disappear and they'd end up back on campus.

Her mouth moved before she knew what she was saying.

Drive us home and I won't call the cops. The words came out louder than she felt, as if someone else had spoken them.

Whoa, such a cock tease. Why else did you think I drove you for a beer run? His disdain was so casual it felt rehearsed, like this was simply the price of entry.

She wanted to spit back, to call him what he was—a predator—but the thought scattered before it could form. He buttoned his jeans. He drove. And she floated in the passenger's seat, detached, weightless, like she could hover above her body until the ride ended. All she wanted was her bed. To bury herself under blankets and cry until there was nothing left in her.

Once they reached the dorm parking lot, she should have run. Straight to her room. Instead, she hovered on the threshold of choice: stairwell or elevator. The stairwell looked haunted, shadowy, like a horror film she didn't want to watch. The elevator meant sharing space, standing too close, pretending civility. And still she'd felt the pull to be polite. That reflex had haunted her ever since, the way she'd acted as if she owed him decency even after what he'd done. As if girls were raised to smile for piggish men, to believe their place was beneath even the worst of them.

Frankie had decided the elevator was her safest bet. Surely someone else would ride the six floors with them, and then she'd never have to be around him ever again. He was visiting campus from out of town, that much she knew; he wasn't even a UC Del Mar student. But when she stepped inside, it felt like climbing into her own coffin. She didn't remember the door closing so much as the darkness of his brown eyes—so near to black the pupil vanished into them—expectant yet certain. As if what he was about to do wasn't violence, just inevitability. Just biology. She felt the crack in her rib cage after he lunged. If tragedy had a texture, pain was bone white, like lightning tearing down the length of her body. The only other time Frankie had experienced pain like that was in labor with her girls, when it felt like her body was being split in two.

When Frankie came to on the gurney, her rib cage throbbed like it was on fire, but even through the pain, she registered that her underwear was down around her ankles. Her skirt was torn. *Too bad*, she'd thought. It had been her favorite, the only one she'd brought to college.

The reality of what might've happened didn't fully sink in until she was in the hospital and someone asked if she wanted a SART exam.

Why would I need one of those? she asked.

A nurse, strikingly beautiful, with her hair swept into a sleek, flight-attendant-style bun, explained, using words so kind they made Frankie's eyes leak water.

But we were only in there for, what, less than thirty seconds? she tried to reason. Besides him slamming her into the handrails and cracking her ribs, how could there have been time for anything more?

This is how we would know for sure, the nurse said gently. Like it was just another step in the trauma protocol, as routine as drawing blood or placing a chest tube. But rape shouldn't be routine. It should never be inevitable.

Frankie refused the SART exam. She just wanted to call

Janey, have her come scoop her out of this nightmare so she could start over. Transfer to UC Blue Ridge, the school she should've chosen in the first place, if she hadn't instead prioritized the juvenile need to punish her sister. Santa Barbara would be her false start. Up north, with Janey and even Mere nearby, she'd be safe. Watched. Anchored.

Though she declined the testing, she was still loaded up on antivirals for potential HIV exposure and given Plan B. Nurses administered intravenous pain meds, and for a few hours, Frankie floated, weightless, cocooned in cotton candy. When Janey came to get her the next day, Frankie tried to explain the floating feeling, how nothing hurt anymore, not really.

In the following weeks, she secured her intradistrict transfer to UC Blue Ridge. All the ugliness tied to Southern California would have to stay behind. Like her father had done with the backyard, she'd torch the memory and walk away from the ashes.

Janey had tried, more than once, to get the full story out of her. But aside from a brief rundown with Pearl while working the Steps, Frankie had kept it buried. She told herself that was recovery—naming it once, then never letting it surface again. She wasn't about to let some nameless stranger live rent-free in her head, not in the sober life she'd fought to build as a mother. But in truth, it still pulsed beneath the floorboards, the kind of secret that seeped through no matter how many rugs she laid over it.

Frankie stepped outside and FaceTimed Janey. She answered on the second ring.

"Hey, where are you?" Janey asked as she held the phone closer to her face, trying to make out any distinguishing landmarks that might give away Frankie's location.

"Waiting outside at an appointment for Chloe."

"She okay?"

"Yeah, she's good. Hey, I don't like what happened with us the other day at my house. I'm sorry I snapped at you about the kids having sex. I haven't been myself since Brie, and I took it out on you," Frankie said, hoping that would be the end of that and Janey wouldn't want to pry into it any further.

"You haven't been yourself," Janey said, her expression hard to read through the blur of FaceTime.

"What's going on with you? What's Jack's version of all this?" Frankie asked, deliberately sidestepping Janey's comment. Janey's husband was the one topic guaranteed to get her ranting.

"Actually, Jack's been like a different person since the camping trip. It's like it finally hit him that if I wasn't around, the whole operation would fall apart. Now he sees me differently. He's even helping with the kids without being asked."

Did Janey expect her to hand out medals for mediocrity? For the bare minimum? He couldn't have transformed overnight. It had been five days since the camping trip. Men did one decent thing and suddenly they were heroes, while mothers did it all, every day, without applause. And now, because Jack remembered to make a grilled cheese and didn't let anyone die, he was a changed man? A better husband? Frankie could barely stomach it. None of them had been paying attention—not when Brie was right there under a pile of blankets. Janey was using Brie's death to bolster her opinion of a man who'd been letting her down for years, allowing grief to give him a redemption arc he hadn't earned. Frankie knew the shine would wear off. It always did. Men were high, distracted, self-absorbed, and then shocked when consequences fell out of the sky. That was negligence, not fate. Why wasn't *he* the one taking their son to buy condoms? Did Jack even know his kid was having sex? Wouldn't a so-called good dad ask those kinds of questions?

Frankie knew her negative spiral was the oxy talking, fueling every sharp, unfiltered thought. So instead of voicing any of it, she swallowed the words down and said, "That's great, J. I'm glad he's stepping up. All of this is so awful—something good should come out of it, at least."

Then she pretended she was getting called back into the office just to end the conversation. Except once she hung up, she couldn't quiet her thoughts.

She hated that she couldn't just say, *Hey, meet me at the doctor's office so I'm not sitting there alone.* But no, that would've been weird. Their teenagers were apparently in love, or in heat, or both, insistent on putting their parts in and out of each other. She hated that she and Janey couldn't just sit in the waiting room flipping through bad magazines, laughing about how they were too young and far too hot to be grandmothers.

Because if they were grandmothers, it wouldn't be equal.

If there were a baby, the child would live at Frankie's house. The cries at three in the morning would echo through her hallway. It would be Frankie up with a bottle, not Janey. Patrick, Patrick and his penis, would be sleeping like a rock in his bed while Frankie stumbled through the dark, trying to be a better grandmother than she'd been a mother. Trying to fix something no one asked her to fix. Because she hadn't been the mother Chloe needed to avoid this in the first place. Was this the punishment for drinking through their childhood?

How the hell had they gotten here?

Frankie needed to text Pearl. She recognized the spiral for what it was.

I know we need to talk about Brie's death. Word had already spread on the group text from their women's meeting after it hit the news. *But I'm future tripping*, she typed out. *My oldest is having sex and I'm here waiting in the waiting room while she discusses birth control options. Yes, I'm grateful we have the kind of relationship where she trusts me enough to tell me, but I also hate that I have no control over the situation.*

Pearl responded immediately: *Sounds like you're having a normal human reaction to a stressful situation you're powerless over. Lucky you don't have to drink over it, because as history shows, that would just make everything a million times worse.*

Frankie's phone rang. Of course Pearl wouldn't let her off the hook that easily.

"Why are you blasting past the miracle that your daughter wants to include you in such an important rite of passage?"

Pearl's wisdom had always reminded Frankie of her mother's. If she was being honest, that was why she'd chosen Pearl to sponsor her. There was something in Pearl's grounded, maternal instinct that matched what Frankie imagined her mother's might have grown into, if she'd lived long enough to see her daughters into adulthood.

It was why she brought Mere along every year to watch Pearl hand her a sobriety birthday chip, then invited her to dinner afterward. She knew Mere saw it too. Pearl wasn't Donna, but she was the closest they'd ever come. And Frankie wanted to share that gift.

"I guess you're right. But Brie is dead," Frankie said, and the words soured the second they left her mouth. She should hang up—the THC and oxy were cresting, just about to hit the sweet spot, and talking to her sponsor while high felt like getting caught by a priest while having sex in church.

"You're right, and it's awful. But nothing about that is going to be resolved right now, and you're missing it."

"Missing what?" Frankie asked as she felt herself start to lift off the floor.

"You're not staying in the miracle. Stay in it."

Stay in it, Frankie repeated to herself, but the only thing she was in was spun sugar, floating somewhere just above the real world, where everything was soft and nothing stuck.

Frankie was impressed by her daughter's driving skills. She'd recovered quickly from the squirrel incident; Frankie had been certain that would set her back weeks. Frankie wanted to say how proud she was, how relieved she felt that everything at the doctor's office was fine. Chloe wasn't pregnant, had her birth control squared away, and even left with a lollipop from the nurses' station, like they'd time-traveled back to when treats could fix everything.

"I didn't mean to tell Auntie Janey about you and Patrick." Frankie was still high, which made broaching the subject of her betrayal feel easier. Chloe was wearing the pale green Aviator Nation ninja-style hoodie Frankie had given her for Christmas. It made her eyes the only thing anyone would see when she wore it.

"I mean, I kind of figured you would. I tell Margaret everything, so I know you tell Auntie Janey everything," Chloe said.

"I still want you to feel like you can trust me," Frankie said. "This relationship only works if we're honest with each other." She hated how half true it was. She wasn't about to tell Chloe she was floating near the ceiling, speaking through a veil of cotton. That fell under the AA guideline of doing more harm than good. But she did make a mental note to stop lying, even by omission.

Chloe looked touched in a way that made Frankie's eyes go glassy.

"Could you guys just not, like, discuss it in gross detail?" Chloe made a face like she'd sucked on something bitter.

"Well, Janey's my best friend. We talk about everything in gross detail." Except, of course, Janey didn't know Frankie was still taking the gummies—or that she'd stolen her husband's prescription pain meds.

"Did she tell you she and Mr. Roberts are like almost back together?"

"She did."

"That whole break thing was really weird."

"Adults are really weird," Frankie said. "Relationships are complicated. Speaking of . . ." She glanced over. "Just because you've started having sex with Patrick doesn't mean it's ever expected of you. Consent is required every time. And mutual respect."

"Mo-om. I'm dying. You did not just say the word *consent*." Chloe covered the side of her face with her hand.

"I did. And I'll say it again. Biology doesn't excuse bad behavior. There are rules, and I'm not sorry for making sure you know them." Frankie stared at the road, then added quietly, "No one ever said that to me. I walked around too long carrying shame that wasn't mine."

At the red light, Chloe gave her mom a rare, concentrated teenage look—the kind that said, *You've got exactly sixty seconds before I mentally check out.* Frankie hesitated. She couldn't believe what was coming out of her mouth. But she didn't want to stop it either. She felt an urgency, like she'd been granted only until midnight to tell the truth before the spell broke.

"I felt shame when it wasn't mine to carry," she said finally, steadying her voice, "because I was sexually assaulted in college. Someone touched me without permission. And for years I thought it was my fault—because of my skirt, or my body language, or something I said. I really believed that."

"I'm sorry, Mom." Chloe's voice softened, sounding a little scared. "That's awful."

Frankie swallowed hard. Hearing it out loud, she realized how much she'd avoided dealing with it—how she'd shoved it aside in her work with Pearl, skimming the surface and leaving the rest to rot. She'd told herself it was buried, but it was still inside her, festering. And now, high as she was, the numbness was thinning, slipping from her grasp. She'd need more. The drugs dulled the edge, but they couldn't silence what she'd refused to face.

"Yes, it is. But it's far too common. I've known too many women who have their own story. Or they know someone who does. It shouldn't be the case, but it is. I know you trust Patrick—I do too. He's a good guy, like your dad. This isn't about saying all men are bad. It's about knowing that pretending this stuff doesn't happen doesn't make it stop. It only makes us less prepared. I wish we didn't have to have this conversation. Believe me."

"Okay. I get it." Chloe nodded, pulling out her phone.

"Not while you're driving."

"I was changing the song," Chloe groaned.

And just like that, the moment vanished. The carriage turned back into a pumpkin.

20

MERE

Thursday, March 21, 2024

Mere couldn't shake the feeling that she needed to see Frankie again—really see her. Last night, Frankie hadn't acted like herself, and who could blame her? Brie's proximity to Frankie—their shared history of alcoholism—terrified Mere.

She asked Frankie to walk the arboretum path with her, the one that curled around the pond. Lily had always been soothed by walks, even as a baby. Frankie took Pancakes' leash while Mere adjusted the stroller. The early evening light filtered through the bare branches, a softer gold now that the snow was nearly gone. It slipped between the trees in fractured beams, catching on the damp ground where the last of the melt still clung.

"This isn't a normal dog, you know that, right?" Frankie said as Pancakes sat patiently beside the stroller. "Do you remember

Janey's old dog Bruno? He'd steal kitchen towels, shred them under the dining room table, then growl at anyone who tried to take them back."

"We got so lucky with her," Mere said, kneeling to stroke Pancakes' ears before double-knotting her sneakers. She handed Lily a cup of Cheerios with one of those magical lids—easy to reach into but nearly impossible to spill.

The walk itself felt familiar, like muscle memory. Back in the early days of new motherhood, all the books insisted it was crucial to get out of the house. Mere had preferred Lily tucked against her chest in the wrap, safer than bumping a stroller along the uneven path. Later, when Lily was bigger and the stroller was easier, Dale had joined them, folding the route into their nightly routine.

"Since Dale was the only one who wasn't messed up, he should know more, right?" Frankie hadn't been able to focus on anything other than Brie since they'd been together. Mere had already explained everything she'd learned from Dale, leaving out the part about the whiteboard. She didn't need her sister thinking Dale was some kind of serial killer.

"I just need to know if it was really an accident," Frankie pressed further. "Or if no one bothered to look—if she was invisible even at the end."

Mere felt her stomach clench. She wanted to tell Frankie to stop, to let the woman rest, to let *them* rest. Picking at the details wouldn't change the outcome. "You're looking for answers that don't exist," she said carefully, though she wasn't sure if she believed it herself.

They came to a stop as Mere pulled out the duck and geese food. She'd done her research and learned that dried mealworms were the safest option, something that wouldn't disrupt the ecosystem. She reached into her backpack, tucked beneath the stroller, and handed a Tupperware container to Lily.

"Are you actually serious right now?" Frankie asked, recoiling. "Are those bugs?"

"Yes," Mere said, smiling to herself. "They're mealworms. Bread and people food are really bad for the wildlife out here, but Lily loves feeding them. And yeah, I'll admit the dried worms are a little creepy, but it makes her so happy. She really loves animals, you know?"

Lily reached over and scooped up a handful of the worms, her face aglow with anticipation. She wandered over to a nearby cluster of wildlife.

"I like to come here when I need a break from the store," Frankie said. "I like the ducks."

After a pause, she added, "I've made up full social dynamics for them. Those ones over there, total bitches. Snooty, judgy, always side-eyeing the brown ones."

Mere laughed softly, shaking her head. "God, that's so you."

"They're also super racist. And fascist, if you can believe it. That one over there with all that unearned attitude and sense of superiority?" Frankie pointed to the largest duck waddling along the pond's edge with bright orange feet. "Total dictator. Militant. Brutal."

Mere shot her a sidelong glance. "You've put way too much thought into this."

"Lately I prefer duck dynamics to people." Frankie sighed theatrically. "I was Brie's sponsor. She was halfway in and halfway out with her relapses."

Mere didn't know Brie had been relapsing. She waited Frankie out in hopes that she would share more.

"It feels like I could have stopped her," Frankie said.

Before Mere could respond, Lily came back for more worms.

"Can I give them to her?" Frankie asked, holding the plastic container at arm's length like the worms might suddenly wriggle up her sleeve.

Mere smiled despite herself, taking a seat on a nearby bench. She watched as Lily settled beside Frankie, her small hand resting lightly on Frankie's knee, eyes tracking her movements with something that looked a lot like trust. It was subtle but unmistakable. There hadn't been many chances for this kind of connection between them. Mere realized, with a quiet pang, that she should've made more room for it sooner.

But it was hard to forget the way Frankie had spoken that night—her last night of drinking, slurred and sharp-edged—about Dale and what their future children might be like. *Those little weirdos wouldn't stand a chance.* Mere hated how deeply that prophecy had rooted itself. She knew better than to let drunken words carry any weight, especially not against the truth of Lily's existence. But motherhood doesn't live in logic. It lives in the raw, tender places, the ones that bruise easily and never stop reaching for answers to questions you wish you never had to ask.

Frankie joined her on the bench. "I know we never talked

about it," Mere began, her voice hesitant, "and I haven't wanted to bring it up since you've been sober. But it still feels like this giant elephant between us, how cruel you were that night we brought the girls back to our house."

Lily reached for more worms, her fingers brushing Frankie's knee again before she scampered back to the ducks. For a second, Mere considered dropping it. But too much had gone unsaid for too long.

"You never made amends to me," Mere said, softer now, but firm. "Not for that night."

Frankie blinked slowly, like the words were hard to absorb. "What?"

"For that night," Mere repeated. "With Dale. With the kids."

"Meredith." Frankie said her name low, a warning.

But Mere held her ground. "It's been a decade. I know amends are part of your program, and maybe you made them to everyone else, but not to me. Not for that final night of drinking."

Frankie exhaled and tipped her head back, eyes scanning the sky like she was searching for patience or maybe just an escape hatch.

"You scared the shit out of me," Mere went on. "You scared the shit out of everyone. I had to explain to your daughters why their mom was screaming at their uncle in the yard, drunk out of your mind. And Dale—"

"You're right. I was awful," Frankie cut in, but her voice was flat and hollow.

"Yes, you were," Mere snapped. "You weren't just mad. You were cruel."

Frankie straightened, her jaw tight. "You don't think Dale had it coming?"

"Jesus, Frankie. This isn't about Dale. This is about you."

Frankie looked away to where Lily was at the pond, which was thankfully protected by fencing that ran along the edge.

"I can't tell you how much it stung, what you said about our future kids," Mere said, her voice tightening. "Like you already knew something would be wrong with them."

She could still picture it, Frankie's girls wrapped around her legs like anchors, trying to hold her upright. Dale had to pry them off. Frankie wasn't steady on her feet.

That image never left her.

In so many ways, she and Frankie had been those girls once, clinging to each other after their mom died, desperate for something solid after the ground cracked open beneath them.

"You were our dad that night," Mere said. "That's what killed me."

Frankie noticeably flinched.

"We never talked about what it was like when you left for college," Frankie said. "When it was just him and me. I know I never brought it up—maybe you were waiting for me to. But if you want to talk about ugly . . ."

Mere saw the shimmer in her sister's eyes, tears threatening but never falling. Frankie tilted her head back, forcing them away. If anyone could muscle their emotions into submission, it was her.

Mere recognized the move. The shift. Frankie trying to redirect, to deflect, to dredge up their shared past so she wouldn't have to sit in the spotlight of her own behavior. It was classic. Their childhood had been hard, no question. But that didn't excuse the things Frankie had done as an adult.

"You want me to float around in your big, empty pool of pity. You act like Mom dying didn't happen to both of us." She paused, her eyes fixed hard on Frankie, waiting for the words to land. "I left because I had the chance to, and what kills me is you would have done the same." Her throat tightened, but she pressed on. "I'm sorry I was the older one and had to make that decision, but I'm done being blamed for our parents' problems. I am your ally in this. I want you to take accountability for your actions." She managed to keep her voice steady.

"Now? You want me to do that right this minute?"

"Why is Pearl the only one who's allowed to call you on your bullshit? It's been a decade," Mere replied. "I think now is as good a time as any."

Frankie didn't answer. She gripped the edge of the bench until her knuckles went white. Mere could see it, the way she teetered between retreat and explosion, how her body readied itself like a cornered animal. She waited for Frankie to lash out, to defend herself, to twist it all around. But instead, Frankie stared down at the plastic container of bugs in her hands, distracted, distant. She looked more like their dad in one of his depressive fogs than the sister Mere used to know.

"You've done a lot of work," Mere said gently. "I see that. But I guess I just needed to hear you say it."

Frankie gave a small nod, barely perceptible. And then, so quietly Mere almost missed it—

"I'm sorry."

It landed lifeless. Performed, not felt. And somehow, that felt worse than silence.

21

FRANKIE

Friday, April 5, 2024
Open Mic Night

It had been more than two weeks since Brie's body was discovered. The official cause of death was ruled hypothermia following a loss of consciousness from an accidental head injury. Based on her location, slumped near a large tree, and the levels of alcohol and drugs in her system, the coroner concluded that she likely struck a low-hanging branch head-on and then fell backward. The impact to the back of her skull hit her brain stem, knocking her unconscious. From there, the snow had done the rest.

Still, the story didn't sit cleanly in town gossip. People knew the guys had been camping near that same spot, and Frankie couldn't shake the thought that whispers were circling. Hosting an event in Brie's honor, opening their arms in support, was supposed to signal they had nothing to hide. But sometimes

Frankie worried that trying too hard to look innocent was the very thing that made you look guilty.

Frankie had been rationing the last of her oxy. She wanted to savor it, even knowing that she could always get more from the sketchier corners of the internet. She'd checked again. It wasn't hard. Still, she figured she'd more likely fake an injury and get a prescription. That way, at least she'd know it wasn't laced with fentanyl. She didn't mean for the hunt for more pills to occupy so much of her headspace lately, but it was either that or spend even more time googling how painful it was to die from hypothermia.

The idea to host an open mic at the bookstore in Brie's honor had been Mere's. Frankie told herself she would've gotten there eventually, but lately her brain was foggy, and she didn't have the bandwidth for much of anything. Janey had set up a GoFundMe for the funeral expenses, and Avery's son, Noah, had decorated printed QR codes with doodles and bright colors. Each one linked to the donation page for guests to scan during the event. Hosting the event felt like the least they could do—something small, something meaningful. Or maybe, Frankie thought, it was also something performative, their way of proving they weren't afraid of being seen. Before finalizing the details, Frankie checked in with Chloe to ask whether she thought Margaret would be okay with it, or if it was still too soon. Brie's family had gone quiet while the press swarmed Big Sky, but recently the media had latched onto another tragedy—a tech billionaire's yacht had capsized in Lake Tahoe, killing six of the eight passengers on board.

For the first time, it felt possible to remember Brie without a camera lens trained on her family.

Frankie glanced around the bookstore, her nerves buzzing as the chairs and couches filled. The place was already close to packed. Sam was on the list again, of course, probably wearing something unnecessarily polished, looking unnervingly handsome. She thought back to the time he'd read a poem in a full three-piece suit, while Caleb sat in the back row with a bemused expression.

Partway through the performance, he'd leaned over and whispered, *What's with the getup?*

Frankie had jumped to Sam's defense without thinking. *It's charming. Part of the performance. You wouldn't understand. It's a creative thing.*

Well, pardon me and my simple mind, Caleb muttered, his pride clearly stung. He'd gotten up and wandered over to the drinks table to join Jack.

As Frankie moved through the room, setting up, she scanned the crowd. She'd suggested making the event dry out of respect, but Brie's membership in AA had never made the papers. Her death had been written off as a cautionary tale, just another overwhelmed, boozy housewife who couldn't handle the pressure. Serving alcohol at an event in her honor felt every kind of wrong, but Brie's family had suggested The Tavern provide all the beer and wine, which told Frankie everything she needed to know about their understanding of the disease. It felt like some kind of hometown loyalty play, as if sentimentality could excuse the optics. Still, Frankie told herself it would have been up to Brie to include her family in her recovery, to make amends, to show them she was changing—if she'd ever made it past Step One.

"Frankie! Frankie!" Eliza, one of the regulars, waved her hand with the urgency of someone flagging down a waitress ready to place an order. "I love these things!" she gushed, gripping Frankie's forearm with an intimacy that felt entirely unearned. Eliza leaned in, her balance precarious.

"Do you know if Sam Heart is performing tonight? Ugh, he's . . ." Eliza trailed off, fanning her face dramatically.

Frankie suppressed a sigh. "Yeah, he's cute," Frankie said, glancing at the sign-up sheet. Sam was fourth in line. She pointed to his name, hoping it would redirect Eliza's attention, but instead, she took it as an invitation for small talk.

"I'll be honest," Eliza said, her words dragging just enough to give her away. "I'm just here for him. Well, him and the wine." She laughed, still clinging to Frankie's arm like it was the only thing keeping her upright. Frankie's patience was wearing thin. Hoping for a quick out, she glanced across the room and waved to her sister, who was standing near the table of food.

"Mere!" she called as her sister bit into a puff pastry. Mere's expression was one of mild confusion, but she weaved her way over, dabbing at her mouth with a napkin.

"Hi," Mere said, voice muffled as she covered her mouth.

Eliza pounced, redirecting her attention, and Frankie barely registered their conversation because Sam was watching her. Their eyes met across the room, and her skin prickled. Without thinking, she moved toward him.

He greeted her with a smile that crinkled the corners of his eyes. He had a few days' worth of stubble, and the casual ruggedness made him even more attractive.

"Hey, are you doing okay? I wanted to check, but your husband seemed pretty, uh, concerned when I dropped you off the other night," Sam said, his head cocked to one side like he'd heard a dog whistle.

"It's all good. Just a misunderstanding." Frankie took a step back; he was standing too close.

Sam quickly changed the subject. "Quite the turnout tonight," he said.

Frankie motioned toward Eliza, who wasn't exactly subtle as she all but drooled over Sam. He was wearing a blazer with tweed elbow patches, so on the nose for a college professor it almost felt ironic, with a crisp white button-down, sleeves rolled just enough to look effortless, and dark slacks that fit too well to be unintentional. His blazer hung open like he didn't take himself too seriously, but everything about him was curated. His glasses caught the warm bookstore light, and under one arm he held a slim black notebook, probably filled with something over-rehearsed but still somehow charming.

"I should be cutting you a percentage of tonight's profits," Frankie said.

He laughed, brushing off the compliment. "It's not me, it's you. That's why people come."

The words hovered, warm and electric. Frankie felt herself lean slightly into the moment, into the heat of his gaze.

"You don't even realize how many admirers you have out

there," she said, glancing again toward Eliza, who was pretending to make conversation with Mere.

"And are you one of them?" he asked, voice low.

The question struck like a match. Her pulse kicked up, just enough to remind her of her body. Just enough to remind her she wasn't supposed to be feeling this.

A warning flared. She'd taken two oxy in her office ten minutes ago and stashed the last one in her desk drawer, saving it for later, her reward for getting through the night. She still had to stand up and say something about Brie, something real. But tonight wasn't the night to show up unguarded. She needed something to smooth the static in her head or she wouldn't make it through. Not after reading how, during hypothermia, the body's final act is often a surge of instinct—shivering, burrowing, desperate movement before the cold takes over. Brie's last moments were probably spent trying to dig herself into the snow like a wounded animal searching for warmth. Terminal burrowing, they called it. Frankie wished she hadn't learned that phrase. And while she was wishing for things, she wished she'd already taken that last pill.

"No, Sam. I'm happily married." There was harmless flirting, the kind that reminded her she was still desirable—that, despite entering the forgotten decade of her forties, where she could no longer compete with twenty-year-olds, she still had some electricity left in her—but she knew that reciprocating *this* kind of attention, even slightly, would push her past the line of what was acceptable. It was beyond what she would be comfortable with Caleb doing with another woman.

"Good luck up there tonight," she added, ensuring her words maintained an appropriate amount of distance between them.

She thought about Pearl's warning: *Go to the barbershop enough times, and you're bound to get a haircut.* The meaning was simple—surround yourself with risk long enough, and relapse becomes inevitable. As Caleb made his way over to them, Frankie strategically headed toward the mic.

Up on their little makeshift stage, she tried to ground herself in the familiar rhythm of hosting, but her mouth moved before her brain could fully catch up.

"Thank you, everyone, for being here tonight," she began, her voice a little too loud. "We're here to celebrate . . . well, not celebrate. That's the wrong word. Honor. We're here to honor Brie Hoover and, um . . . her family."

She paused, blinking at the crowd. "Let's start with a moment of silence. For Brie. And for, you know . . . all of it."

Frankie dipped her head, heat creeping into her cheeks as a few awkward coughs filled the silence. Whatever she'd meant to say slipped away, swallowed by the lump in her throat. She backed off the stage with a sheepish nod, more than ready to pass the mic to the first performer, whom she proceeded to completely tune out while she gathered herself.

Next came a lanky university student whose hands flitted like birds every time the crowd responded. The room moved with him, falling into rhythm, offering a wave of silent, shimmering ASL applause when he asked for it. From the back, Frankie watched Mere more than the performance. Her sister sat rigid, shoulders tense, leaning forward like she was bracing for a punch. Like it was Lily up there, fifteen years in the future, and every stranger's reaction might shape the way she saw herself.

The next woman wasn't as rehearsed as the university student had been. She was nervous and it showed, reading from her phone, a sweet story about a dog that became the family's anchor while their child battled cancer.

By the time Sam's name was called, Eliza was practically vibrating, inching closer until she slid into an empty seat right up front. Sam shrugged off his jacket, draping it neatly over the stool before stepping to the mic.

"This one's called 'Green with Envy,'" he said.

Frankie's fingers moved instinctively, twisting her wedding ring until the emerald was pressed flush into her palm. She closed her hand around it, making a fist so tight it pulsed with a nervous ache. Caleb stepped in beside her, wrapping his arm around her lower back, his body warm and steady as he drew her into him.

Heat crawled up Frankie's neck as Sam read the poem intended for her. The subtleties and nuances spelled out in a language only she would understand. A private declaration of want disguised as art.

Even with the oxy dulling her limbs and loosening her thoughts, guilt pricked at her like glass in her shoe. Caleb stood beside her, unaware. That was the worst part. Sam had become a secret she never meant to have, humming beneath her skin like a low-grade fever she couldn't sweat out. Because some days she felt like she was fading from her own life, and

Sam represented the promise of something thrilling and a little dangerous. Brie had mentioned that same thing before she vanished, about how in the beginning, everything felt vivid, like magic—but then it all dulled. Or maybe you dulled. And suddenly, you were stuck inside a version of yourself that didn't quite fit.

That's what scared Frankie. Not becoming Brie exactly, but becoming whatever Brie had seen on the horizon.

But then what? No one gave out medals for endurance. For staying rooted in a life that kept asking more of you than you knew how to give. Staying meant letting go of the fantasy of escape. It meant choosing Caleb again and again, even when the love between them had become something that only counted because it endured.

She thought of the old Raymond Carver stories she used to devour in college, how everyone drank too much and mistook disaster for depth. How in "What We Talk About When We Talk About Love," they end up sitting in the dark, having talked themselves into silence, into the space where connection used to be. The light fades, and no one moves. The more they tried to define love, the further it slipped away.

Frankie used to think that scene was romantic, in a beautifully tragic way. But now, with her thoughts murky and guilt creeping in, she saw it differently. Not as poetic, but as paralyzing. A room full of people so desperate to feel something true that they'd wrung it dry. Self-destruction masquerading as meaning.

She didn't want to die like Brie Hoover.

As Sam made eye contact, reading his last lines, his lyrical voice and easy pull were poison in a prettier bottle. She leaned into Caleb, her grip tightening around his arm like a latch. Her throat was dry. Her pulse uneven. Here she was in a room full of people and yet her own thoughts could be just as dangerous as any substance.

As she retreated to the back office, she couldn't stop the gnawing thought: Alcohol had become the engine of these open mic nights. It hadn't always been that way. When she first launched the series, she'd kept it dry, not to push sobriety on anyone, but because she liked the idea of creativity being shared unfiltered. Then The Tavern had sponsored an evening, and it had been their most successful yet. Frankie had reluctantly admitted that booze helped people loosen up. They stayed longer, spent more at the register, and kept coming back. But it still gnawed at her. Alcohol created the illusion of bravery, but at the cost of clarity. In AA, there was no buffer. You spoke, or you didn't. But when you did, the words were yours—raw, unpolished, undeniable. That was the kind of truth she'd wanted these nights to be.

And tonight, with The Tavern's logo plastered on the flyer, it felt like a betrayal. Brie had died with alcohol in her system, and still everyone wanted to pretend it wasn't dangerous. Frankie knew better—or at least she thought she did, though the oxy had her drifting, her conviction swelling and slipping all at once. Alcohol didn't make people brave—it made them vanish.

22

MERE

Friday, April 5, 2024
Open Mic Night

Mere had surprised even herself by signing up to read at Frankie's open mic night. But if ever there was a time to step outside her comfort zone, it was now. She hadn't known Brie, but the least she could do was be brave in her honor. She'd asked Dale to keep an eye on Lily while she was up there, even though it was past bedtime. She wanted her daughter to see her at the front of the room, doing something she loved, something entirely her own, separate from the role of mother or wife.

No three-year-old, neurotypical or otherwise, would remember the words Mere said up there. She knew that. But she hoped the moment would plant itself somewhere inside Lily anyway, the way a thousand quiet memories of her own mother still found her when she needed them most.

Except, when she stepped up and took the microphone, the

words evaporated. How could she convince Lily she could be anything, do anything, if she didn't believe it herself? If she didn't start shedding the guilt she carried like a second skin?

She adjusted the mic, buying time. From the stage, she spotted Dale sitting on the rug by the kids' corner, crouched beside Lily. They were lining up wooden blocks in quiet tandem. No one else seemed to notice, but Mere did.

That kiss on his palm during their first date at the Lock Bridge had seemed like nothing back then. But now it felt like the first domino in a chain of choices that had led to this moment. To Lily.

Dale didn't co-regulate like she did. He didn't emote the way she wished he would. But Lily responded to his calm the way trees bent toward light: slow, instinctive, and sure. Maybe he wasn't falling short. Maybe she'd been measuring him against a version of partnership that never quite matched the man he was.

She started reading.

"I used to think the wall was the problem. It was too high, too thick, too stubborn. I imagined the wall had been built by others. By circumstance. By disappointment. But lately I've started to wonder if I built it myself—brick by brick, with every 'I'm fine' I didn't mean, with every truth I swallowed out of fear it might make me too much, or not enough. The wall kept things out. But it also kept things in. Joy. Grief. Longing. Love. It turns out walls don't just protect you from hurt. They protect you from being known. And not being known is its own kind of loneliness. Then I became a mother and thought I was meant to build you your own wall. Because people aren't always kind, and pain doesn't wait its turn. I'm so terrified of you being misunderstood that I didn't take the time to ask you if you even care. So here I am, tapping at the bricks, a little softer now, to see what happens when I stop hiding behind them. I thought I needed to build a wall, when what I really needed was a bridge."

Applause erupted, and when Mere finally had the courage to look up from her paper, she saw that Lily's arms were flapping out in front, in happiness, not fear. Mere stepped away from the microphone and gave a small curtsy, catching Frankie's joyful shrieks, just like the ones she used to let out on warm summer nights when they were kids, chasing bunnies around the yard, trying to round them up before it got too dark to see or the sprinklers kicked on.

Mere looked at her little family again, father and daughter, heads still bent close as Dale squeezed the tops of Lily's shoulders. What if Mere stopped waiting for them to become different people and started trusting who they already were?

Mere, Janey, and Avery had insisted on staying to help Frankie clean up. She'd tried to wave them off, but her resistance only made Mere more determined. Sam had offered too, but Janey had practically shoved him out the door.

"Why'd you do that?" Frankie snapped, sharper than Mere had ever heard her be with Janey.

Janey didn't flinch. "You'd better believe you're playing with fire there. You need to tell him to back off."

"Oh, so that's how it is?" Frankie barked. "You're back with Jack for five minutes after a trial separation and now you're a marriage expert?"

"We aren't back together. We had another fight," Janey admitted, her voice flattening.

Mere glanced at Avery, who busied herself with stacking napkins, clearly staying out of it.

Frankie folded her arms across her chest, her eyes flickering with that brand of defensiveness that always showed up when she felt cornered. "People talk about gray area drinking, right? Well, I think there's such a thing as gray area marriage. It's not broken, just dulled. You coexist like pack animals. No chase, no thrill. Just the slow erosion of wanting." She scanned the room, her voice rising. "And don't act like you don't miss it. That feeling when we'd walk into a party and lock eyes with the most magnetic person there. Just because we could."

Mere and Avery exchanged a glance. Mere felt heat flood her face but didn't look away.

Frankie kept going. "You're really going to tell me boredom had nothing to do with your separation?"

Her gaze bounced from Janey to Avery to Mere, searching for someone to validate her. But something about the way she spoke, too slippery, too self-justifying, put Mere on edge.

Janey's jaw tightened. "Of course there's tedium. That's what love becomes over time. Things wear in. That comfort? That's the real thing. Sam Heart isn't magic, Frankie. He's just a distraction. And he's bad for your sobriety."

"He's harmless," Frankie snapped. "He's like caffeine. My last vice. You want to take away my coffee too?"

"Nothing is harmless with you, Frankie. You don't do anything halfway. For better or worse," Janey said. The room stilled. Mere had the sense she'd wandered into the middle of something much deeper than she understood.

Frankie didn't respond. She turned abruptly, heading for her office like she'd remembered something urgent.

"Where are you going?" Janey called after her. "What's in your office, Frankie?"

Mere watched her sister head toward the door to her office, a knot of dread tightening in her chest.

"What is going on?" Mere finally asked. "You're both speaking in code."

"Do you want to tell your sister, or should I?" Janey said.

"Tell me what?" Mere pressed.

"I'm going to get the pill I hid in my desk," Frankie called out after a long pause.

A pill?

The word barely registered before it shattered something in Mere, like glass between them she hadn't known was there until it cracked. Frankie didn't look like she was drinking again. That would've been easier to spot, easier to name. But now Mere could see it. The erratic behavior, the apology that had barely made it out. She hadn't been drunk at the arboretum—she'd been high.

Frankie vanished behind the door. Janey met Mere's eyes

and gave the smallest nod. Not permission, exactly, but acknowledgment. This was Mere's moment. Her responsibility. Except Mere knew she wouldn't be just walking into her sister's office. She'd be walking into a room crowded with both of their demons.

She entered and shut the door behind her. "How long have you been taking pills?" Mere asked gently, keeping her voice level. One wrong note and she'd lose her.

"You know where I learned my best coping skills?" Frankie said, not gentle at all. "When you left me alone with him at sixteen, Dad taught me the easiest way to check out of my feelings. I picked it up quick. And after the assault, I was a goner."

The words landed like a gut punch. One Mere had braced for but still couldn't absorb.

She reached for the desk to steady herself.

"I know you told me you were leaving for school, but you never asked me. We talked about everything. You made the decision to leave for college alone, and we were a team!" Frankie's voice cracked. Her tears were falling now, fast, steady. It reminded Mere of the character Alice, who cried so hard in Wonderland that her own tears nearly drowned her.

"You're right," Mere said. "I could have stayed. But I honestly thought I was blazing a trail for you to follow. I really did." She wasn't sure the words would land.

"Bullshit. You didn't know what you were doing. The house was on fire, and you left me there to burn."

Frankie opened the drawer and pulled something out, her fingers curling tightly around it. Mere's heart pounded.

"We got out," Mere said, voice shaky. "Both of us. Just in time."

Mere didn't miss the metaphor for what it was—a pointed reminder. Had she waited even one more day, Mere might've been the only Gilmore left in their family.

"Please don't take it," Mere said. "I'm sorry. I am so, so sorry I left you. I was doing the best I could with the same limited tools you had. What was I supposed to do, pull you out of high school and take you to college?"

"It would've saved me a sexual assault, three broken ribs, and a SART exam," Frankie said, meeting Mere's eyes with a glare that dared her to look away.

Mere swallowed hard. "You never told me you had the SART exam."

"I didn't," Frankie said, no longer meeting her eyes. "At the hospital, they asked if I wanted one. I still don't know what happened in the elevator. But . . ."

Mere knew only the barest details of what happened to her sister. Her transfer to UC Blue Ridge had always felt like a gift. Like something sacred that was not to be questioned. She could see now how naive that had been. Mere couldn't help but think of all the ways she'd misunderstood the people she loved most. How she projected her own needs onto Dale and Lily. Waiting for everyone else to meet her where she was, when maybe she needed to take the first step.

"I'm sorry the world is broken," she said quietly. "I wish I could protect you from all of it. But I can't. I never could."

She reached for Frankie's hand, the one not clenched around

the poison that threatened to take her only sister, and pressed a kiss into its center. Frankie's shoulders softened. She handed over the tin.

"It isn't your fault. None of this is your fault," Frankie whispered. "Goddamn it. There are bigger things at play. Bigger bombs than mine."

"Except yours is the only one that ends in life or death."

"It's not that serious. It doesn't have to be that serious," Frankie muttered.

While Mere still held Frankie's hand, she whispered, "Tell that to Brie."

After they left the bookstore, Mere brought Avery back to her house for tea and to process everything that had unfolded that night. She left Avery in the kitchen to start the kettle and slipped down the hall to peek into Lily's room. That's when she saw Dale curled up beside their daughter and Pancakes, looking absurdly large, like a grown man trying to fold himself onto dollhouse furniture. The sight made Mere smile. Lily must've had trouble falling asleep without her at home, and this was Dale's way of showing up.

Back in the kitchen, Avery was perched on one of the barstools.

"I'm thinking Earl Grey, unless you need to get back to the boys?" Mere asked, hoping she'd stay.

Avery twisted her dark hair into a loose topknot. "They're at Tom's mom's place in Sacramento for the night."

Mere turned to the stove. The burner coils were already glowing. She reached for two mugs hanging from hooks beneath the cabinet. "I appreciate you coming. My head's spinning. I can't believe I missed the signs with Frankie."

"Why is that your job?" Avery asked gently. Her only-child confidence showed in flashes. "You're not her keeper. You're her sister."

That was true, but it wasn't something Mere could explain. They sat in silence as the kettle began to steam.

"Hey, I liked what you read tonight," Avery said, letting the compliment land without needing to dress it up.

"Thanks. It's the start of something. Just an idea I've been circling, trying to figure out what it wants to be." Mere noticed a bottle of wine near the fridge. "I could open a bottle . . ."

She trailed off, then shook her head. "Actually, no. I want to keep my wits about me. In case Frankie needs me."

They moved to the couch with their mugs. Avery pulled a throw blanket across their laps. Mere curled her fingers around the tea, letting the heat settle into her hands.

She studied Avery's face, the quiet beauty of it, the way her cheekbones caught the light. There was a softness to her, a sense of ease that had felt out of reach since Lily was born. The saying "A mother is only as happy as her unhappiest child" took on a different weight when you were raising a child with a disability. The grief came laced with guilt. Guilt for wanting it to be easier. For mourning the version of motherhood you thought you'd have. For feeling any of that when you loved your child more than anything.

Mere leaned toward Avery, as if she could borrow just a little of her calm.

"Why do you look so peaceful?" she asked, near desperate to feel that kind of peace herself.

Avery reached out to touch Mere's free hand, her fingertip tracing an absent pattern across her skin, a gesture so small yet intimate, Mere couldn't help but wonder what it meant.

Avery smiled slowly, settling back against her. "Wouldn't it be lovely if it could be us, in that way, instead of our husbands?"

Mere swallowed, not because she hadn't thought of it, but because she had.

"Except we are married to men," she said with a small chuckle that didn't feel funny. She understood exactly what Avery was suggesting—the appeal of a friendship folded inside a partnership. She had yearned for that with Dale, but for it to exist, he would have to be someone entirely different. And it didn't help that she was drawn to women, which made the idea of Avery feel all the more desirable. And lately she'd found herself wondering what was really happening inside Avery and Tom's marriage, the quiet questions that lingered whenever Avery let a silence stretch too long, but before she could give voice to them, Avery pulled closer.

"What if there's more we could feel here, between us?" Avery said.

Mere let herself imagine it, just for a second. The fantasy

bloomed fast and bright: running away with Avery, leaving the demands of caretaking behind, being chosen by someone who understood her without explanation. Another baby had held that same allure—a vision of fullness, of rewriting the story. But both were the same kind of dream—beautiful in the imagining, impossible in the living. She thought of her sister and the way drugs had pulled at her and somehow tricked her into believing they were the solution. The tug she felt now wasn't so different.

If Mere leaned in, she could pretend this was that kind of connection. But it wasn't. It was an escape dressed up as intimacy. She had learned not to mistake being seen for being loved, not to confuse desire with clarity. Avery did see her, and maybe even loved her in a way Dale never could. But that truth didn't have to negate the love she still had for Dale. Her needs were being met in different ways, across very different bridges.

Mere pulled back, though she didn't look away.

She took a breath. "Sometimes I think about escape—new communes, new babies, new lives. But none of it's real. Not for me."

She glanced down the hallway, imagining Dale and Lily still sleeping in their shared cocoon.

"Dale and Lily both claim what they need when they need it. Without apology. It's made me rethink how I want to move through this life from now on too. And maybe that's the point. There's not just one right way to be okay."

Avery studied her.

"I need us to keep this as what it is," Mere said gently.

"Those afternoons we spend together, the four of us, they fill me up more than I ever expected."

Avery nodded, her gaze steady. "I hear you," she said. "And I'm not disappointed. What you said—it matters. Maybe it's less about us and more about me realizing I've been wanting something different in my own life. That pull I've felt? It probably says something about the cracks I've been ignoring with Tom."

She took a sip, then set down the mug. Neither of them spoke. The quiet didn't feel awkward. It felt honest.

23

FRANKIE

Sunday, April 7, 2024

Frankie asked Pearl to connect with her at their women's meeting—the same one she'd wished Brie had come to, because maybe then everything would've turned out differently. The room was full, every chair taken, which didn't surprise her. Just as the holidays always drew a crowd—they had a way of stirring up grief you thought you'd already put to bed—a town tragedy did the same. Especially when the tragedy involved someone like Brie. One of their own.

Their meeting took place in the choral room of a church. Frankie had liked it immediately. The space felt intrinsically cheerful, which couldn't be said for most of the other AA meeting rooms she'd sat in. She could still conjure the sour, stale sips of coffee during those first brutal weeks, when she was convinced she'd rather hang herself than get sober. Yes, they all had a problem with alcohol, but did the rooms themselves have to feel so depressing?

She used to roll her eyes at the secrecy, the hush-hush reputation. Why did everyone treat AA like Fight Club, where the first rule was not to talk about it? If they wanted to grow membership, shouldn't they be advertising on supermarket corkboards or plastering billboards along the freeway? *There is an easier, softer way!*

It wasn't until she actually worked the program that she understood. The anonymity, the privacy—it wasn't secrecy. It was reverence. Part of a spiritual practice that had saved millions of lives. AA didn't need a marketing campaign. People would always find their way to the rooms when they were desperate enough.

And right now, Frankie felt about as desperate as she had on Day One.

Sue was the speaker that night, and Frankie was glad. She'd always loved hearing Sue share. A former English teacher, Sue couldn't help but find meaning between the lines, naturally weaving lessons into every story. They sat around a large rectangular table, with Sue and the meeting secretary, Candice, at the head.

As usual, they began with readings from *How It Works* and *Twelve Steps and Twelve Traditions*. Then Sue began, the way every speaker did: "Hi, I'm Sue, and I'm an alcoholic."

"Hi, Sue," the group responded.

Sue cleared her throat and looked around the room. Brie had never had a designated seat when she came, but she almost always sat to the left of the speaker, and Frankie noticed Sue's eyes drift to that side more than once.

"I don't know where else it's safe to say this, because I don't want to break Brie's anonymity," Sue began gently. "But I feel like we understand a bigger part of who Brie was because she came here."

Her gaze landed again where Brie would have sat. "Of course, we don't know exactly how or why it happened. All we know is that she wasn't sober in the end. And I keep thinking about Mrs. Dubose from *To Kill a Mockingbird*." She lifted her water for a slow sip.

Frankie had recently reread Harper Lee's famous novel, working her way through all the books she'd skimmed in high school. This time she'd found quiet comfort in them, a reminder of why she'd opened the store. There weren't many places that still felt safe, but books had always offered her a way out, and they always would.

"Mrs. Dubose, the old woman Atticus made Jem read to, was addicted to morphine," Sue continued. "And even though she knew she was dying, she chose to go through withdrawal. She wanted to die clean."

Pearl coughed, the sound jagged, like a fist pounding from the inside. Frankie twisted open a bottle of water and set it in front of her. Pearl sipped and gave Frankie a small, grateful wink.

"I don't know exactly what happened with Brie," Sue said. "I'm not here to judge. None of us are. We're already hard enough on ourselves without the world piling on." She glanced down at the wrinkled tissue in her hands, then back to the group. "It just made me think about what it means to keep your sobriety intact, even at the end. Not perfectly. Not even bravely. Just honestly and with dignity. Still showing up for myself when it matters most. That's the kind of sober I want to be."

Sue's voice steadied. "All we really have is today. Right now. Either this disease will take us out, or we'll put in the work and stay in recovery."

Frankie let herself go quiet. Her mind was never safe terrain, thoughts ricocheting like loose change in a dryer. But here, in this circle, the weight was shared. Women carried one another through their lowest points. Mothers, daughters, friends—these women could hold your grief when you couldn't. That collective strength was its own kind of medicine. Its own kind of magic.

For once, Frankie let herself settle into it. Let herself feel safe enough to just be. She'd sat in these chairs for years, but usually with her guard up, cataloging other people's stories instead of letting herself belong to them. She had never truly surrendered to the idea that she deserved to be carried too. And maybe even to be proud. She'd stepped up for their dad, kept their house from collapsing in every sense of the word. She'd pieced herself back together after her assault, built a marriage, a family, a business, a life. She'd found these rooms and stayed sober for ten years. That mattered.

She hadn't done it all cleanly, and the shame of some of those missteps still lingered—the blackouts at bedtime, or worse, at bath time, when she'd narrowly avoided tragedy with her daughters. She couldn't remember the exact words she'd hurled at Mere and Dale when they came to pick up the girls on her final night of drinking. But she knew she'd wanted to wound, in the way only a sister could.

She'd let her anger at Mere's absence calcify, let it reshape how she remembered things. She'd focused on the cracks instead of the light. And there had been so much light. But she'd pressed the rest down—abandonment, grief, all the hurt she never named—until Brie went missing and it rose back up. Because pain doesn't vanish. No matter how deep you shove it, it claws its way to the surface.

This time, though, she wasn't shoving it. She was letting it rise, and letting the women around her hold it. That was new. That was surrender. She hadn't let go of everything—not fully. She still gripped her anger, her guilt, the illusion of control. But she had entrusted herself to the rooms, to sobriety, to the belief that her life was worth rebuilding. And maybe that was the only way healing really worked: in layers, some deeper than others, unfolding when you were finally ready. But that was the progress, not perfection, portion of the program. And Brie was dead, maybe because she couldn't surrender, maybe for a hundred other reasons. Frankie would never know. But she did know that surrender wasn't just about staying sober. It was about unburdening herself of old wounds, the assault she'd tried to minimize, the rage she'd never voiced, the grief she'd carried like contraband. Letting go meant finally putting it down, even if only for this hour.

After Sue finished and opened the floor, Frankie knew she had to speak before fear took over.

"My name is Frankie, and I'm an alcoholic."

She paused, glancing at Pearl, ashamed this was how she'd hear it—at group level, not one-on-one. Of all the people in Frankie's life, Pearl was the one she'd been fully honest with. Frankie had never taken for granted the quiet holiness of being her truest self with another woman.

"The first thing I need to say is that I have nowhere to put the guilt I feel about Brie. I was her sponsor, and I can't stop feeling like I failed her. I know in this program we're only responsible for our own sobriety, but guilt and shame are my most dangerous emotions. The ones I used to drink over. And I know this is a space for alcohol, but I need to say this out loud or I'm afraid of what might happen. Actually, that's not true. I already know what will happen."

She stopped, the image of Brie's frozen body flashing in her mind. Her voice dropped.

"I started experimenting with other substances. Just here and there. Trying to re-create the feeling alcohol used to give me. The scariest part was that, for a moment, I actually convinced myself I'd discovered something new. Something better, because I didn't wake up sick the next day."

Her knee bounced under the table. She pressed her palms flat to still it.

"But it got me. Oh my god." Her voice cracked as tears came fast. "Addiction got me again. I can't believe I didn't see it coming. After all these years, after all the work I've done, the meetings, the Steps, I still got taken down."

The woman to her left—someone Frankie couldn't name but who reminded her of a young Meryl Streep—pushed the tissue box toward her. Frankie didn't want to be one of the blubbering criers, but the tears wouldn't stop.

"You know what's wild? I thought I'd outsmarted it. I said I was going to get sober. At first, I thought my family bullied me into it, but eventually I saw it for what it was: an immeasurable gift. I liked who I became without alcohol. For the first time, I was who I said I was. Honest. Reliable. Trustworthy with my kids."

She drew in a shaky breath.

"But then I thought I'd found a loophole. A way to detach just a little. Just enough to blur out the scary feelings. My husband unknowingly triggered a memory of my sexual assault, and after that, it was like I was off to the races."

She turned toward the space where Brie used to sit.

"And after everything that happened with Brie, I became obsessed. I couldn't stop thinking about it, what I could've done differently, what might've changed things. I thought if I just thought about it hard enough, I could rewrite the outcome. That's how I spiral. The obsession itself becomes the addiction. My thoughts—they're my new substance. Just as toxic, just as dangerous."

She swallowed as she steadied herself.

"I used to think sobriety was about the drink. But I wasn't just addicted to alcohol. I was addicted to anything that filled the void, anything that let me disappear from myself. And now I see that the real work isn't just about putting down the glass. It's about staying present when every part of me wants to escape."

Frankie's gaze circled the table. Her tears had stopped, replaced by a bone-deep weariness.

"Everywhere I go, there I am," she whispered. Then, with a humorless laugh, she added, "I guess I've got a lot to process with my sponsor."

Her eyes found Pearl's. Pearl met her with a steady, unflinching look. No judgment, no panic. Just quiet strength. Already understanding.

Afterward, Frankie stayed behind to face the music with Pearl. They borrowed the keys from Candice and promised to lock up. Frankie had been the treasurer for this meeting for years, which meant she was responsible for all the donation money, making sure rent got paid to the church and contributions were sent to the other AA entities. It was wild, really, the kind of responsibility a bunch of recovering drunks could handle in sobriety. Trusted with keys to a church, no less. And everyone knew they'd guard them like their sobriety depended on it. Back in the day, they'd have sold those keys to the highest bidder with the best booze, no questions asked.

"So apparently, I'm also a drug addict now," Frankie said, dropping her forehead to the table. Just saying it out loud felt like a release, like naming it had finally loosened whatever had been cinched tight around her ribs. For the first time in weeks, she could breathe. It meant she was out, really out, of the hell she'd fallen back into. The lying, the hollow apologies, the blame. The way she'd let things with Sam inch too far, chasing a makeshift dopamine hit. At what cost? Her marriage to a man who loved her.

She lifted her head to lean on Pearl's shoulder. "Do I lose my sobriety?"

"Some people in the room would argue yes. But you haven't lost all that you've learned from a decade's worth of work," Pearl offered as Frankie pulled away, reaching for the tissue box again, adding a new tissue to the crumpled pile in front of her on the table. "Old trauma has a way of rearing its ugly head just when you least expect it."

Frankie thought about the pain she'd tried to ignore, Caleb exposing himself in the car, Brie disappearing and then dying. It made sense, in a way, that she'd turned to drugs. She already knew alcohol wasn't an option, so she went with what was in front of her.

"You are going to call me every day. Meetings, let's say ninety in ninety like you're a newcomer, and you will definitely need to rework the Steps with another woman in the program around this."

Frankie was stunned. "Why another woman in the program? Why not you?" She didn't want to work with someone else.

"It'll help you branch out. Find someone else who understands both alcohol and drugs."

"But you're still my sponsor, right? You're not breaking up with me because I slipped?"

"This has nothing to do with that," Pearl said. "I promise."

She rubbed the top of Frankie's hand, still clenched around a tissue.

At home, the kitchen smelled like melted butter and chocolate. Chloe stood half inside the refrigerator.

"We need more eggs." Chloe poked her head out from behind the fridge door. "Oh, and the garbage disposal is making that scary sound again."

As Frankie entered the kitchen, Chloe made her way over to the island with the KitchenAid mixer and proceeded to dump the remainder of what had been a full bag of chocolate chips into the bowl. "By the time I get to the end of the dough, the last few cookies always have, like, zero chocolate chips left," she said, popping one into her mouth.

"I wonder how that happens," Frankie teased, leaning on the counter.

"I can't help it if the dough tastes so much better than the cookies themselves."

Frankie let out a short laugh. "It must be genetic, because when I used to make cookies with your grandma and Aunt Mere, by the time the actual cookies came out of the oven, I was too full of raw dough to eat a single one."

Chloe grinned, the kind of smile that started in her eyes before spreading to her mouth. She reached out her hand, offering a carefully curated ball of dough. There was a spot on the tray, empty and ready, but Frankie met her daughter's gaze and popped the gooey blob directly into her mouth.

"Rayna's not here?" Frankie glanced around, and Chloe shook her head. Caleb already handled all of Rayna's sports practices as one of the coaches; they'd divided and conquered when it came to the girls, though Frankie knew she needed to circle back and spend more time with Rayna soon. "I feel like I haven't seen your sister in too long," she admitted. She'd been so distracted but was grateful for Caleb as her teammate in parenting and life.

"Yeah, we talked last night," Chloe said, a shy smile tugging at her mouth. "We both agreed we need you never to die."

Frankie laughed, her throat tightening at the same time. "I'll do my best."

As Frankie savored the dough, she braced herself for what needed to come next. "Mmm, these are good. Hey, I have to tell you something," she began. "I never apologized for breaking your trust. It's not an excuse, but I slipped back into active addiction, and I wasn't myself. I'm sure you noticed."

Saying it out loud made her stomach twist. It was one thing to admit to her addiction in a room full of sober women, but telling her teenage daughter was something else entirely.

"What do you mean?" Chloe stopped rolling the ball of dough she had in her hand.

Frankie took the ball from Chloe and removed a little glob to eat. Chloe playfully swatted at her hand before grabbing what was left of the ball and placing it on the last empty spot on the baking sheet.

"Well, you know I have a problem with alcohol, and I've been sober since you were about six." Frankie waited until Chloe gave some sort of signal of understanding. They had discussed the subject ad nauseam. Frankie and Caleb decided it was best to share openly about the girls' genetic predisposition to addiction and allow them to ask any questions. Frankie wasn't under any disillusionment that Chloe hadn't tried alcohol or weed, but she hoped that by being honest with her girls, it would potentially spare Chloe the kind of experimenting Frankie did when she was her age. "I started taking THC gummies, and that led to me taking your dad's prescription painkillers—which, turns out, are also totally addictive." Frankie paused, giving Chloe a moment to absorb this.

She tried to imagine a version of her life where her own mother had sat a sixteen-year-old Frankie down and admitted she was a drug addict. But the image wouldn't come. Her mom still lived in her mind as someone impossibly put together, untouched by the kinds of messes Frankie now found herself in. She wondered if Mere saw their mom the same way. She made a mental note to ask her next time they were together.

"Mom, that's crazy. Why would you do that?" Chloe asked. The oven was beeping, but Chloe wasn't moving, so Frankie went over to pull out the first batch of cookies.

"I got addicted to them, and luckily, because I already had enough recovery running through my system, I was able to stop before something really horrible happened." The wave of heat from the oven blew her hair back as she reached for the oven mitt from the hook on the wall. When she placed the tray next to the raw batch, Chloe yanked the mitt off Frankie's hand and went to slide in the final tray.

Frankie clocked the roughness in Chloe's exchange.

"Are you upset?" Frankie asked. She tried to remind herself that she was the parent in this situation and not the child, but the role reversal was making it impossible to shake off the shame of somehow letting down her oldest daughter. "I just came from a meeting. I've asked for help. I'm going upstairs to talk to Dad right now."

"Dad doesn't know about this yet?" Chloe couldn't hide her exasperation. "You're telling me before Dad?"

"Well, I saw you first. And I want you to trust me—to be honest with me—the way I'm trying my hardest to be with you." Frankie poked at the cookies still cooling on the tray. They were perfectly gooey. "I taught you well, my child," she said, nodding toward the cookies.

Chloe made a face, half sniff, half eye roll, but then her expression softened. "Okay, well . . . if we're being totally honest with each other, I told Patrick I'm not ready. I thought I was, but now I want to wait. With everything going on, Margaret's mom and all, it just doesn't feel right, right now." Her voice dropped. "What you said in the car . . . I don't know, I just . . ." Chloe trailed off, staring ahead like she was back in the car. And maybe, for her daughter, that was the safest place to be. Frankie tried her best to stay present, *stay in it*, as Pearl would say. She was so proud of Chloe, proud of her maturity, that she nearly teared up. But she knew better. So instead, she asked the one question she was most afraid to hear answered.

"And Patrick? How did he respond?"

"He's been great. Totally gets it. He's bummed, obviously, he's a guy, but he said he wants it to feel right for both of us. Plus, his parents are being really dumb lately and still fighting a lot. I think it's messing with his head."

Frankie took that in, one piece at a time. Relief bloomed at the news that Patrick was being respectful, as she'd always hoped and expected he would be, but the second half caught her off guard. Janey and Jack were fighting a lot? It sounded familiar but foggy, like something she'd half registered and then let slip away. Janey always confided in her when things got hard with Jack. Frankie had been such a terrible friend lately, drifting through life like a shadow of herself. But not anymore.

That was the gift of being here, in this body, with an unaltered mind. She could show up. She *would* show up. Janey deserved that. So did Chloe.

"I'm really proud of you, Chloe," Frankie said, doing her best to hold back a sniffle.

"Yeah, well," Chloe said, rolling her eyes, then softening. "I'm really proud of you too."

"I wanted to talk to you about something," Frankie called to Caleb from inside their walk-in closet. It was still early afternoon, but Frankie shed her normal outside-world clothes and pulled on her 4XL T-shirt—the one that felt like a sigh of relief. Oversized, shapeless, and absolutely necessary for the conversation she needed to have with Caleb.

She felt almost giddy with relief: The pills were gone, the tin emptied and tossed, and she was no longer beholden to anything. Sobriety had never felt this easy before. It was as if every tool she'd gathered over the years had resurfaced, reminding her that the same rules applied to drugs as they had with alcohol.

Maybe this was the pink cloud, that early stage of recovery when everything feels euphoric, deceptively easy, when dopamine tricks you into believing you're already healed. She'd felt that lightness before. Still, she leaned into it, the empathy and recognition she'd felt in the meeting, letting it carry her forward before fear had the chance to catch up.

"Mm-hmm," Caleb replied from his side of the bed, where he was sitting on top of the covers, still scrolling through his phone. He looked up when she returned, tucking herself under the covers beside him. The routine steadied her. Ruby, their little black dog, jumped up between them and settled in, like she sensed something important was coming.

"Do you remember when I drove you home from the dentist?" Frankie asked tentatively.

Caleb shook his head. "I don't even remember getting in the car, to be honest."

She shifted closer. That's what she'd assumed. So she told him. Everything. What happened in the car. How seeing him in that altered state, pants undone, disoriented, had triggered something she'd worked hard to bury. Something she wasn't sure she could anymore.

As the words left her, shame burned hot in her chest. She hated even implying a parallel between Caleb and her attacker. They weren't the same. Not even close. Caleb was the safest man she'd ever known, the one who had stood steady while she stumbled, who never asked her to be anything other than herself. The look on his face now—confused, wounded—twisted her stomach.

She knew then she had to own it. Her reaction wasn't his fault. He didn't need to carry the weight of every predator simply because he was a man. She'd been the one who let old ghosts bleed into the present, who reached for pills instead of reaching for him. He deserved honesty, not blame. He deserved a wife who could separate the past from the man in front of her.

She pushed back against the old reflex, the one that whispered to numb it all with a fistful of pills.

"I also stole your pain meds," she said flatly, the way Pearl had suggested. "The ones you were prescribed after your appointment. I didn't throw them away. I stole them."

Caleb froze. She forced herself to hold his gaze.

"You stole my prescription pain meds?" he asked, voice quiet, like he was still buffering the information. Of everything she'd just admitted, she knew that line would echo the loudest. Caleb still struggled to understand how addiction rewired her brain. To him, the world was made of solvable problems. But her brain, her past, her chaos—none of it fit into that kind of order.

"Where are they now?" he asked finally.

"Dissolving in the toilet at The Open Book."

"You took them?" His face twisted, like the words themselves were toxic.

Her cheeks burned. It took her right back to her late twenties, when the girls were still small and Caleb would catch her lying about drinking. Like that Tuesday afternoon he came home early with takeout pizza and found her drunk by four. She hadn't even bothered with an excuse. Just the hot, skin-prickling shame of being caught, of having to explain something she already regretted.

"The point is," she said, steadying herself, "I know now I have a problem with any substance. THC, prescription meds, NyQuil. From now on, I'll be sober. Completely clean."

Caleb's mouth tightened. "Uh-huh. Just like that."

"No, not just like that," she said gently. "I'll go back to in-person meetings. I'll talk to my sponsor. I'll ask for help. But the difference this time is . . . I feel relief. Not fear. Not dread. Just . . . relief."

If she were talking to Janey, they would already be knee-deep in parsing the trauma, her relapse, the shame, how Caleb had unknowingly triggered something buried. But this was Caleb. He needed time, order, logic. And if she wanted their marriage to survive, she had to let him process the conversation his way.

Caleb rubbed a hand across his face, like he was trying to scrub something away. Finally he sat up straighter, exhaling through his nose.

"Well," he said quietly, "I'll certainly never do drugs again."

That wasn't him dismissing her—that was Caleb's way of connecting. It was him trying to make sense of it, trying to meet her where she was. That was how he showed up: through routines, through stillness, through being the one who kept the wheel steady when she couldn't. And she loved him for it.

"While I wish that were everything," he said, watching her closely, "I can tell there's more. I know you. Just say it."

Frankie tensed. "Are you asking if I put our kids in danger again?"

The memory of Step Nine slammed into her, the moment she had made amends and confessed to Caleb that she once drove drunk with the girls in the car. If she hadn't done the steps leading up to that one, she never would have survived it. She would have twisted it into a story where she was the victim, not the one who had done the harm.

"I was high the other day," she said quietly. "In the passenger's seat, when Chloe drove us home from the doctor's office. I wouldn't exactly win any parenting awards for that."

Caleb shot her a sharp look. "Are you trying to make jokes right now?"

She dropped her gaze to the floor.

"No," she said. "I'm not."

She took a deep breath and continued, "I was high when Sam dropped me off the other night too. Nothing happened. But I never should have put myself in that position, out of respect for our marriage."

Caleb's face dropped. Of everything she could have done, that crossed a line. He stood and began pacing the room. Early in their relationship, he'd made it clear how important respect was between them, not in some outdated "honor and obey" way, but by never creating situations where trust could be questioned.

Years ago, a guy in the program had developed feelings for Frankie. She hadn't exactly shut it down right away. She liked the attention. It made her feel wanted. When he finally asked her out for coffee, she said no, told him she was happily married—but this wasn't all that different. Attention had always been its own kind of drug.

Caleb studied her carefully.

"I'm grateful you quit drinking and stayed committed to that. But the other night, I knew something was off," he said, shaking his head. "You weren't yourself. I know what you look like when you're wasted, Frankie. And then you get in the car with him?"

She felt herself bristle, an old instinct to deflect rising fast. She wanted to remind him what he had looked like in the car after the dentist, but she stopped herself. This part was on her—her choice to numb, her choice to flirt, her choice to lie. He was allowed his reaction. He deserved her accountability.

"Here I was thinking I was going crazy, that I wasn't reading the situation right," he said, still pacing. He was growing more agitated, and Frankie wanted so badly to say something that would get him to climb back into bed.

"There's more," she said softly, eyes on the floor. "That poem Sam read? It was about me."

Caleb froze. "Why would it be about you?"

She hadn't planned on telling him everything. Just fragments. But once she started, she couldn't stop. Pearl had told her many times before that she no longer needed to be the hero in every story. Sometimes, she had to be okay with being the villain.

She moved to the edge of the bed and reached for his hand. His fingers brushed her wedding ring, and she watched realization flash across his face—the title of the poem slotting into place with a sickening click.

Caleb sucked in a breath and let her hand go as he stepped back.

"I want to punch that guy," Caleb said. "I've never felt such a strong urge to hit someone."

The shame of it nearly knocked her breathless. This was her doing—not his, not Sam's alone, but hers. She had let pills cloud her judgment and let attention blur her boundaries. Addiction didn't fire a single bullet; it emptied the whole magazine into everyone she loved. She saw that now, in the pain stamped across Caleb's face.

"You're my wife," Caleb said. "Not that I own you. But there's a line. And you don't cross it with another man's wife."

Caleb wasn't violent. She'd seen him get physical only once, in college, when a guy dressed as the Energizer Bunny wouldn't stop harassing her. Caleb had stepped between them, calm but firm, and shoved the guy hard enough to make him stop. Then he walked her home, slept on the couch, and picked up coffee in the morning. That was the moment she knew. Not all men were like the ones from Santa Barbara. Or like her father, unpredictable and sometimes terrifying. Caleb was different. And she had treated him as if he weren't. That wasn't just unfair—it was wrong.

"You're right," Frankie said quietly. "I'm sorry. I never should have done that."

She meant it. But she also knew her apologies didn't land the same anymore. That was the problem with addiction. The switch flipped, and suddenly little lies didn't feel like lies at all. Before she knew it, she was living a life she didn't recognize, standing in a bed of lies she had to lie down in.

Eventually Caleb paced out of the room, probably into his office. She knew he needed space. He'd come back when he was ready. In the meantime, she tried to read, but every word blurred. The truth was, all she really wanted to do was get high.

Instead, she texted Pearl. *Fighting with Caleb. It's my fault and I feel like shit. Wish I could take something. But I won't. Figured texting you was the next right thing.*

Pearl replied almost immediately. *Good. See, all those years of recovery being put to good use.*

Okay, but now what?

You're not alone. Stay in it.

She clutched the phone like it was a lifeline, reread the words twice, then set it face down before she could spiral further.

Eventually Caleb came back. His shoulders had softened. He sat next to her on the bed.

"Why?" he asked, voice low but steady. "Why do you need attention from someone who's not me?"

"I want everyone to love me enough so they won't leave me," she said. "The problem is, there's no such thing as enough. If there were a way to measure love, Pearl would be the standard, because I've never performed for her. I've just existed. And that's always felt so good."

She glanced at Caleb to see if he was following. His brows

were furrowed, a deep line down the center of his forehead like someone had taken a knife to him and he'd refused to get it stitched up.

"Back in the fall," she said, "Brie got drunk at a school dance. I let her sleep it off in my truck. She was curled in the back seat, totally out of it, and she mumbled something I'll never forget. She said she felt invisible. I knew exactly what she meant. That feeling of being looked through. Attention feels like proof you still exist."

"But Brie wasn't sober," Caleb said quietly. "She wasn't sober when she said that, and she wasn't sober when she died."

He was right. The words stung, but she needed him to say them. She shifted to rest her head beneath his chin, testing whether he was open to touch. He leaned his head against hers. His breathing steadied her. She nestled in closer.

These were the moments that reminded her why she'd fallen in love with him in the first place.

"I am clean and sober," she whispered. "And I don't want my addiction to die with me. I want to be free from it."

So Frankie waited. Sat in the discomfort. She didn't take anything, not just because there was nothing in the house, but because she had reached out, and she wasn't alone. Her husband was beside her. He couldn't live inside her head, but he lived inside her heart, and that was always going to be enough.

"Can you forgive me?" she asked, sitting beside him in the home they built together.

"You're a lot," he said.

"Some might argue I'm too much."

"I'd never say that." He smiled faintly. For a second, she saw the boy he'd been when they first met. The one she'd hoped could calm the storm inside her. But that was never his job, and she couldn't put it on him anymore.

"I'm so sorry," she said. "It's done. I won't let it happen again. Everything feels heavier since Brie died."

"The guilt," he said softly. "I can't believe we were right there."

"You didn't know."

She saw it in his eyes. He was back in the woods. Back in that blank, drugged confusion where something irreversible had happened.

"I saw her before she died," Frankie said. "I haven't told you that. I wanted to be mad at her. For giving in. For choosing the thing I'm trying so hard to fight."

She paused, the admission catching in her throat.

"I wanted to save her. But I know it doesn't work that way. You'll drive yourself crazy trying to save people who don't want to be saved."

Caleb said nothing, but he didn't pull away.

After a long silence, his voice cracked. "I hate drugs. I hated them before. But now, knowing what I know, I hate them even more."

"What do you mean?" she asked, hoping Caleb would keep talking.

"If we hadn't been high, we could've saved her. Me and the guys. We just let her lie there, dying, because we didn't understand what we were seeing. That's not an excuse. But it's the truth."

Frankie's breath caught. His grief carved her open.

"It's not your fault," she whispered.

He shook his head, but she held his face, made him look at her.

"No, Caleb. It's not your fault. The drugs, the alcohol, those aren't the root. They're the symptom."

She wasn't trying to preach. Just trying to give him what had helped her survive.

"Brie died because Brie was going to die," she said gently. "You're not God."

She needed him to believe it. So she could believe it too.

"It's not your fault."

Caleb exhaled, his chest trembling under her hand.

"I don't know how to forgive myself."

She wrapped her arms around him. For once, she wasn't the one unraveling. This time, she would be the one to hold him steady. And in that stillness, she understood something new: Just like he wasn't God, she wasn't a monster. But she was responsible—for her choices, for the hurt she'd caused, and for what came next. Accountability was the only way forward.

24

MERE

Sunday, April 7, 2024

Lily sat cross-legged on the rug, her globe purse propped in front of her like a sacred object. She tapped the globe once, then tilted it, watching the tiny cars circle the bridge as if she could will them into new patterns. Mere leaned against the doorframe, arms folded, that familiar prickle of protectiveness stirring in her chest.

"Careful, Lil," she said automatically, though the purse had cushioned the globe through dozens of tumbles. Lily hummed, unbothered, her focus absolute.

Dale wandered in from his office, still in his work clothes, though the workday was long over. He crouched beside their daughter, watching the cars whirl around with the same rapt attention. Then he glanced up at Mere. "You know," he said slowly, "I could 3D print her something sturdier. A case with a padded insert, maybe even a clasp she can open herself."

Mere raised her eyebrows. He had suggested something like this before and she'd dismissed him. This time she wanted to do better. "A case for her comfort object? That's very . . . you."

Dale blinked, tilting his head. "What do you mean?" His tone was genuinely curious, not defensive. "You said 'very me.' Do you mean because I like to build things? Or because I think about safety a lot?"

He grinned faintly, continuing, "Very me? If you mean practical, then yes. I think it would help. The globe is glass, and statistically speaking it will eventually break. But if she had a case, she'd still get the sensory input from carrying it, and it would reduce the risk. That seems like a good trade-off."

"Exactly," she said. But this time there was no edge in her voice. Instead, she let herself imagine it: Lily slipping the globe into something her dad had designed just for her, safe and snug, a little world inside a little invention.

Lily tapped the purse again, murmuring, "Soft," her shorthand for anything that made her feel steady. Mere walked over and knelt on the other side of their daughter. She touched the strap of the makeshift purse she'd fashioned—Velcro fraying, fleece poking out from one corner—and smiled at how far it had gotten them. Then she looked at Dale. "Maybe you should," she said softly. "Print her something. Not to replace this. Just . . . an upgrade."

Dale's eyes flickered, revealing his surprise, then warmed. "Lily, you can pick the shape and color or pattern."

"Would you like that, Lily?" Mere asked. Lily glanced up,

her cheeks flushed with the intensity of her play, and gave the smallest nod before returning to her globe. For once, Mere didn't feel the need to translate or push for more. That nod was enough.

She leaned back on her heels, meeting Dale's gaze over their daughter's head. There had been years when she thought connection had to come in speeches, in hashing everything out until it was clear and symmetrical. But maybe connection looked more like this: small, practical acts of care. Accepting what Lily needed. Letting Dale contribute in the way he knew best.

She felt the old reflex tugging—the one that always placed her in the caretaker role. First with their mother, then their father, now with Lily. And wasn't there some echo of it in regard to Dale too? Not that he needed caretaking in the same way, but he had his own blind spots, his own pockets of absence, places where she felt she had to pick up the weight. She thought of Frankie, who had dumped so much of their father's care onto her, and realized the pattern: Her sister had been both—someone who had leaned on her, but also someone who hadn't seen how heavy it was to hold it all. Her life had been marked by the people she'd loved deeply who required everything from her, and the others—her father and even Frankie, to an extent, and now Dale—who never seemed to notice how heavy it had all been. But Dale's quiet was not neglect. It was difference, the same way Lily's silences were. It reflected an interior world she wasn't always invited into but was lucky to glimpse on occasion. What she had long called absence might, in truth, be another kind of presence, love expressed in a language she was still learning to hear.

Watching Dale tonight, crouched beside Lily, offering not a grand gesture but a simple, tangible solution, Mere let herself release the tally sheet. He wasn't Ed, and he wasn't Frankie. He was here, trying in the way he knew how. Maybe partnership wasn't about efficiency. Maybe it wasn't about perfection. Maybe it was about building a life that could hold the fragile things—together.

25

FRANKIE

Saturday, June 1, 2024
Two Months Later

Frankie met Janey at her gym, wanting to check in. Things hadn't been going well again with Jack.

"Unsurprisingly, whatever honeymoon phase we hit after that camping trip is officially over," Janey said. "He's back to being completely unhelpful, and I'm so tired of this cycle."

She looked exhausted.

"I'm sorry, J," Frankie said, and meant it. She listened as Janey listed everything that still hadn't changed. Frankie had heard most of it before, probably more than once, but she didn't care. If Janey needed to say it a thousand times, Frankie would show up for each one of them. Because this version of her, the one who was clean and sober, understood the value of being there for the people who mattered.

Later that afternoon, the weight of everything came rushing

back. Brie's case had blown up, snatched up by national true crime podcasts and turned into a spectacle. Their quiet little town had become background noise for strangers dissecting every detail of a woman they didn't know. The truth was simple: The men had been high, and in their altered state they hadn't understood what they were seeing. They hadn't hurt Brie. They hadn't touched her. They just hadn't helped her.

But online, that wasn't enough. The guys were offered interviews, even money, in exchange for telling their version of the night she went missing. The police report had been made public, and her husband, along with Jack, Tom, and even Dale, was dragged through the court of public opinion. Conspiracy theories sprouted like weeds—claims that the men had drugged and murdered Brie, despite the complete lack of evidence. If they'd been anyone else, it might have cost them their jobs. But these were established, middle-aged white men, tucked inside institutions that closed ranks around them. There was plenty of backlash over their drug use, which was fair enough, but even that was eventually whittled down to "locker room" and "boys will be boys" excuses. Their careers were rattled but not undone, though the whispers and sidelong glances followed them into every meeting.

But the majority of people clung to the easier, more palatable narrative: Brie's death was a tragic accident. Easier to paint her as a struggling woman who couldn't handle motherhood, who turned to substances and sealed her own fate. Easier to believe that as long as *they* drank responsibly, nothing like this could ever happen to them. That what happened to Brie was her own fault, not a reflection of how quickly the ground could drop out from under anyone.

Frankie had tried to stay above it, but she got sucked in. She scrolled through Reddit threads late at night. Listened to a podcast that speculated Brie's unraveling had to do with raising a deaf child. It made her stomach turn. She finally picked up the phone and called Pearl.

"I already know what you're about to say," Frankie said as they sat on their usual bench in the arboretum, watching ducks bob along the pond. "You don't even have to say anything."

Pearl raised an eyebrow. "And what exactly am I going to say?"

"Tell me what you think I think you're going to say."

"Can you cut the shit and get to the point? I don't have all day," Pearl said.

Frankie let out a breath. "I need to stay off the internet and quit bingeing true crime."

"Ding, ding, ding," Pearl said, her voice dripping with sarcasm, like Frankie had just won the grand prize on some twisted sobriety game show.

Frankie stared at the pond, her reflection blurred by ripples. "I've been trying to figure out why I can't stop. Why I keep going back to stories about crimes against women, the ones that end in horror. It's like my brain is searching for proof that my gut was right all along—that monstrosities do happen to women, regularly, brutally. Worse than what happened in Santa Barbara. And still, we're told we're too sensitive. Too dramatic. Always overreacting."

She gripped the edge of the bench. "True crime scratches that itch. It gives shape to the darkness. It makes the senseless feel . . . if not understandable, at least real. Like I'm not crazy for being scared all the time. Like the fear has evidence."

Her voice dropped. "Because of what happened to me in Santa Barbara, I think I've spent years burying it. And sometimes I wonder . . . if I'm one of the lucky ones, then what right do I have to be upset?"

"Who says you're one of the lucky ones?" Pearl asked.

"I survived," Frankie said. "Some women don't."

"So because your attacker left you alive, that makes you lucky?" Pearl grimaced as she adjusted her position on the bench. "I just want to make sure I'm hearing that right."

Frankie considered asking if she was okay, but she knew better. Pearl would wave her off and tell her to stop deflecting.

Frankie's words tumbled faster, agitation tipping toward panic. "What's the alternative? Become an angry, bitter feminist and hate all men, because statistically almost all crimes come at their hands? And then what? How do I live with the fact that the majority of sex crimes against women—even with overwhelming evidence—end with no conviction? What do I do with that?"

Her throat tightened. "I need the world to be fair. To be just. Otherwise none of this makes sense. Because if even when I'm sober, even when I'm clean, there's no rule of law to anchor me, then everything unravels. Everything. And I'm back in that upside-down place. Disoriented. Unmoored. Unsure what's real. The same way it felt when I was drunk or high."

"Who says the world has to be fair and just? When has that ever been true?" Pearl asked.

Frankie felt her blood pressure rise. This was the part in her discomfort where she'd usually bolt, where the urge to flee would take over. The injustice of it all, the silent fury lodged deep in her bones, was only growing, especially as she imagined the world her daughters were inheriting.

"I feel like I can't breathe," she said, leaning forward with her forearms on her knees, trying to ground herself in a slow, steady inhale, followed by a deliberate exhale.

"There you go," Pearl said gently. Her own breathing was labored, but she still tried to guide Frankie through it. "My dear, I wish it wasn't always the same lesson we had to learn, over and over and over again. But it is. It always is."

Frankie kept her eyes on the ground, still focused on her breath. She knew—just as surely as she knew that if her mother were here, she'd kiss the inside of her palm—that Pearl was about to say something she needed to hear. Something that would carry her through this moment and into whatever came next.

"Acceptance is the key," Pearl whispered. "You have no control over people, places, or things. As much as we wish we did have control. And believe me, I know. My god, do I know."

She looked out at the ducks on the pond while Frankie sat up, her breath finally steady. When Pearl turned back to her, her face had changed. It was the kind of shift that happens when a woman stops pretending, when she lets the full weight of sadness show. And sometimes, that kind of honesty isn't pretty. "What makes you think you have control over any of the things that happen in this life?" she asked.

Frankie shook her head. She thought of her mother's death, their father's mental illness, Mere leaving, her sexual assault, her alcoholism, and now Brie's death.

"I don't, but . . ." Frankie started to protest, then looked up and saw Mere walking with Lily and Pancakes about twenty yards ahead on the path.

"Mere!" Frankie called out, raising her hand in a wave.

"I thought you might be here," Mere said as she approached. She carried the bag of bugs she often brought for Lily on their arboretum walks. Frankie made room for her on the bench and felt a flicker of relief—her sister's timing had always been uncanny.

"Hello, Pearl. I'm so happy to see you again," Mere said warmly.

"Hello, ladies," Pearl beamed, her eyes landing on Lily, who was crouched beside Pancakes.

Lily didn't make eye contact, just let out a small grunt and pointed at the printed arboretum pictures that Mere had made for their walks to request bugs. Pearl smiled, unfazed, but Frankie watched her closely. This was the first time she'd seen Pearl and Lily meet directly. Frankie wasn't sure how Pearl would respond to the lack of eye contact, the grunting, the sharp laser focus.

There was a generational gap when it came to understanding neurodiversity. Even Frankie sometimes felt behind, not nearly as informed as she wanted to be, for Lily's sake and for

Mere's. She trusted that Pearl wouldn't judge or assume Lily was being rude, but still, traces of that old-school thinking lingered in people. The idea that children like Lily just needed stricter boundaries or more discipline. Pearl didn't fall into that camp, not at all, but something about Frankie's two worlds colliding so suddenly made her shoulders tense. She wanted to protect Lily from being misunderstood. And she wanted to protect Pearl from the ache of misinterpreting. She realized this must be how Mere felt all the time.

"I'm so happy we ran into you," Pearl said. "I wanted to invite you both to my house tomorrow night for dinner. Daniel's doing up the barbecue, and I know it's a little early for your sobriety birthday, Frankie, but I'd love for you to come."

"Both of us?" Frankie tried not to sound like the favorite child.

"I don't want to intrude on your sponsor-sponsee time. I can just catch you at the meeting next Sunday," Mere offered, her voice low as she gave Frankie a look of quiet apology.

Frankie kept her gaze soft. Whatever Pearl was planning, it wasn't Mere's doing.

"Yes, both of you," Pearl said. "I'll tell you more when I see you. Six o'clock. And, Mere, please bring Lily. And Pancakes," she added with a wink. "I actually must be going, but you two sit and catch up. I've got things to do with Daniel, who's meeting me downtown."

"But can you—" Frankie started.

"People, places, and things, my dear," Pearl said, offering a knowing smile as she pulled Frankie in. There was no force in the hug, just quiet comfort. Frankie returned it with an embrace that tried to say all the things she didn't yet have words for. Pearl let go first, then nodded at Mere, a silent cue with the steady certainty of someone who had always helped Frankie find the right path.

After Pearl left, Mere pulled out the bag of bugs for Lily, who immediately crouched near the ducks.

"Your chip meeting is still June ninth, right?" Mere asked. "That's your ten-year?"

Frankie nodded, distracted. "Yeah, that's right."

"Is Pearl going to be out of town or something?" Mere asked, her mind clearly trying to piece together why Pearl wanted them both over one week earlier.

"It's weird. I have no idea."

Frankie was still thinking about Pearl's strange energy when she looked up and saw Lily standing next to her, waiting. Her hand hovered near the bag of bugs, eyes flicking to Frankie, then to the ducks.

Rayna and Chloe had always been so vocal at this age. *Mommy, look at this! Mommy, watch me do it.* But Lily wasn't like that. She wasn't focused on Frankie or even on Mere. Her attention was locked on the ducks, throwing handfuls of bugs and giggling as the birds pecked furiously at the ground. She flapped her arms out in front of her, and Frankie remembered from Mere's "Lily handbook" that it meant she was happy and excited.

Frankie glanced at her sister. Mere watched Lily with a kind of serene, quiet pride that took Frankie by surprise. On Lily's next round of scattering bugs, she tugged gently on Frankie's hand and guided it toward the bag.

"She wants you to join in," Mere said.

Frankie had hoped that was what Lily meant, but hearing her sister say it out loud, interpreting Lily's invitation in a language that now included Frankie, stirred something deep within. It felt like a part of herself she thought had been invisible was now quietly coming back. Light and quick. Like a duck's webbed feet padding along the muddy shore. And for the first time in a long while, there wasn't anywhere else she'd rather be.

26

BRIE

Saturday, March 16, 2024
The Day of Brie's Disappearance

Brie had a plan.

It started as a fantasy during lockdown, when she'd fallen into a pit of darkness so deep, she struggled to know daylight hours from night. Stuck in a pattern of coming to in the morning only to scoop herself into her different roles as wife and mother, while the family scattered within the house to their separate corners for online learning, Zoom worship for her husband, and nothingness for Brie. Never had she been so categorically useless.

A silly thought broke through: *It's five o'clock everywhere.* She'd seen the meme on social media, promoting wine morning, noon, and night because, after all, the world was coming to an end. She thought of it as a temporary sabbatical from her real life. A welcome reprieve. She'd bounce back after the world did.

Everything became second to drinking. She wasn't really held accountable for anything because the majority of her role was shuffling her girls around to their various activities, which were now canceled. She became a master of lying to her family.

Each morning, desperation clawed at her, an unbearable need for relief from the monotony and agony of—what, exactly? She had no idea. Only that she no longer recognized the face staring back at her in the mirror. She couldn't muffle the sound of her retching; it echoed back from the toilet, reverberating through the small space. And on the worst mornings—those violent, punishing hangovers—the toilet water would splash up, smacking her cheek like a final blow. The kind you see in movies, when the defeated man is already curled on the ground, bloodied, yet the victor lands one last hit just to make it sting.

Something about that death knell to her face made her open her phone and message Frankie Marino. She was the only woman Brie knew who was open about being sober. Brie had seen Frankie post pictures of her family with captions about her recovery, and they'd always made her roll her eyes. But her daughter Margaret adored Chloe Marino, and her daughter was an excellent judge of character. How bad could Frankie be? One night when she was in a blackout, she DMed Frankie on Instagram and asked if she had a meeting she could recommend for her to try out. It wasn't the first meeting Brie ever attended—she'd gone to a few with her previous sponsor—but it was the first time she reached out to Frankie directly. Nothing serious. Nothing permanent.

She'd attended meetings and attempted the deal, said the

prayers and had a version of quiet that never quite seeped into the marrow of her bones. But she'd never fully committed because she wanted everyone to know that there was something about her that was different from all of them. Others described the ache and the longing, the reprieve that drinking provided from the mental obsession, the hardness of motherhood, and that sense of being a square peg jammed into a round hole. She listened, but she didn't believe those words belonged to her—not really. Her pain was sharper, more particular.

Humiliation in relapse continued when Frankie had to rescue her at a school dance. Brie had arrived to the '80s-themed event too drunk, and she needed to sleep it off in Frankie's truck. Brie asked Frankie to be her sponsor afterward because she figured that if anyone could help someone who wasn't easily teachable, it was Frankie.

But after working with Frankie, she knew she didn't want sobriety to swallow her whole the way it had with Frankie. Recovery seemed to be all Frankie talked about, all she built her identity around—every slip of life turned into a lesson, every ache forced to mean something. It was exhausting just to watch. And yet, beneath the exhaustion, there was a sting of envy, because Frankie made it look like she had found a system, a scaffolding, something that kept her upright. Brie wanted that steadiness, but she hated how it came packaged. She didn't want her pain to be a parable, or Margaret's progress to be recast as some higher purpose. The way Frankie had linked her daughter finally hearing a sound to the "gift" of recovery left Brie feeling cornered, like her own motherhood was being folded into someone else's sermon.

They lived close enough to downtown that one night, she decided she'd grown tired of drinking alone. A voice—one that started deep in her gut and crawled up to her head—told her to stay home, but she had long since stopped listening.

The Tavern in downtown Big Sky catered equally to townies and college students. When she walked in, the place wasn't particularly busy. She slid onto a stool at the far left corner of the bar, near the restrooms, already more than a little buzzed.

Through the thick haze of alcohol, she was aware of how she must have looked to the two men sitting a few seats down. They weren't the size of regular men, but rather appeared to her as two wild rhinoceroses. Still, in that moment, cloaked in the warmth of her buzz, she felt like the ignited version of herself, the one from before. Before she became a preacher's wife. Before she became a mother. Before she was seen as anything but a sexual being.

She smiled into her glass when the bartender slid her a fresh drink. "From the gentlemen across the bar."

The body shields a woman's mind during a rape. Brie found herself perched above her flesh as one of the men held her down and the other forced his way inside.

She'd once read that thousands of rape kits sat untested, women left in a backlog that felt like a conveyor belt, shuffled along, anonymous, forgotten. In that instant, she swore she would not be reduced to another case file gathering dust, another woman in line whose pain was processed instead of believed.

Afterward Brie was all nerve and skin, nothing but the vessel they'd used, when she wanted to be anything but. Any warm and gooey protection the alcohol provided had long since left her when she was dragged to the parking lot. Since then, Brie hadn't been able to outdrink the loneliness she felt.

The idea came the way a dream can unfold in a blurry, illogical mirage. Brie had been holding on to a plan—one she kept tucked away just in case. She wanted one last blaze of glory, a controlled descent into oblivion. She would throw herself down the stairs, twisting her ankle just enough to secure a prescription for pain meds from her doctor. Nothing too dramatic, just effective.

She'd supplement the pills with the THC tincture she kept hidden in her bathroom cabinet, pairing them with the gummies she bought on her last trip to the dispensary. She'd even handed those gummies to Frankie yesterday, a crooked kind of offering—half cry for help, half dare. But Frankie hadn't seen it. All she'd done was encourage another meeting, like recovery was a cure-all she could paste over everything.

So Brie doubled down. She would calibrate the perfect mix—painkillers, weed, alcohol—until she reached complete oblivion, convinced that this time she could control it, bend it to her will. And after that? And after that? She'd play her last hand. Rehab. Not surrender, but strategy. She'd check herself into rehab in the Bay Area and somehow begin piecing herself back together. She already had the plan in place when she saw Frankie at the arboretum. She wanted to tell her, but then Frankie would have reminded her of Step One and how she was powerless over alcohol. Except Brie refused to believe that. With her plan, she'd take the power back. The power those men had stolen from her, the power Frankie kept trying to reframe into slogans. Brie would prove that she wasn't powerless. That she could use the very thing the program warned against and still come out on top. That would show everyone. Then she would quit for good.

So she took an Uber with her remaining oxy—four pills she had been saving for a final explosion. A single pill had been disappointing, which was when she turned to vodka. If she was going to relapse, she wanted to go out with a bang. That had always been her plan. She never did anything halfway. And she was a nature girl—always had been. That's why they lived where they did. She had loved the snow before motherhood, before she realized the exhausting effort of dressing small children for the cold. For a time, it had almost ruined winter for her completely. But eventually she found pleasure in it again. And now she wanted to be immersed in it.

She had packed as if she were going camping, though she didn't have a tent. Just a backpack with an extra blanket for warmth and a fifth of vodka she'd been gifted years ago, one she had kept all this time, knowing it would be there when she needed it. That was the most terrifying part. She didn't need it for any reason other than the fact that she was no longer needed.

There was an ultimate loneliness in being essential yet

unseen. Always on the outside of her own life, looking in. And when she swallowed the liquid again, it felt like the only way she knew to come home to herself. As if it curled around her brain and whispered seductively in her ear, *Welcome back. Oh, how I've missed you.*

The Uber driver had been too chatty, too bright-eyed for Brie's liking, oblivious to how deeply she had already retreated into herself. Only two pills in, just a swallow of the clear liquid from the bottle, and she was already slipping. She couldn't wait to be recklessly off the grid. That was the thing about a quiet undoing—she didn't want to be gone forever, just long enough to light the "away" sign for a few hours.

It was still early. No one in her house was awake yet. Her husband was in the middle of leading a group of teens through their confirmation process. Soon she would come clean to him and her children too. She would finally force herself to say the awful thing she had never spoken aloud. The thing she couldn't tell another living soul. Because part of her believed they would see her as a willing participant—for wearing a dress, for being drunk all alone at a bar.

While the driver talked on and on, Brie's thoughts drifted to Margaret's deafness—how sound had created an invisible barrier between them for the first sixteen years of her daughter's life. Brie had done all the research, weighed every option, and in the end, it had been her decision to present them to Margaret. Her husband had deferred to her, as he always did with major parenting choices, even though they had been parents for exactly the same amount of time.

They had agreed it would be Margaret's choice. That was why they waited. She had already found her place in the deaf community and was thriving, but as she prepared for college, she wanted to be fully immersed in the hearing world. Brie had encouraged her—selfishly, if she was honest—because she hated that her daughter lived in a space where she couldn't fully follow. The implant became a bridge, a way for them to meet in the middle. A gateway to each other.

Brie had been to Hollow Ridge often during her Spartan training last year. Training had kept her grounded, kept her sober. There was something about the event itself, especially the charged moment before the starting pistol fired. Runners packed in tightly, muscles pressed shoulder to shoulder, their collective energy like a live wire snapping against the air. It reminded her of those rare AA meetings where the chemistry of women aligned, where she could feel the "we" that everyone spoke of with such reverence. The Spartan emcee would lead them in chants, their voices grunting in unison, as if they truly were Spartans. That sensation of being huddled together, part of something bigger, a single mass with a shared purpose . . . Brie wished she could bottle it up and drink it down forever. And yet, she could still hear Frankie in her head, always turning those moments into lessons, into proof of recovery. Frankie seemed to live for that kind of alchemy, while Brie resented how small it made her feel in comparison—resented it and envied it, both at once.

Hollow Ridge was one of her favorite places, though she had never shared that with anyone. She liked keeping something just for herself. Now, she had come here with a singular intention: to check out completely before she knew she would have to check back in. This final act of defiance would set her recovery back, but she had relapsed before. She could find her way back again.

But something about this time felt different. She wasn't just falling—she was on a quest, a journey of self-discovery, convinced that the answers she sought lay hidden in the snowy ridges, buried beneath the haze of booze. She had a plan.

This would be her final test, the last indulgence before she closed that door once and for all. It was reckless, she knew. Insane, even. But she needed to try, just to be certain that no corner of her "problem" was left unexplored. Her last day of "research," as the program called it, just to make sure she did, in fact, have the disease of alcoholism. This one last indulgence before she surrendered.

The bed at Our Lady of Mercy Treatment Center was ready and waiting. Because she was the wife of a youth minister and they had a religious affiliation, she had secured a spot for that coming Sunday. There had never been a follow-up appointment for Margaret's cochlear implants in San Francisco—that had all been a ruse. The plan was to have the family drive her down under that pretense, and once they were together, she would sit them down and finally explain everything. She imagined herself clearheaded, able to articulate exactly what had been weighing on her. But she'd reassure them there was no need to worry. As with everything else, she had a plan. And rehab was the final box to check, the last step that would set her firmly on the path to resolution, once and for all.

Brie had rolled up a quilted down comforter stitched together from pieces of her children's baby clothes. She had found someone on Etsy who specialized in turning sentimental clothing into quilts—items that had once been stuffed away in storage, gathering dust in the garage. Now, wrapped in it, she felt cocooned in their memories, swaddled in the fabric of their earliest years. Even the familiar scents came rushing back.

She had forgotten to pack food, but it didn't matter—she hadn't planned to stay out past morning. But once she started walking, she didn't want to stop. Eventually she found a ridge with a rock overhang, sheltered from the wind, overlooking a snowy meadow below. It seemed as good a place as any to rest. She took another pill and had another drink.

Despite the snow and the cold, she was warm enough. She had dressed for a hike, bundled like a Russian nesting doll—layer upon layer, bulky and misshapen, unmooring into the landscape.

Brie had no idea how long she'd been asleep—only that when she awoke, it was night. The darkness was absolute, pressing in from every side. She hadn't packed a flashlight. There was one on her phone, but she'd turned it off before she left the house, and now, in her fumbling panic, she couldn't remember which button to press to turn it back on. Her fingers, clumsy and frozen, scraped against the screen, but nothing happened.

A sharp pang of fear shot through her, but whatever was

still in her system dulled it, numbing her in a way she hadn't been able to achieve since that night in the parking lot of The Tavern. The cold was seeping in now, stiffening her legs. She had to move. Had to get back to the parking lot—or at least head in the direction she thought it was.

She started running. Faster and faster, her breath coming in quick, shallow gasps. The blanket was still wrapped around her, dragging at her limbs. Snow clung to her face, stinging her cheeks, burning her nostrils. Each step was a battle, her legs lifting high, trying to break free from the grasp of it. But it was like running through molasses—every effort swallowed by the deep, unrelenting white.

Thwap.

The impact came out of nowhere. One second she was pushing forward; the next—stars.

Not real ones. Not the pinpricks of light she'd seen earlier, scattered across the vast sky as if they had been placed there just for her. No, these were sharp, bursting behind her eyes, exploding in rapid succession. A silent fireworks show in the blackness of her mind.

Then came the pain, slow and creeping. A throbbing ache radiated from her skull, spreading like ink. She blinked, vision swimming, struggling to make sense of what had just happened. The ground was cold beneath her, the snow dropping down on her face until she couldn't remember that she ever had a face. For a moment, she just lay there, disoriented, wondering how exactly she'd arrived in that spot.

Then, blackness again.

When she tried to open her eyes, ice crystals had landed on her lashes and she couldn't lift her arms to wipe them away. Pain continued pulsing from the back of her head in slow, merciless waves. At first, it was a dull ache, but then it sharpened, spreading like fire down her neck, curling around her spine. She tried to move, to lift her head, but her body refused. The force of the cold pressed her into the ground, the snow affixing her so she'd become one with the ground.

She blinked up at the sky—the same sky she had used to distract herself from what was happening down below, at the hands of those rhinoceros-sized men.

A thought surfaced, unbidden.

This is how it happens. How a person disappears. How a woman vanishes into the night.

Not all men, she had told herself.

There were good ones. There had to be.

Like her husband. A man of faith. A man of conviction.

And yet, wasn't that the point of the Flannery O'Connor story she'd read in English lit? In "A Good Man Is Hard to Find," the grandmother clings to the idea, desperate to believe—despite all evidence to the contrary—that goodness still exists in the world. Even as she listens to her family being murdered and stares down the barrel of a gun, she tries to reach the Misfit with a final plea for grace. Brie tried to retell the story to herself from the beginning, remembering as many details as she could to help herself stay awake.

She didn't want to die, not now, not when her daughter had only just begun to hear her voice.

Not all men. But how could you ever really know?

The wind howled through the trees, bending the branches, whispering something she couldn't quite make out.

Then, footsteps. Heavy, slow.

Two voices, deep and indistinct, calling out just as sleep began to pull her under again. Her face was too cold to tell if she was grinning, but she had found it: the languid, euphoric oblivion she had been seeking.

They will help me, she thought.

The men are coming to save me.

27

MERE

Sunday, June 2, 2024

Mere had checked with Frankie twice to confirm that she should bring Lily and Pancakes to Pearl's house for dinner. Frankie insisted that Pearl and her husband loved dogs and children and that it would be fine. Still, Mere had tried to decode the subtext of the invitation, squinting for some hidden meaning, but had come up empty. When Mere, Lily, and Pancakes arrived at Pearl's, Frankie was just pulling in along the side of the road across from the house.

While Mere helped Lily out of the car—steadying her and adjusting the strap of her globe purse—Pancakes hopped down, and Frankie crossed over to meet them. Her expression softened as Lily reached out her empty hand and hooked her fingertips around Frankie's, a gesture she'd never offered before. In the slant of evening light, Frankie's face glowed, her smile catching in the golden hue of the setting sun. For a breathless moment, it looked to Mere as if Lily were holding Donna's hand.

"Why don't you walk Pancakes up and back, let her go potty before we head in," Mere suggested. She could see the gratitude on Frankie's face for those extra few minutes she'd offered.

As Frankie started to lead them away, Lily instinctively looked back at Mere but then quickly turned to face forward, still holding the tips of her aunt's fingers.

The front porch had two hand-carved wooden rocking chairs, so quaint and inviting that Mere had to resist the urge to sit and start rocking. She pictured Pearl and Frankie there over the years, swapping war stories, and the image of her sister having a mother-like presence all this time made her unexpectedly emotional.

Her hand hovered near the railing. "Mere, wait," Frankie said, voice catching. "Before we go in, I need to tell you something."

Mere turned, brows lifting in quiet question.

"On my last night drinking, I said the ugliest thing I've ever said to you." Frankie's voice started to break. "It was cruel, and it was wrong. I was sick, and I used that sickness to wound you. I need you to know, standing here clean and sober, that I regret it more than almost anything."

Mere's eyes softened, but she stayed silent, letting Frankie go on.

"You're the best mom I know. And Dale is steady in a way

I didn't understand back then. And Lily . . ." Frankie gazed down at her niece. "Lily is light. Pure light. She's proof of everything I couldn't see that night—that love doesn't need fixing, it just needs protecting."

Mere nodded, no words needed, the kind of quiet forgiveness that traveled deeper than speech. For a beat they lingered, until Mere saw Lily give a little tug on Frankie's finger, and Pancakes bounded ahead, pulling them all forward.

At the top of the steps, Frankie bent to Lily's level, guiding her hand to the bell. The chime echoed, and a moment later the door creaked open. Daniel stood there—older than Pearl, maybe late seventies, with a kind face weathered like driftwood.

"Is Pearl manning the barbecue?" Frankie joked, though her voice carried a nervous edge as she leaned in to embrace Daniel. His eyes crinkled into slits as he smiled, wrapping her in a hug and resting his hand gently on the back of her head, holding her there for a beat with quiet affection.

"This must be Mere, Lily, and the famous Pancakes!" Daniel said as he knelt to their level. His movement was stiff, and a faint wince crossed his face—enough for Mere to wonder if it was worth the effort. He gave a little wave, as did Lily, and Mere appreciated that Frankie had likely given them a heads-up that Lily wasn't big on physical contact with strangers.

"Where's Pearl?" Frankie asked again, her tone lighter than her eyes, which flicked quickly past Daniel into the house as if needing proof.

The house was warm and charming, just as Mere expected.

Hand-carved wood details echoed the rocking chairs on the porch, cozy touches softening the space. But beneath it all, Mere caught a faint, unsettling scent. Not unpleasant exactly, but clinical, sharp, the kind of smell that once clung to their mother's hospice room. Her chest tightened. She glanced at Frankie, wondering if she noticed it, too, or if Mere was just overlaying memory onto the present.

"Frankie tells me you're a budding engineer," Daniel said, speaking to Lily. "I set up some blocks in the corner—my grandson's, actually. He's about Lily's age, so we've got a good collection."

Mere blinked. She hadn't thought Pearl had children, let alone grandchildren, but before she could ask, Daniel added, as if reading her mind, "My daughter from my first marriage stayed with us last week. They were visiting from Hawaii, so we still have some of their things out."

As they rounded the corner, Mere exhaled with relief. There was a full foam ball pit, plus age-appropriate blocks just like the ones they had at home. Lily let go of Frankie's hand—Mere noticed, with a pang, that she had been clinging to it the entire time—and dashed straight for the ball pit.

"This is so thoughtful of you and Pearl. Lily might never want to leave," Mere said, a shaky laugh slipping out with the breath she hadn't realized she'd been holding. She rarely brought Lily to unfamiliar homes—too many unknowns, too many chances for sensory overload and the kind of public meltdown that still left her rattled for hours, like the one at the store a couple of months back.

"Why don't you two head in and say hi to Pearl?" Daniel offered. "I'll stay out here with Lily and Pancakes. She's just through that door, waiting."

Frankie looked puzzled, and Mere felt it too—a current of unease slipping between them, unspoken but undeniable. Still, Frankie headed toward the door, Mere following close behind.

28

FRANKIE

Sunday, June 2, 2024

Pearl looked like she was being swallowed whole by the king-sized bed. Frankie had never really acknowledged how small she was. In her mind, Pearl had always filled a room, commanding, grounded, impossible to overlook. But now, with the portable oxygen tube running into her nose and the plastic tank resting beside her, she looked fragile. The setup reminded Frankie of the breast pump she'd once been tethered to when her girls were babies.

Pearl's eyes were closed, and for a second, Frankie half expected her to pop up, rip the tubes from her nose, and start jumping on the bed like a sugar-hyped kid refusing to sleep.

"Pearl?" Frankie's voice cracked. "Pearl?" she repeated and went over to sit in the chair next to the bed. Mere had followed but stood near the dresser by the door. Pearl opened her eyes as a smile quickly morphed into a cough. She positioned her body upright as best she could.

"Oh good. You're here," Pearl said, her voice tight. "I'm going to cut right to it." She paused to suck in air, adjusting the tubing like she needed it to flow more freely in order for her to breathe. "I was never one for bullshit, as Frankie knows." Pearl tried to adjust her body again, but stopped when her breathing became too strained. She took in one sharp inhale and started speaking again. "We found out it was cancer a while back, terminal shortly thereafter. I have no interest in making a fuss. At this point they say it's maybe a week."

Frankie turned to look at Mere. Was she in on this? Mere was leaning against the dresser, her hands folded out in front of her. When Frankie saw the devastation in her sister's face—the same look that had told her their mother was dying—she knew this was real.

Frankie slipped from the chair, crouching low, trying to make herself as small as Pearl so she could curl into the familiarity of her arms. Maybe if Frankie tucked herself away, stayed very still and quiet, nestled into a perfect sphere beneath Pearl's chin, maybe a week could be longer, and Pearl wouldn't have to leave. In Frankie's efforts to shrink herself down, she tried not to interfere with Pearl's tubing, but Frankie was too big and took up too much of the bed. "My dear, dear girl," Pearl whispered into her ear. "Settle down here a moment. Take up all the space you need. Stop apologizing for being too much." Frankie's sadness spilled over, welling up until it was overflowing. She'd never allowed herself to envision a universe without Pearl as her voice of reason. Her touchstone who was always able to level her out.

"I'll just leave you two to have a minute alone," Mere said. "Pearl, I'm so sorry. I'm just—"

"That small velvet box on the dresser." Pearl lifted her hand off Frankie's back to point, but Frankie stayed put. "Could you bring it on Sunday to the meeting?"

"This?" Mere asked. Frankie didn't see what they were talking about. She had found the perfect curve where she could rest her head, tucked into the quiet comma between Pearl's neck and shoulder, and she didn't dare move. She was terrified that if she did, time would pass by too quickly.

"Yes," Pearl said.

"I'll just be out there with Lily and Daniel, if you need anything. I am so sorry, Pearl. Thank you for everything, truly."

Frankie heard the door close gently behind Mere and knew it was just the two of them now. She listened to the oxygen flowing into Pearl, the sound like steam at the start of a kettle, like it was announcing that soon they'd be sitting out on Pearl's porch, teacups in hand, as Frankie tried to maneuver the jigsaw pieces of her mind into something that made sense. Pearl always showed her where to start, and even if it took a while, she waited patiently as Frankie figured out which way they fit together.

But she had been dying? For how long? Frankie wanted to scream, *Why didn't you rush me to move faster when the time you had left was all so precious?* But even lately, Pearl's patience with her had been unwavering.

As they'd sat alone in the choir room after that meeting, the one where Frankie finally shared everything that had been going on, Frankie had tried to make sense of why she'd turned to pills. Pearl and the program had taught her better. She kept thinking that if she could just trace it back, follow the thread, she'd see how one thing had led to the next. How she'd buried the feelings she couldn't face, the ones she deemed the ugliest, under layers of snow so densely packed she might've hidden beneath them completely.

Don't you ever get tired up there in your mind? Pearl asked as Frankie analyzed and dissected as best she could. Pearl had chuckled softly but hadn't laughed. Frankie was much too fragile to recognize that being angry with her own thoughts didn't change a damn thing. Pearl knew that too. But she let Frankie work through it on her own. Pearl never pushed.

"You know if I wasn't so spiritually fit, I'd be angry with you for keeping this from me for so long and find a way to make this all about me." Frankie sat up, finally allowing herself to take Pearl in, to see with her own eyes that she was still here, still real, still in the room.

"What kind of drugs they got you on? The good stuff?" Frankie asked. Her comment made Pearl cough into a laugh and Frankie instantly regretted her joke. "I'm sorry. That was inappropriate," she said, trying to pull up the duvet around Pearl since her hands felt ice cold.

"Why—do you want to steal them from me?"

"Okay, now *that* was inappropriate!" Frankie said, the laughter only serving as a catalyst to make the tears fall harder.

"Can I get you anything? Water?"

Pearl ignored her question and started talking. "I considered what Sue said at our meeting the other day about dying with our sobriety intact, dying with dignity. I don't want to go out all foggy and looped out of my head, as tempting as that sounds not to be in pain and to remove this two-thousand-ton elephant sitting on my chest. I don't want my addiction to die along with me. I want to die free from it. I want to show that it's possible."

"That what's possible?" Frankie whispered.

But Pearl plowed ahead, determined to get through what she needed to say without another coughing fit. "Do I hate that I'm dying when I just now figured out that I look good with bangs? Of course I do. I'm too young and I have so much more I wanted to do. But frankly, now I can say that I see what's possible, and not everyone can say that," Pearl said, pressing the plastic tubing hard into her nostrils while taking a deep inhale through her nose.

"That what's possible?" Frankie repeated, desperate to know now.

"Acceptance. True acceptance. Like I've always said, we have no control over people, places, and things. Turns out that is also true of our own death."

Frankie let the tears slip down the corners of her eyes and get absorbed by the green-and-cream floral duvet cover.

"Could you stop trying to teach me something, for once in your life?" Frankie let the anger rise up in her throat. It was much easier than sadness, which was heavy and lurking underneath, along with the fear of realizing this could be the last lesson Pearl would ever teach her.

29

Saturday, June 8, 2024

Mere had chosen the kind of test that spelled it out clearly: *Pregnant* or *Not Pregnant*. No guessing, no squinting at lines. When she found out she was pregnant with Lily, the two faint lines on the first test had been too ambiguous for Dale. She'd ended up sending him back to the store for the digital kind, and the wait nearly broke her.

Now, she was late. They still hadn't been preventing it, but neither had they the night she knew she was ovulating—and she'd gotten her period last month, so why would this month be any different? She felt queasy, but she couldn't tell if it was from anxiety or the sense that death was hanging over Big Sky, the way a storm presses down before the first drop falls. Dale had taken Lily and Pancakes to the park, giving Mere an hour alone.

Since they'd started communicating more intentionally, Dale had been better about carving breaks into their days. He made sure she had uninterrupted writing time, a quiet acknowledgment that her needs mattered too. More often than not, she'd look up to find Pancakes' wet nose pressed against her knee and realize a full sixty minutes had passed. Usually, she only managed ten pages, but still—she'd learned that progress wasn't always measured in volume but in consistency.

She peed on the stick, snapped the plastic cover back into place, and set it on her desk beside the clock to wait the required three minutes. Wrapping a blanket around her legs, she had barely settled in when the doorbell rang.

Mere stood, heart pounding, and made her way to the door. When she opened it, Frankie was on the other side, eyes swollen and wet, collapsing into her arms.

"She's gone," Frankie whispered. "She's gone."

Mere had known that Pearl only had days, but still, she had hoped—not for herself, but for Frankie—that time would stretch just a little longer.

They stood on the porch, wrapped in a quiet embrace, until Frankie finally pulled away, wiping at her cheeks.

"What are you doing now?" Frankie asked. "Is this a bad time?"

"No, no, come in. I'm so glad you came." Mere's heart swelled; it was true. Of all the places Frankie could have gone with the news, she came to her. They made their way over to the couch and sat knees touching. "Can I make you tea or coffee?"

"I'll take coffee," Frankie said, then stopped. "You know what, water. I should drink water." She sniffed.

Mere busied herself in the kitchen, wishing there were

words that could take away the pain. But she knew—just as Frankie did—that nothing could be said on days like this, when women like their mother, like Pearl, were no longer here.

When she made her way back with a glass of water, Mere said the only thing that could be said that was true. "You were lucky to have her. And she was lucky to have you."

Tears streamed down Frankie's face as she nodded. Mere used the corner of her sweatshirt to dry her sister's eyes. It was so unfair. Frankie needed Pearl.

"I went to sit with her today. She asked me to take her out to the porch. She had been waiting for me to come so I could carry her. Daniel wasn't able to—his back is bad from years of tennis."

"And did you?" Mere blinked over at Frankie, her breath catching as she pictured what that must have entailed.

Frankie nodded. "She wanted to die in her rocking chair, even though it made no medical sense for her to be sitting up. But she was stubborn." A soft, tear-laced laugh escaped. "Daniel wheeled the oxygen behind us while I scooped her up like a child. I hadn't realized how small she'd gotten. I was so busy getting high, I didn't even notice my sponsor was dying."

Mere saw the pain written on her sister's face, the regret, etched into the tears that kept welling in her eyes.

"I carried her to what became her deathbed. We sat out there for about an hour. The hospice nurse said it wouldn't be long, and I knew it should be Daniel with her at the end. So I sat in my car, in your driveway, and waited." Her voice broke. "He just called."

As heartbreaking as it was, the image struck Mere as profoundly beautiful—her sister, steady and strong, carrying the woman who had once steadied her to the very end of her life. Mere thought of their mother in her hospice bed and how rare, how bittersweet, it was that they both had been given the gift of being able to carry someone they loved across that final threshold. She reached for Frankie, pulled her into an embrace, and rested her head against her shoulder, her hand moving slowly up and down her back in quiet comfort.

Frankie tilted her head and leaned in, putting her weight into Mere. "It got me thinking. If Pearl was able to die free from her addiction, knowing it was coming, that her death was inevitable and imminent, surely I can move forward in the rest of whatever time I have clean and sober. I can live with my dignity intact as Pearl died with hers." Frankie swiped at her eyes, but she was smiling.

"I know you can," Mere whispered, and Frankie remained in Mere's arms until eventually Frankie pulled her head up. She wiped at Mere's shirt, which was dark with tears.

"Sorry about that," Frankie said as she tried to blot it dry.

"Leave it, don't worry." Mere batted her hand away.

"Were you in the middle of something? Where are Lily and Dale?"

The question reminded Mere of the test on her desk, which had long since ticked down its three minutes. She hadn't wanted to take it with Dale, not because he wouldn't love her through any answer, but because she would've had to manage her reaction to his reaction. For years, she'd lived in that loop—

interpreting, caretaking, smoothing. First for her mom, then for Lily, often for Dale, too, even though he never asked her to. It was a pattern, a reflex she couldn't quite turn off. Mere realized she had been running the same anxious circuits for years—thought patterns that fed off one another, controlling, correcting, carrying everything as if vigilance itself were enough. But right now she didn't want to translate or manage. She wanted one moment that was hers.

Regardless of the answer, she had everything she needed already. Her expectation of motherhood was exactly that: an expectation. Not an exact science, and another baby wasn't going to fill a void that never existed. If she were to have another child like Lily, if she was being fully and truthfully honest, she was terrified she would disappear completely.

"I'm afraid I did the wrong thing, and now it's too late," Mere said, bringing her hands up to her mouth. It wasn't until she touched her own face that she realized they were shaking. "I know I was meant to be Lily's mom. I know it in the way I know you were meant to be my sister. If we were in a wide-open field and suddenly didn't have our hearing or sight or touch, I'd be able to find you both, I know I would. Just as Mom would be able to find us. Just as Pearl would be able to find you."

Frankie nodded in hesitant understanding.

"Will you come with me? I need to check on something in the back room."

"Okay," Frankie said, standing before Mere could. Frankie had to help lift Mere off the couch as her legs had apparently stopped working and become like Jell-O. Soon Dale and Lily would return with Pancakes, and the rhythm of caretaking would spool back up. But this was her window, one she had finally found the words to ask for. If there was a baby, there would be no window anymore. Possibly ever again if the baby's needs were more challenging than Lily's. Beautiful still, always, but surely, if they had another baby, then she worried she would only be able to exist as a body.

Mere led them back into her office, her sister gently taking her hand as they crossed the room. The short walk from the doorway to her desk stretched out like an infinite runway—one she was grateful not to walk alone, her sister right there beside her.

Not Pregnant it read. Mere dropped to her knees. Frankie joined her on the floor, searching her eyes for meaning, but Mere wasn't ready. Frankie wrapped her arms around Mere and let her rest her head on her shoulder, just as Mere had done for her minutes earlier. Frankie waited for Mere to be the one to speak first. If only Pearl could be here to witness Frankie's growth. The volatile, selfish version of Frankie that reared its ugly head when she was in active addiction, the impatient version from open mic night where she couldn't wait for everyone to leave, had given way to the Frankie who had nothing but time and love to give and wasn't rushing Mere to tell her what she was feeling.

With it being Frankie there and not Dale or Lily on the floor, Mere needed only to exist. There was nothing for her to do or perform, no acts of service to offer anyone but herself, which she was finally learning how to do.

"I am so relieved," Mere said finally.

30

FRANKIE

Sunday, June 9, 2024

She couldn't have stayed one more day to hand Frankie her chip. It was perfectly Pearl to orchestrate one last gift from beyond—a divine nudge, insisting that this next portion of Frankie's sobriety be carried out without her. She knew better than to call it coincidence.

Frankie used to waste hours during their early Step work trying to convince Pearl that everything leading up to her sobriety had been an accident, a fluke of timing. And everything beautiful that came after—her relationships with her daughters, her husband, her sister, Janey, and Pearl herself—was just lucky fallout.

Pearl used to listen with quiet amusement, like Frankie was a teenager irritated by a magic trick. She couldn't accept that it might be real—it had to be sleight of hand, a stacked deck, something hidden up the magician's sleeve. Pearl never said it outright, but today, more than ever, Frankie understood: The magic had been in her all along. It wasn't alcohol that made her the best version of herself. Quite the opposite. Alcohol only stirred her demons and dulled the signals from the people who were meant to help her heal. The same way the drugs had dulled the memories of her assault, numbing her instead of freeing her. But Pearl had always said, *You've got to feel it to heal it.* And Frankie was feeling it now, all the bad, but also the good, in its full, unfiltered weight.

Mere slid in next to Frankie just before the meeting started. She was wearing a dress, jewelry, and even makeup. She looked rested and lovely—lighter, more herself, no longer the woman crushed beneath invisible weight. Frankie was grateful she'd lived long enough in sobriety to see this version of her sister.

The meeting proceeded as it always did. Since it was an anniversary meeting, and Marta was the anniversary chair, she had brought cake. More specifically, carrot cake. Had Pearl tipped off Marta that it was Frankie's favorite? She and Caleb had even chosen it as their wedding cake. Normally the woman with the longest amount of sobriety in the room celebrating an anniversary got to pick the cake flavor, but Frankie smiled thinking of the chain of events that must have transpired: Pearl dictating to Daniel that she needed to text Marta and make sure she picked carrot this time for Frankie. *That's what happens in a long line of custody of thoughts*, Frankie mused. *When one person thinks of another, and passes it on to yet another—it's like everyone out there cares that we exist.* There was something special about knowing that others were looking out for her, ensuring she had everything she needed.

Marta started by asking if anyone wanted a twenty-four-hour chip. She held one up. All chips typically had messages or slogans from the program written on them, something like *Keep Coming Back* or *To Thine Own Self Be True*, as well as the length of sobriety they recognized. The twenty-four-hour chip, the smallest denomination, was something anyone could ask for. It really just acknowledged a willingness to go a full day without drinking. Even if the person requesting it didn't reach that goal, the token provided a symbol of hope.

Up until this point, Frankie had received a total of 18 chips, each special because they had belonged to Pearl at one point, and before that belonged to other women on the same journey as them. Instead, it would be the first time that the anniversary person would have to pull a chip from the anniversary box. It would still be special, because Frankie would pass it on to one of her sponsees someday. But Brie had been her only one. The idea gutted her, pulling her into a pit of loneliness where Brie was gone and now Pearl too. Only then could Frankie see how her thoughts kept circling the same fears, again and again—worry dressed up as logic, repetition she had mistaken for vigilance, not recognizing how much of it was being fueled by old addictive patterns.

Her sister stood up and made her way to the front of the room.

"You don't know how much I wish it were Pearl standing up

here right now. This is the second time in recent months that I'm engaging in a form of public speaking, and quite frankly, I'd rather set myself on fire," Mere said with a half laugh. Frankie sniffled, smiling, knowing it was true.

This Mere was different—reading at open mic nights, taking a creative writing class, carving space for herself in ways she never had before. The old Mere would have stayed hidden, the quiet doer of everything. This one wanted to be seen. Frankie loved that she got to witness it.

"But from what I've learned about this program through watching my sister thrive in sobriety, sometimes we have to do the things that make us most uncomfortable and just be in it."

Mere pulled a small velvet box from her coat pocket and held it up in her hand.

"Pearl asked me to give this to you, Frankie. From what I understand—and someone correct me if I'm wrong, as I'm just an honored bystander here today—it once belonged to Pearl, and now this ten-year chip belongs with you," Mere said, holding the box up higher, balanced in the center of her palm as if it were the tiniest of crowns waiting to be placed upon a worthy head.

Frankie was flooded with feeling. An entire ocean of emotion was rising up in her chest. Gratitude, mostly, for being given the gift of sobriety and for finding her way back to recovery again when she just as easily could have lost it for good.

She had to swallow the lump that rose in her throat, reminding herself that she was worthy. Even though Pearl wasn't there, she was. As of today, Frankie had gone ten years without a drop of alcohol. Ten years sober and sixty-five days clean.

Mere signaled for Frankie to join her up front, and so Frankie stood and walked to the front while Mere removed the chip from the box and clutched it in the palm of her hand. As the room filled with applause, Frankie reached for the coin, but Mere pressed her lips into Frankie's palm before replacing the kiss with the coin.

It was the kind of gesture that only surfaces when love and memory collide in a moment too tender to name. Frankie felt the warmth of it in her palm and hoped she'd have the chance to pass it on one day. But she didn't want to jump ahead. That had been the problem with her thoughts—always wasted in the waiting, rushing toward the next thing, mourning the last. Never staying in the now.

It wasn't Pearl's voice she heard this time.

Stay in it.

31

MERE

Sunday, June 9, 2024

Mere left the meeting quietly after presenting Frankie with her chip. Technically it was an "open" meeting, family members welcome, but she wanted to give Frankie space—space to be held by the circle of women who knew the terrain of her heart in a way Mere never fully could.

In the guest room at Pearl's house, before she stepped aside to let Frankie say goodbye, Mere had opened the velvet box. Pearl had given her a small, solemn nod. That was all. No grand instructions. Just trust.

After Pearl's door had closed behind her, Mere found Lily on the floor, happily building a bridge with her wooden blocks. Daniel moved quietly through the kitchen, busying himself. Mere stood still, watching as Lily aligned the pieces with careful focus, the way Dale would if he were there alongside her—precise, patient, steady. Connecting one side to the other until they met in the middle.

There can be opposing forces, she thought. *Neither entirely right nor entirely wrong. They just have to stand, equal or not, depending on how well they're supported.*

If she was meant to take anything from Pearl's final offering—her generosity in inviting Mere into her last days—it was this: Pearl had known what was best for Frankie, and now she had entrusted Mere to carry it forward. That chip in Frankie's hand held more than time. It held the weight of connection. It was the kind of inheritance passed quietly between women. Between mothers and daughters. Between the family we're born into and the one we choose. A handoff not of possessions, but of presence. A reminder that showing up was enough.

Dale and Lily probably didn't see bridges the way Mere did—poetic, symbolic. So she took a page from their book and simply enjoyed watching Lily build. *A bridge doesn't need to mean something. It just needs to hold.*

Pearl had trusted Mere to be that bridge. Between what was and what could still be. Between memory and presence, silence and care, loss and the choice to go on. Because something is passed between women. It tells us—whispers, really, whenever we are ready to listen—that as long as we don't allow ourselves to fully disappear, as long as we keep looking out for one another, as long as we stay present, we are never really alone.

AUTHOR'S NOTE

Dear Reader,

Thank you for diving into my second novel, *Both Can Be True*. Like my debut, *Between the Devil and the Deep Blue Sea*, this story was born from the collision of lived experience and imagination, what my agent lovingly called "autofiction." Writing has always been part of my healing. In sobriety, it became a release—a way to pull apart shame, to study its threads, and to stitch them into something whole.

As a mother to three daughters, and as a survivor of sexual assault, I experience days when the weight of their safety feels unbearable. What I cannot carry in silence, I write. My voice is the power I can offer them, the inheritance I can leave. I hate how easily our culture absorbs assault into the fabric of everyday life. I cannot accept that as the reality of my daughters' world. This book is my defiance, my refusal of quiet.

I write novels to hold up mirrors to the soul, to reflect what hides in plain sight: how women vanish inside marriages, motherhood, and trauma, and how, again and again, we rise to be seen. My intention is to keep the conversation alive, to name what I once wanted to bury, and to insist that disappearance is never the answer.

AUTHOR'S NOTE

I chose to name Alcoholics Anonymous in this book because it felt paramount to show the loving, sometimes maternal nature of the sponsor-sponsee relationship. That relationship was a cornerstone of my sobriety. I am alive today because my first sponsor, Meg, carried me to safety, just as I carried her to what became her final resting place. In *Between the Devil and the Deep Blue Sea*, I lovingly refer to AA only as "The Program," which is meant to honor its spiritual principle of anonymity. Yet part of my own recovery has been learning that secrecy and silence are not the same as privacy. By naming AA, I do not presume to represent it; I can only speak from my lived experience. While this is a fictionalized story, the collective healing that transpires within AA is cause for celebration. My intention is to shine a light on the ways the program has evolved—especially in honoring women's roles within a framework that was created by and for men at its origin. My goal is that by writing openly, I extend a hand to anyone who might feel alone in their struggle and remind us all that recovery, in whatever form it takes, is possible.

Sobriety gave me the gift of language; fiction gave me the distance to say aloud what I once could not. Through Frankie, Mere, and the people who surround them, I wanted to explore how survival can be both fractured and communal, private and shared—and how, ultimately, connection is our greatest hope in healing.

With gratitude,
Jessica

ACKNOWLEDGMENTS

Writing *Both Can Be True* stretched me in ways I wasn't prepared for. It demanded honesty, stamina, and a willingness to revisit parts of myself I once believed were fully healed. I could not have stayed inside this story, especially when it pressed on every tender bruise, without the people who walked beside me and reminded me why the work mattered.

First and always, to my husband of fifteen years, Clark, my steadfast partner and home. You have allowed me to evolve into every version of myself as I uncover difficult truths, never asking me to be smaller for the sake of comfort. Thank you for holding the center while I chased these characters across drafts, deadlines, and doubt.

To my daughters—Charlotte, Maddie, and Joey—you make me braver simply by being yourselves. Every heartfelt word I write carries a trace of you three. Charlotte, I hope one day you smile when you notice the Gilmore sisters' name woven into this book, a small homage to our nights rewatching *Gilmore Girls* with bowls of ice cream and the kind of laughter that only belongs to us.

To my sister, Cara Cutter—thank you for being the kind of sister who makes me want to write toward the best parts of us: the complicated love, the shared history, and the unspoken understanding only sisters truly know. *'For there is no friend like a sister / In calm or stormy weather.'* Dad, your love has wrapped around me in ways words can't even hold, and Peggy, thank you for showing up in all the ways you do. Mom and Toni, thank you for your enduring love and support, and Mom for always nurturing my love of books. Maureen and Dennis, Mom and Dad, thank you for the family you built and for the place you made for me within it.

To Meg, I wish more than anything that you were still here to see what happened when I finally ceased fighting. Your presence changed the course of my life, and I carry you with me always. Grammy, thank you for welcoming me with such open arms and an open heart. I'm forever grateful for you. To Katie Layton, my original best friend, who helped lay the foundation.

To the GVG—I never could have imagined all the places our friendship would take us, but I can't picture a single day of motherhood without you all. Thank you for trusting me with pieces of your stories that found their way into my fictional ones. I'll keep repaying you the only way I know how: our annual girls' trip to Mexico and an endless supply of well-earned sarcasm.

To Allison Olson, thank you for a decade of ride-or-die friendship, laughter, and loyalty that has carried me through every season of motherhood. Cristina Buss, your brilliance and presence have shaped me into a stronger version of myself in every way. Laura McLively, thank you for your vulnerability and bravery and for trusting me to lovingly fictionalize pieces of your lived experience; your honesty is a gift. Sara Kadoch, watching you mother Charlie and Bobbi with fierce, unwavering love inspires me every day; your devotion to your family, your friends, and your faith shaped the truest, most tender parts of Mere, and I borrowed only the very best from the way you show up for the people you love. Heather Jones, thank you for rallying your Napa book club and for being a constant cheerleader and bright light through life. Molly DeSantis, thank you for your friendship and for being the world's greatest pediatrician. Breidi Truscott Roberts, thank you for being a constant source of warmth and optimism and the kind of person who lifts everyone around her. Nora Roos, thank you for sharing your passions and your unrelenting desire for justice. To Anais Foley-Kennedy, thank you for showing up for me in countless ways and for the deep generosity you carry so naturally in your heart.

To my agent, Ismita Hussain, who continues to be a lighthouse through every uncertain season, thank you for advocating fiercely, protecting my voice, and guiding me with a steadiness I rely on more than you know. I appreciate the entire team including Liz Nealon at Great Dog Literary.

To my Guerrieri, Scheiber, and Adams families, thank you for supporting this journey, for loving me fully, and for stepping into this next chapter on our country property together. Aunt Karen Clark, your generosity of spirit and unwavering warmth are a constant reminder of how fortunate I am to belong to such an extraordinary extended family.

To Laura Wheeler, thank you for the editorial letter that cracked this story open and helped me understand what it truly wanted to be. Your insight revealed the emotional architecture beneath the plot and gave me the courage to dig deeper than I thought I could.

To Whitney Bak, who went above and beyond as my line editor, thank you for your precision and the gentleness with which you approached every sentence. You honored the nuance of this story while helping me shape it with intention and clarity.

To Kimberly Carlton, Sicily Lippincott, Caitlin Halstead, and the entire Harper Muse team, thank you for championing this book from the inside out and for believing in complicated women who hold multiple truths at once.

To the marketing, publicity, BookSparks, sales, audio, design, and production teams, your work transforms a Word document into something that can live in a reader's hands, ears, and heart, and I am endlessly grateful for your dedication.

Our narrators: Mia Hutchinson-Shaw, thank you for returning to lend your voice to this book; whenever I write characters who mirror pieces of myself, it's your voice I hear in my head now. Rebecca Lowman, you were in my ear while narrating Lily King's *Heart the Lover* as I moved through deep edits and toured for *Between the Devil and the Deep Blue Sea*, and having you read Mere fills me with profound joy. Helen Laser, I love that you became the voice of Brie; her passage is one of my favorite chapters I've ever written, and you gave her breath and presence even in her death.

The Writing Coven, thank you for creating a space where honesty and creativity could coexist. Alexis Hatcher, thank you for fielding every frantic call and for believing in this work long before it felt real. Gina Banks Daly and Kym Summers, thank you for showing up for events with such enthusiasm. Thank you to Laura Klein Mullen and Meredith Riley for being early readers whose feedback strengthened this manuscript. Mere, thank you for letting me borrow your name and for your thoughtful design feedback on the cover. To Nicole Mirchandani, thank you for throwing one unforgettable Seattle book launch and for celebrating this story with the same heart you bring to uplifting other women.

Kristen Bear (@creativesobriety), thank you for joining me across cities for our literary salons and for being an extraordinary conversation partner whose presence inspires creative sobriety in action. To Kat Rhadans, thank you for opening your home, your city, and your platform to me with such generosity. Thank you to Amy Davidson and Ashley Jones for believing in my work in a very special way. To my favorite high school English teacher from Carlmont, Mr. Joey Hill—you helped foster my love of literature.

To the Peloton Moms Book Club, a community of more than 46,000 readers who show up with fierce support, thank you for championing my journey as an author. To my recovery community and my sponsor, MarySue Benz, thank you for teaching me how to stay, how to tell the truth, and how to keep choosing the next right thing. The language of accountability and grace are shaped by the spaces we hold together. Michelle Flowers and Lola, you are both an inspiration to me. Thank you to the fellowship of women in AA, especially Wednesday nights in Woodland and Davis. The sanctity of those spaces heals in ways few will ever fully witness, and opening this window onto the story is my way of offering hope to those still suffering. This is how I carry the message. To the Sober Mom Collective, specifically thank you for creating safety, belonging, and community for mothers choosing to live awake. Your community changes lives, including mine.

Thank you to Holly Snyder Thompson at the Avid Reader in Davis, California, for your unwavering support of both my book launches—and for helping make me an official bestseller. Thank you to Stacy Gould at Ruby's Books in Folsom and to Hanna Nakano of The Dirt for your encouragement and enthusiasm. Lizz Schumer at *People* magazine, thank you for your thoughtful support of my work and voice.

To my wellness and support team—Dr. Vi Liu-Ha; Gwen Morgana Poggi; Christina Stokke, RN; Bryanna Ferguson; Ian Marrow; Dr. Andrea Sherman; and Fit4Mom Davis-Woodland—thank you for helping me sustain the mental, physical, and emotional stamina required to finish this book.

Kerri Maher, I'm so grateful we connected and for how our paths have crossed. Amy Neff, thank you for reading early and for your gorgeous blurb. Celeste Yvonne (@theultimatemomchallenge), thank you for your support in the sober community online. It means so much. Thank you to Elizabeth Hamilton and the Carmel, Indiana, community for welcoming me with such warmth. To Marie Bostwick, thank you for your kindness and encouragement. Annie Harnett, thank you for granting permission to use the name Pancakes for Lily's dog, a small tribute to one of my favorite books, *The Road to Tender Hearts*. Sarah

Damoff, Emily Lynn Paulson, Barbara Samuel-O'Neal, and Virginia Evans, thank you all for your support. Lara Love Hardin, thank you for showing up for me in this business as both a sober woman and a true friend. Your generosity and presence at my book launch will stay with me forever.

To the Clark, Ferragamo, and Bevier families, thank you for supporting this dream and for showing up for me in ways both loud and quiet. To the community of Davis, California, as well as my alma mater, UC Davis. To my daughters' wonderful teachers and our neighbors. If I've left anyone out, please know the gratitude is still there. There are far too many incredible bookstagrammers to name, but I see you and I thank you.

And finally, to the women who will see themselves in these pages—the sisters, the mothers, the survivors, the friends, the partners who carry more than anyone ever sees—thank you for reading, for staying, and for reminding me every day that our stories matter.

DISCUSSION QUESTIONS

1. How does the novel explore duality—motherhood and selfhood, love and resentment, sobriety and craving, care and erasure? Which character embodies this contradiction most?

2. The prologue suggests: *"Sometimes the body stays. But the woman is already gone."* Where in the story do you see women disappearing—emotionally, physically, or socially? Which disappearance (Mere's, Frankie's, or Brie's) felt most haunting?

3. Mere and Frankie share old wounds, loyalty, rivalry, and tenderness. How do they save each other? How do they wound each other? Did your allegiance shift between them as the story unfolded?

4. Frankie struggles with the language of Step One, especially the word *powerless*. How does the novel complicate the idea of surrender for women? How do trauma and addiction show up in the body?

5. Mere is constantly translating Lily's needs for a world not built for her. What does the novel reveal about the invisible labor of mothering a neurodivergent child?

6. Mere and Frankie carry the long, unspoken weight of caring for a mentally ill father—a burden that began in childhood and continues into adulthood. How does the novel portray the emotional labor, resentment, love, and guilt intertwined in caretaking a parent who cannot care for themselves? In what ways do the sisters cope differently with this inherited heaviness, and how does it shape the women they become?

7. What did you make of the men's drug-altered encounter with Brie? Do you see their inaction as fear, negligence, moral failure, or something more complex? Did your view shift as the story progressed?

8. Frankie's near-relapse moments—the pain meds, the flirtation with Sam, the emotional overload of motherhood—illustrate how recovery rarely moves in a straight line. What commentary is the author making about the ongoing nature of sobriety? Did Frankie feel close to slipping, and what ultimately anchors her when she's at her most vulnerable?

9. Throughout the novel, Frankie's most profound moments of growth happen in connection—with Pearl, with her Sunday women's group, and even with Brie. What does the story reveal about why healing often requires the presence of others who have been there themselves? How does being witnessed, guided, or challenged by peers in recovery shape the choices Frankie makes?

10. Caleb's undressing post-anesthesia, Frankie's near-kiss with Sam, Brie's obsession with following along with her "plan"—each scene explores blurred boundaries. What does the novel suggest about how women internalize or override discomfort?

11. Throughout the novel, women's bodies are used, emptied, abandoned, misunderstood, or expected to withstand too much. Where did you see this pattern most powerfully illustrated?

12. Brie struggles with addiction, isolation, motherhood, and chronic self-erasure. How do you parse responsibility: Brie herself, the husbands, her community, or the systems around her?

13. In her author's note, Jessica Guerrieri shares her lived experiences with sexual assault and recovery. Why do you think she chose to explore these themes through a *fictional* narrative rather than memoir? How might fiction create a safer doorway for readers—and the author—to engage in conversations about trauma, secrecy, shame, and healing?

14. Did the ending feel hopeful, unresolved, devastating, or all of the above? What future do you imagine for Mere and Frankie five years after the final page?

ABOUT THE AUTHOR

With over twelve years of sobriety, Jessica Guerrieri is the author of *Between the Devil and the Deep Blue Sea* (Harper Muse, 2025), which won the Maurice Prize for Fiction from her alma mater, UC Davis. Her essays have appeared in *People*, *HuffPost*, and *Writer's Digest*, and she is a frequent voice in the recovery and mental health communities. She lives in Davis, California, with her husband, three daughters, and a small parade of pets.